T.S. Arthur

The Good Time Coming

T.S. Arthur

The Good Time Coming

1st Edition | ISBN: 978-3-73406-513-2

Place of Publication: Frankfurt am Main, Germany

Year of Publication: 2019

Outlook Verlag GmbH, Germany.

THE GOOD TIME COMING.

BY

T. S. ARTHUR.

BOSTON:
PHILADELPHIA:
1855.

PREFACE.

LIFE is a mystery to all men, and the more profound the deeper the striving spirit is immersed in its own selfish instincts. How earnestly do we all fix our eyes upon the slowly-advancing future, impatiently waiting that good time coming which never comes! How fast the years glide by, beginning in hope and ending in disappointment! Strange that we gain so little of true wisdom amid the sharp disappointments that meet us at almost every turn! How keenly the writer has suffered with the rest, need not be told. It will be enough to say that he, too, has long been an anxious waiter for the "goodtime coming," which has not yet arrived.

But hope should not die because of our disappointments. There is a good time coming, and for each one of us, if we work and wait for it; but we must work patiently, and look in the right direction. Perhaps our meaning will be plainer after our book is read.

THE GOOD TIME COMING.

CHAPTER I.

THERE was not a cloud in all the bright blue sky, nor a shadow upon the landscape that lay in beauty around the lovely home of Edward Markland; a home where Love had folded her wings, and Peace sought a perpetual abiding-place. The evening of a mild summer day came slowly on, with its soft, cool airs, that just dimpled the shining river, fluttered the elm and maple leaves, and gently swayed the aspiring heads of the old poplars, which, though failing at the root, still lifted, like virtuous manhood, their greenest branches to heaven.

In the broad porch, around every chaste column of which twined jessamine, rose, or honeysuckle, filling the air with a delicious fragrance beyond the perfumer's art to imitate, moved to and fro, with measured step and inverted thought, Edward Markland, the wealthy owner of all the fair landscape spreading for acres around the elegant mansion he had built as the home of his beloved ones.

"Edward." Love's sweetest music was in the voice that uttered his name, and love's purest touch in the hand that lay upon his arm.

A smile broke over the grave face of Markland, as he looked down tenderly into the blue eyes of his Agnes.

"I never tire of this," said the gentle-hearted wife, in whose spirit was a tuneful chord for every outward touch of beauty; "it looks as lovely now as yesterday; it was as lovely yesterday as the day my eyes first drank of its sweetness. Hush!"

A bird had just alighted on a slender spray a few yards distant, and while yet swinging on the elastic bough, poured forth a gush of melody.

"What a thrill of gladness was in that song, Edward! It was a spontaneous thank-offering to Him, without whom not a sparrow falls to the ground; to Him who clothes the fields in greenness, beautifies the lily, and provides for every creature its food in season. And this reminds me;" she added in a changed and more sobered voice, "that our thank-offering for infinite mercies lies in deeds, not heart-impulses nor word-utterances. I had almost forgotten poor Mrs. Elder."

And as Mrs. Markland said this, she withdrew her hand from her husband's arm, and glided into the house, leaving his thoughts to flow back into the channel from which they had been turned.

In vain for him did Nature clothe herself, on that fair day, in garments of more than usual beauty. She wooed the owner of Woodbine Lodge with every enticement she could offer; but he saw not her charms; felt not the strong attractions with which she sought to win his admiration. Far away his thoughts were wandering, and in the dim distance Fancy was busy with half-defined shapes, which her plastic hand, with rapid touches, moulded into forms that seemed instinct with a purer life, and to glow with a more ravishing beauty than any thing yet seen in the actual he had made his own. And as these forms became more and more vividly pictured in his imagination, the pace of Edward Markland quickened; and all the changing aspects of the man showed him to be in the ardour of a newly-forming life-purpose.

It was just five years since he commenced building Woodbine Lodge and beautifying its surroundings. The fifteen preceding years were spent in the earnest pursuit of wealth, as the active partner in a large mercantile establishment. Often, during these busy fifteen years, had he sighed for ease and "elegant leisure;" for a rural home far away from the jar, and strife, and toil incessant by which he was surrounded. Beyond this he had no aspiration. That "lodge in the wilderness," as he sometimes vaguely called it, was the bright ideal of his fancy. There, he would often say to himself—

"How blest could I live, and how calm could I die!"

And daily, as the years were added, each bringing its increased burdens of care and business, would he look forward to the "good time coming," when he could shut behind him forever the doors of the warehouse and counting-room, and step forth a free man. Of the strife for gain and the sharp contests in business, where each seeks advantages over the other, his heart was weary, and he would often sigh in the ears of his loving home-companion, "Oh! for the wings of a dove, that I might fly away and be at rest!"

And at length this consummation of his hopes came. A year of unusual prosperity swelled his gains to the sum he had fixed as reaching his desires; and, with a sense of pleasure never before experienced, he turned all his affections and thoughts to the creation of an earthly paradise, where, with his heart and home treasures around him, he could, "the world forgetting, by the world forgot," live a truer, better, happier life, than was possible amid the city's din, or while breathing the ever-disturbed and stifling atmosphere of business.

And now his work of creation at Woodbine Lodge was complete. Everywhere the hand of taste was visible—everywhere. You could change nothing without marring the beauty of the whole. During all the years in which Mr. Markland devoted himself to the perfecting of Woodbine Lodge, there was in his mind just so much of dissatisfaction with the present, as made the looked-for period, when all should be finished according to the prescriptions of taste, one in which there would be for him almost a Sabbath-repose.

How was it with Mr. Markland? All that he had prescribed as needful to give perfect happiness was attained. Woodbine Lodge realized his own ideal; and every one who looked upon it, called it an Eden of beauty. His work was ended; and had he found rest and sweet peace? Peace! Gentle spirit! Already she had half-folded her wings; but, startled by some uncertain sound, she was poised again, and seemed about to sweep the yielding air with her snowy pinions.

The enjoyment of all he had provided as a means of enjoyment did not come in the measure anticipated. Soon mere beauty failed to charm the eye, and fragrance to captivate the senses; for mind immortal rests not long in the fruition of any achievement, but quickly gathers up its strength for newer efforts. And so, as we have seen, Edward Markland, amid all the winning blandishments that surrounded him on the day when introduced to the reader, neither saw, felt, nor appreciated what, as looked to from the past's dim distance, formed the Beulah of his hopes.

CHAPTER II.

A FEW minutes after Mrs. Markland left her husband's side, she stepped from the house, carrying a small basket in one hand, and leading a child, some six or seven years old, with the other.

"Are you going over to see Mrs. Elder?" asked the child, as they moved down the smoothly-graded walk.

"Yes, dear," was answered.

"I don't like to go there," said the child.

"Why not, Aggy." The mother's voice was slightly serious.

"Every thing is so mean and poor."

"Can Mrs. Elder help that, Aggy?"

"I don't know."

"She's sick, my child, and not able even to sit up. The little girl who stays with her can't do much. I don't see how Mrs. Elder can help things looking mean and poor; do you?"

"No, ma'am," answered Aggy, a little bewildered by what her mother said.

"I think Mrs. Elder would be happier if things were more comfortable around her; don't you, Aggy?"

"Yes, mother,"

"Let us try, then, you and I, to make her happier."

"What can I do?" asked little Aggy, lifting a wondering look to her mother's face.

"Would you like to try, dear?"

"If I knew what to do."

"There is always a way when the heart is willing. Do you understand that, love?"

Aggy looked up again, and with an inquiring glance, to her mother.

"We will soon be at Mrs. Elder's. Are you not sorry that she is so sick? It is more than a week since she was able to sit up, and she has suffered a great deal of pain."

"Yes, I'm very sorry." And both look and tone confirmed the truth of her words. The child's heart was touched.

"When we get there, look around you, and see if there is nothing you can do to make her feel better. I'm sure you will find something."

"What, mother?" Aggy's interest was all alive now.

"If the room is in disorder, you might, very quietly, put things in their right places. Even that would make her feel better; for nobody can be quite comfortable in the midst of confusion."

"Oh! I can do all that, mother." And light beamed in the child's countenance. "It's nothing very hard."

"No; you can do all this with little effort; and yet, trifling as the act may seem, dear, it will do Mrs. Elder good: and you will have the pleasing remembrance of a kind deed. A child's hand is strong enough to lift a feather from an inflamed wound, even though it lack the surgeon's skill." The mother

5

said these last words half herself.

And now they were at the door of Mrs. Elder's unattractive cottage, and the mother and child passed in. Aggy had not overdrawn the picture when she said that everything was poor and mean; and disorder added to the unattractive appearance of the room in which the sick woman lay.

"I'm sorry to find you no better," said Mrs. Markland, after making a few inquiries of the sick woman.

"I shall never be any better, I'm afraid," was the desponding answer.

"Never! Never is a long day, as the proverb says. Did you ever hear of a night that had no morning?" There was a cheerful tone and manner about Mrs Markland that had its effect; but, ere replying, Mrs. Elder's dim eyes suddenly brightened, as some movement in the room attracted her attention.

"Bless the child! Look at her!" And the sick woman glanced toward Aggy, who, bearing in mind her mother's words, was already busying herself in the work of bringing order out of disorder.

"Look at the dear creature!" added Mrs. Elder, a glow of pleasure flushing her countenance, a moment before so pale and sad.

Unconscious of observation, Aggy, with almost a woman's skill, had placed first the few old chairs that were in the room, against the wall, at regular distances from each other. Then she cleared the littered floor of chips, pieces of paper, and various articles that had been left about by the untidy girl who was Mrs. Elder's only attendant, and next straightened the cloth on the table, and arranged the mantel-piece so that its contents no longer presented an unsightly aspect.

"Where is the broom, Mrs. Elder?" inquired the busy little one, coming now to the bedside of the invalid.

"Never mind the broom, dear; Betsy will sweep up the floor when she comes in," said Mrs. Elder. "Thank you for a kind, good little girl. You've put a smile on every thing in the room. What a grand housekeeper you are going to make!"

Aggy's heart bounded with a new emotion. Her young cheeks glowed, and her blue eyes sparkled. If the pleasure she felt lacked any thing of pure delight, a single glance at her mother's face made all complete.

"When did you hear from your daughter?" asked Mrs. Markland.

There was a change of countenance and a sigh.

"Oh! ma'am, if Lotty were only here, I would be happy, even in sickness and suffering. It's very hard to be separated from my child."

"She is in Charleston?"

"Yes, ma'am,"

"Is her husband doing well?"

"I can't say that he is. He isn't a very thrifty man, though steady enough."

"Why did they go to Charleston?"

"He thought he would do better there than here; but they haven't done as well, and Lotty is very unhappy."

"Do they talk of returning?"

"Yes, ma'am; they're both sick enough of their new home. But then it costs a heap of money to move about with a family, and they haven't saved any thing. And, more than this, it isn't just certain that James could get work right away if he came back. Foolish fellow that he was, not to keep a good situation when he had it! But it's the way of the world, Mrs. Markland, this ever seeking, through change, for something better than Heaven awards in the present."

"Truly spoken, Mrs. Elder. How few of us possess contentment; how few extract from the present that good with which it is ever supplied! We read the fable of the dog and the shadow, and smile at the folly of the poor animal; while, though instructed by reason, we cast aside the substance of to-day in our efforts to grasp the shadowy future. We are always looking for the blessing to come; but when the time of arrival is at hand, what seemed so beautiful in the hazy distance is shorn of its chief attraction, or dwarfed into nothingness through contrast with some greater good looming grandly against the far horizon."

Mrs. Markland uttered the closing sentence half in reverie; for her thoughts were away from the sick woman and the humble apartment in which she was seated. There was an abstracted silence of a few moments, and she said:

"Speaking of your daughter and her husband, Mrs. Elder; they are poor, as I understand you?"

"Oh yes, ma'am; it is hand-to-mouth with them all the time. James is kind enough to Lotty, and industrious in his way; but his work never turns to very good account."

"What business does he follow?"

"He's a cooper by trade; but doesn't stick to any thing very long. I call him the rolling stone that gathers no moss."

7

"What is he doing in Charleston?"

"He went there as agent for a man in New York, who filled his head with large ideas. He was to have a share in the profits of a business just commenced, and expected to make a fortune in a year or two; but before six months closed, he found himself in a strange city, out of employment, and in debt. As you said, a little while ago, he dropped the present substance in grasping at a shadow in the future."

"The way of the world," said Mrs. Markland.

"Yes, yes; ever looking for the good time coming that never comes," sighed Mrs. Elder. "Ah, me," she added, "I only wish Lotty was with me again."

"How many children has she?"

"Four."

"One a baby?"

"Yes, and but three months old."

"She has her hands full."

"You may well say that, ma'am; full enough."

"Her presence, would not, I fear, add much to your comfort, Mrs. Elder. With her own hands full, as you say, and, I doubt not, her heart full, also, she would not have it in her power to make much smoother the pillow on which your head is lying. Is she of a happy temper, naturally?"

"Well, no; I can't say that she is, ma'am. She is too much like her mother: ever looking for a brighter day in the future."

"And so unconscious of the few gleams of sunshine that play warmly about her feet—"

"Yes, yes; all very true; very true;" said Mrs. Elder, despondingly.

"The days that look so bright in the future, never come."

"They have never come to me." And the sick woman shook her head mournfully. "Long, long ago, I ceased to expect them." And yet, in almost the next breath, Mrs. Elder said:

"If Lotty were only here, I think I would be happy again."

"You must try and extract some grains of comfort even from the present," replied the kind-hearted visitor. "Consider me your friend, and look to me for whatever is needed. I have brought you over some tea and sugar, a loaf of

8

bread, and some nice pieces of ham. Here are half a dozen fresh eggs besides, and a glass of jelly. In the morning I will send one of my girls to put everything in order for you, and clear your rooms up nicely. Let Betsy lay out all your soiled clothing, and I will have it washed and ironed. So, cheer up; if the day opened with clouds in the sky, there is light in the west at its close."

Mrs. Markland spoke in a buoyant tone; and something of the spirit she wished to transfer, animated the heart of Mrs. Elder.

As the mother and her gentle child went back, through the deepening twilight, to their home of luxury and taste, both were, for much of the way, silent; the former musing on what she had seen and heard, and, like the wise bee, seeking to gather whatever honey could be found: the latter, happy-hearted, from causes the reader has seen.

CHAPTER III.

"WALKING here yet, Edward?" said Mrs. Markland, as she joined her husband in the spacious portico, after her return from the sick woman's cottage; and drawing her arm within his, she moved along by his side. He did not respond to her remark, and she continued:—

"Italy never saw a sunset sky more brilliant. Painter never threw on canvas colours so full of a living beauty. Deep purple and lucent azure,—crimson and burnished gold! And that far-off island-cloud—

'A Delos in the airy ocean—'

seems it not a floating elysium for happy souls?"

"All lovely as Nature herself," answered Mr. Markland, abstractedly, as his eyes sought the western horizon, and for the first time since the sun went down, he noticed the golden glories of the occident.

"Ah! Edward! Edward!" said Mrs. Markland, chidingly, "You are not only in the world, but of the world."

"Of the earth, earthy, did you mean to say, my gentle monitor?" returned the husband, leaning towards his wife.

"Oh, no, no! I did not mean grovelling or sordid; and you know I did not." She spoke quickly and with mock resentment.

"Am I very worldly-minded?"

9

"I did not use the term."

"You said I was not only in the world, but of it."

"Well, and so you are; at least in a degree. It is the habit of the world to close its eyes to the real it possesses, and aspire after an ideal good."

"And do you find that defect in me, Agnes?"

"Where was thought just now, that your eyes were not able to bring intelligence to your mind of this glorious sunset?"

"Thought would soon become a jaded beast of burden, Agnes, if always full laden with the present, and the actually existent. Happily, like Pegasus, it has broad and strong pinions—can rise free from the prisoner's cell and the rich man's dainty palace. Free! free! How the heart swells, elated and with a sense of power, at this noble word—Freedom! It has a trumpet-tone."

"Softly, softly, my good husband," said Mrs. Markland. "This is all enthusiasm."

"And but for enthusiasm, where would the world be now, my sweet philosopher?"

"I am no philosopher, and have but little enthusiasm. So we are not on equal ground for an argument. I I don't know where the world would be under the circumstances you allege, and so won't pretend to say. But I'll tell you what I do know."

"I am all attention."

"That if people would gather up each day the blessings that are scattered like unseen pearls about their feet, the world would be rich in contentment."

"I don't know about that, Agnes; I've been studying for the last half hour over this very proposition."

"Indeed! and what is the conclusion at which you have arrived?"

"Why, that discontent with the present, is a law of our being, impressed by the Creator, that we may ever aspire after the more perfect."

"I am far from believing, Edward," said his wife, "that a discontented present is any preparation for a happy future. Rather, in the wooing of sweet Content to-day, are we making a home for her in our hearts, where she may dwell for all time to come—yea, forever and forever."

"Beautifully said, Agnes; but is that man living whose heart asks not something more than it possesses—who does not look to a coming time with vague anticipations of a higher good than he has yet received?"

10

"It may be all so, Edward—doubtless is so—but what then? Is the higher good we pine for of this world? Nay, my husband. We should not call a spirit of discontent with our mere natural surroundings a law of the Creator, established as a spur to advancement; for this disquietude is but the effect of a deeper cause. It is not change of place, but change of state that we need. Not a going from one point in space to another, but a progression of the spirit in the way of life eternal."

"You said just now, Agnes, that you were no philosopher." Mr. Markland's voice had lost much of its firmness. "But what would I not give to possess some of your philosophy. Doubtless your words are true; for there must be a growth and progression of the spirit as well as of the body; for all physical laws have their origin in the world of mind, and bear thereto exact relations. Yet, for all this, when there is a deep dissatisfaction with what exists around us, should we not seek for change? Will not a removal from one locality to another, and an entire change of pursuits, give the mind a new basis in natural things, and thus furnish ground upon which it may stand and move forward?"

"Perhaps, if the ground given us to stand upon were rightly tilled, it would yield a richer harvest than any we shall ever find, though we roam the world over; and it may be, that the narrow path to heaven lies just across our own fields. It is in the actual and the present that we are to seek a true development of our spiritual life. 'Work while it is to-day,' is the Divine injunction."

"But if we can find no work, Agnes?"

"If the heart be willing and the hands ready," was the earnestly spoken answer, "work enough will be found to do."

"I have a willing heart, Agnes,—I have ready hands—but the heart is wearied of its own fruitless desires, and the hands hang down in idleness. What shall I do? The work in which I have found so much delight for years, is completed; and now the restless mind springs away from this lovely Eden, and pines for new fields in which to display its powers. Here I fondly hoped to spend the remainder of my life—contented—happy. The idea was a dreamy illusion. Daily is this seen in clear light. I reprove myself; I chide the folly, as I call it; but, all in vain. Beauty for me, has faded from the landscape, and the air is no longer balmy with odours. The birds sing for my ears no more; I hear not, as of old, the wind spirits whispering to each other in the tree tops. Dear Agnes!—wife of my heart—what does it mean?"

An answer was on the lip of Mrs. Markland, but words so unlooked for, swelled, suddenly, the wave of emotion in her heart, and she could not speak. A few moments her hand trembled on the arm of her husband. Then it was softly removed, and without a word, she passed into the house, and going to her own room, shut the door, and sat down in the darkness to commune with her spirit. And first, there came a gush of tears. These were for herself. A shadow had suddenly fallen upon the lovely home where she had hoped to spend all the days of her life—a shadow from a storm-boding cloud. Even from the beginning of their wedded life, she had marked in her husband a defect of character, which, gaining strength, had led to his giving upbusiness, and their retirement to the country. That defect was the common one, appertaining to all, a looking away from the present into the future for the means of enjoyment. In all the years of his earnest devotion to business, Mr. Markland had kept his eye steadily fixed upon the object now so completely attained; and much of present enjoyment had been lost in the eager looking forward for this coveted time. And now, that more than all his fondest anticipations were realized, only for a brief period did he hold to his lips the cup full of anticipated delight. Already his hand felt the impulse that moved him to pour its crystal waters upon the ground.

Mrs. Markland's clear appreciation of her husband's character was but a prophecy of the future. She saw that Woodbine Lodge—now grown into her affections, and where she hoped to live and die—even if it did not pass from their possession—bartered for some glittering toy—could not remain their permanent home. For this flowed her first tears; and these, as we have said, were for herself. But her mind soon regained its serenity; and from herself, her thoughts turned to her husband. She was unselfish enough not only to be able to realize something of his state of mind, but to sympathize with him, and pity his inability to find contentment in the actual. This state of mind she regarded as a disease, and love prompted all self-denial for hissake.

"I can be happy any, where, if only my husband and children are left. My husband, so generous, so noble-minded—my children, so innocent, so loving."

Instantly the fountain of tears were closed. These unselfish words, spoken in her own heart, checked the briny current. Not for an instant did Mrs. Markland seek to deceive herself or hearken to the suggestion that it was but a passing state in the partner of her life. She knew too well the origin of his disquietude to hope for its removal. In a little while, she descended and joined her family in the sitting-room, where the soft astral diffused its pleasant light, and greeted her sober-minded husband with loving smiles and cheerful words. And he was deceived. Not for an instant imagined he, after looking upon her face, that she had passed through a painful, though brief conflict, and was now possessed of a brave heart for any change that might come. But he had not thought of leaving Woodbine Lodge. Far distant was this from his imagination. True—but Agnes looked with a quick intuition from cause to effect. The elements of happiness no longer existed here for her husband; or, if they did exist, he had not the skill to find them, and the end would be a searching elsewhere for the desired possession.

"You did not answer my question, Agnes," said Mr. Markland, after the children had retired for the evening, and they were again alone.

"What question?" inquired Mrs. Markland; and, as she lifted her eyes, he saw that they were dim with tears.

"What troubles you, dear?" he asked, tenderly.

Mrs. Markland forced a smile, as she replied, "Why should I be troubled? Have I not every good gift the heart can desire?"

"And yet, Agnes, your eyes are full of tears."

"Are they?" A light shone through their watery vail. "Only an April shadow, Edward, that is quickly lost in April sunshine. But your question is not so easily answered."

"I ought to be perfectly happy here; nothing seems wanting. Yet my spirit is like a aged bird that flutters against its prison-bars."

"Oh, no, Edward; not so bad as that," replied Mrs. Markland. "You speak in hyperbole. This lovely place, which everywhere shows the impress of your hand, is not a prison. Call it rather, a paradise."

"A paradise I sought to make it. But I am content no longer to be an idle lingerer among its pleasant groves; for I have ceased to feel the inspiration of its loveliness."

Mrs. Markland made no answer. After a silence of some minutes, her husband said, with a slight hesitation in his voice, as if uncertain as to the effect of his words—

"I have for some time felt a strong desire to visit Europe."

The colour receded from Mrs. Markland's face; and there was a look in her eyes that her husband did not quite understand, as they rested steadily in his.

"I have the means and the leisure," he added, "and the tour would not only be one of pleasure, but profit."

"True," said his wife, and, then her, face was bent down so low that he could not see, its expression for the shadows by which it was partially concealed.

"We would both enjoy the trip exceedingly."

"Both! You did not think of taking me?"

"Why, Aggy, dear!—as if I could dream for a moment of any pleasure in which you had not a share!"

So earnestly and tenderly was this said, that Mrs. Markland felt a thrill of joy tremble over her heart-strings. And yet, for all, she could not keep back the overflowing tears, but hid her face, to conceal them, on her husband's bosom.

Her true feelings Mr. Markland did not read: and often, as he mused on what appeared singular in her manner that evening, he was puzzled to comprehend its meaning. Nor had his vision ever penetrated deep enough to see all that was in her heart.

CHAPTER IV.

THE memory of what passed between Mr. and Mrs. Markland remained distinct enough in both their minds, on the next morning, to produce thoughtfulness and reserve. The night to each had been restless and wakeful; and in the snatches of sleep which came at weary intervals were dreams that brought no tranquillizing influence.

The mother's daily duty, entered into from love to her children, soon lifted her mind into a sunnier region, and calmed her pulse to an even stroke. But the spirit of Markland was more disturbed, more restless, more dissatisfied with himself and every thing around him, than when first introduced to the reader's acquaintance. He eat sparingly at the breakfast-table, and with only a slight relish. A little forced conversation took place between him and his wife; but the thoughts of both were remote from the subject introduced. After breakfast, Mr. Markland strolled over his handsome grounds, and endeavoured to awaken in his mind a new interest in what possessed so much of real beauty. But the effort was fruitless; his thoughts were away from the scenes in which he was actually present. Like a dreamy enthusiast on the sea-shore, he saw, afar off, enchanted Islands faintly pictured on the misty horizon, and could not withdraw his gaze from their ideal loveliness.

A little way from the house was a grove, in the midst of which a fountain threw upward its refreshing waters, that fell plashing into a marble basin, and then went gurgling musically along over shining pebbles. How often, with his gentle partner by his side, had Markland lingered here, drinking in delight from every fair object by which they were surrounded! Now he wandered amid its cool recesses, or sat by the fountain, without having even a faint picture of the scene mirrored in his thoughts. It was true, as he had said, "Beauty had faded from the landscape; the air was no longer balmy with odours; the birds sang for his ears no more; he heard not, as of old, the wind-spirits whispering to each other in the tree-tops;" and he sighed deeply as a half-consciousness of the change disturbed his reverie. A footfall reached his ears, and, looking up, he saw a neighbour approaching: a man somewhat past the prime of life, who came toward him with a familiar smile, and, as he offered his hand, said pleasantly—

"Good morning, Friend Markland."

"Ah! good morning, Mr. Allison," was returned with a forced cheerfulness; "I am happy to meet you."

"And happy always, I may be permitted to hope," said Mr. Allison, as his mild yet intelligent eyes rested on the face of his neighbour.

"I doubt," answered Mr. Markland, in a voice slightly depressed from the tone in which he had first spoken, "whether that state ever comes in this life."

"Happiness?" inquired the other.

"Perpetual happiness; nay, even momentary happiness."

"If the former comes not to any," said Mr. Allison, "the latter, I doubt not, is daily enjoyed by thousands."

Mr. Markland shook his head, as he replied—

"Take my case, for instance; I speak of myself, because my thought has been turning to myself; there are few elements of happiness that I do not possess, and yet I cannot look back to the time when I was happy."

"I hardly expected this from you, Mr. Markland," said the neighbour; "to my observation, you always seemed one of the most cheerful of men."

"I never was a misanthrope; I never was positively unhappy. No, I have been too earnest a worker. But there is no disguising from myself the fact, now I reflect upon it, that I have known but little true enjoyment as I moved along my way through life."

"I must be permitted to believe," replied Mr. Allison, "that you are not reading aright your past history. I have been something of an observer of men and things, and my experience leads me to this conclusion."

"He who has felt the pain, Mr. Allison, bears ever after the memory of its existence."

"And the marks, too, if the pain has been as prolonged and severe as your

15

words indicate."

"But such marks, in your case, are not visible. That you have not always found the pleasure anticipated—that you have looked restlessly away from the present, longing for some other good than that laid by the hand of a benignant Providence at your feet, I can well believe; for this is my own history, as well as yours: it is the history of all mankind."

"Now you strike the true chord, Mr. Allison. Now you state the problem I have not skill to solve. Why is this?"

"Ah! if the world had skill to solve that problem," said the neighbour, "it would be a wiser and happier world; but only to a few is this given."

"What is the solution? Can you declare it?"

"I fear you would not believe the answer a true one. There is nothing in it flattering to human nature; nothing that seems to give the weary, selfish heart a pillow to rest upon. In most cases it has a mocking sound."

"You have taught me more than one life-lesson, Mr. Allison. Speak freely now. I will listen patiently, earnestly, looking for instruction. Why are we so restless and dissatisfied in the present, even though all of earthly good surrounds us, and ever looking far away into the uncertain future for the good that never comes, or that loses its brightest charms in possession?"

"Because," said the old man, speaking slowly, and with emphasis, "we are mere self-seekers."

Mr. Markland had bent toward him, eager for the answer; but the words fell coldly, and with scarce a ray of intelligence in them, on his ears. He sighed faintly and leaned back in his seat, while a look of disappointment shadowed his countenance.

"Can you understand," said Mr. Allison, "the proposition that man, aggregated, as well as in the individual, is in the human form?"

Markland gazed inquiringly into the questioner's face. "In the human form as to uses?" said Mr. Allison. "How as to uses?"

"Aggregate men into larger or smaller bodies, and, in the attainment of ends proposed, you will find some directing, as the head, and some executing, as the hands."

"True."

"Society, then, is only a man in a larger form. Now, there are voluntary, as well as involuntary associations; the voluntary, such as, from certain ends, individuals form one with another; the involuntary, that of the common society in which we live. Let us look for a moment at the voluntary association, and consider it as man in a larger form. You see how all thought conspires to a single end and how judgment speaks in a single voice. The very first act of organization is to choose a head for direction, and hands to execute the will of this larger man. And now mark well this fact: Efficient action by this aggregated man depends wholly upon the unselfish exercise by each part of its function for the good of the whole. Defect and disorder arise the moment the head seeks power or aggrandizement for itself, the hands work for their good alone, or the feet strive to bear the body alone the paths they only wish to tread. Disease follows, if the evil is not remedied; disease, the sure precursor of dissolution. How disturbed and unhappy each member of such an aggregated man must be, you can at once perceive.

"If it is so in the voluntary man of larger form, how can it be different in the involuntary man, or the man of common society?"

"Of this great body you are a member. In it you are sustained, and live by virtue of its wonderful organization. From the blood circulating in its veins you obtain nutrition, and as its feet move forward, you are borne onward in the general progression. From all its active senses you receive pleasure or intelligence; and yet this larger man of society is diseased—all see, all feel, all lament this—fearfully diseased. It contains not a single member that does not suffer pain. You are not exempt, favourable as is your position. If you enjoy the good attained by the whole, you have yet to bear a portion of the evil suffered by the whole. Let me add, that if you find the cause of unhappiness in this larger man, you will find it in yourself. Think! Where does it lie?"

"You have given me the clue," replied Mr. Markland, "in your picture of the voluntarily aggregated man. In this involuntary man of common society, to which, as you have said, we all bear relation as members, each seeks his own good, regardless of the good of the whole; and there is, therefore, a constant war among the members."

"And if not war, suffering," said Mr. Allison. "This man is sustained by a community of uses among the members. In the degree that each member performs his part well, is the whole body served; and in the degree that each member neglects his work, does the whole body suffer."

"If each worked for himself, all would be served," answered Mr. Markland. "It is because so many will not work for themselves, that so many are in want and suffering."

"In the very converse of this lies the true philosophy; and until the world has learned the truth, disorder and unhappiness will prevail. The eye does not see for itself, nor the ear hearken; the feet do not walk, nor the hands labour for themselves; but each freely, and from an affection for the use in which it is engaged, serves the whole body, while every organ or member of the body conspires to sustain it. See how beautifully the eyes direct the hands, guiding them in every minute particular, while the heart sends blood to sustain them in their labours, and the feet bear them to the appointed place; and the hands work not for themselves, but that the whole body may be nourished and clothed. Where each regards the general good, each is best served. Can you not see this, Mr. Markland?"

"I can, to a certain extent. The theory is beautiful, as applied to your man of common society. But, unfortunately, it will not work in practice. We must wait for the millennium."

"The millennium?"

"Yes, that good time coming, toward which the Christian world looks with such a pleasing interest."

"A time to be ushered in by proclamation, I suppose?"

"How, and when, and where it is to begin, I am not advised," said' Mr. Markham, smiling. "All Christians expect it; and many have set the beginning thereof near about this time."

"What if it have begun already?"

"Already! Where is the sign, pray? It has certainly escaped my observation. If the Lord had actually come to reign a thousand years, surely the world would know it. In what favoured region has he made his second advent?"

"Is it not possible that the Christian world may be in error as to the manner of this second coming, that is to usher in the millennium?"

"Yes, very. I don't see, that in all prophecy, there is any thing definite on the subject."

"Nothing more definite than there was in regard to the first coming?"

"No."

"And yet, while in their very midst, even though miracles were wrought for them; the Jews did not know the promised Messiah."

"True."

"They expected a king in regal state, and an assumption of visible power. They looked for marked political changes. And when the Lord said to them, 'My kingdom is not of this world,' they denied and rejected him. Now, is it not a possible case, that the present generation, on this subject, may be no wiser than the Jews?"

"Not a very flattering conclusion," said Markland. "The age is certainly more enlightened, and the world wiser and better than it was two thousand years ago."

"And therefore," answered Mr. Allison, "the better prepared to understand this higher truth, which it was impossible for the Jews to comprehend, that the kingdom of God is within us."

"Within us!—within us!" Markland repeated the words two or three times, as if there were in them gleams of light which had never before dawned upon his mind.

"Of one thing you may be assured," said Mr. Allison, speaking with some earnestness; "the millennium will commence only when men begin to observe the Golden Rule. If there are any now living who in all sincerity strive to repress their selfish inclinations, and seek the good of others from genuine neighbourly love, then the millennium has begun; and it will never be fully ushered in, until that law of unselfish, reciprocal uses that rules in our physical man becomes the law of common society."

"Are there any such?"

"Who seek the good of others from a genuine neighbourly love?"

"Yes."

"I believe so."

"Then you think the millennium has commenced?"

"I do."

"The beginning must be very small. The light hid under a bushel. Now I have been led to expect that this light, whenever it came, would be placed on a candlestick, to give light unto all in the house."

"May it not be shining? Nay, may there not be light in all the seven golden candlesticks, without your eyes being attracted thereby?"

"I will not question your inference. It may all be possible. But your words awaken in my mind but vague conceptions."

"The history of the world, as well as your own observation, will tell you that all advances toward perfection are made with slow steps. And further, that all changes in the character of a whole people simply indicate the changes that have taken place in the individuals who compose that people. The national character is but its aggregated personal character. If the world is better now than it was fifty years ago, it is because individual men and women are becoming better—that is, less selfish, for in self-love lies the germ of all evil. The Millennium must, therefore, begin with the individual. And so, as it comes not by observation—or with a 'lo! here, and lo! there'—men are not conscious of its presence. Yet be assured, my friend, that the time is at hand; and that every one who represses, through the higher power given to all who ask for it, the promptings of self-love, and strives to act from a purified love of the neighbour, is doing his part, in the only way he can do it, toward hastening the time when the 'wolf also shall dwell with the lamb, the leopard shall lie down with the kid; and the calf, and the young lion, and the fatling together; and a little child shall lead them.'"

"Have we not wandered," said Mr. Markland, after a few moments of thoughtful silence, "from the subject at first proposed?"

"I have said more than I intended," was answered, "but not, I think, irrelevantly. If you are not happy, it is because, like an inflamed organ in the human body, you are receiving more blood than is applied to nutrition. As a part of the larger social man, you are not using the skill you possess for the good of the whole. You are looking for the millennium, but not doing your part toward hastening its general advent. And now, Mr. Markland, if what I have said be true, can you wonder at being the restless, dissatisfied man you represent yourself to be?"

"If your premises be sound, your conclusions are true enough," answered Markland, with some coldness and abstraction of manner. The doctrine was neither flattering to his reason, nor agreeable to his feelings. He was too confirmed a lover of himself to receive willingly teaching like this. A type of the mass around him, he was content to look down the dim future for signs of the approaching millennium, instead of into his own heart. He could give hundreds of dollars in aid of missions to convert the heathen, and to bring in the islands of the sea, as means of hastening the expected time; but was not ready, as a surer means to this end, to repress a single selfish impulse of his nature.

The conversation was still further prolonged, with but slight change in the subject. At parting with his neighbour, Markland found himself more disturbed than before. A sun ray had streamed suddenly into the darkened chambers of his mind, disturbing the night birds there, and dimly revealing an inner world of disorder, from which his eyes vainly sought to turn themselves. If the mental disease from which he was suffering had its origin in the causes indicated by Mr. Allison, there seemed little hope of a cure in his case. How was he, who all his life long had regarded himself, and those who were of his own flesh and blood, as only to be thought of and cared for, to forget himself, and seek, as the higher end of his existence, the good of others? The thought created no quicker heart-beat—threw no warmer tint on the ideal future toward which his eyes of late had so fondly turned themselves. To live for others and not for himself—this was to extinguish his very life. What were others to him? All of his world was centred in his little home-circle. Alas! that its power to fill the measure of his desires was gone—its brightness dimmed —its attraction a binding-spell no longer!

And so Markland strove to shut out from his mind the light shining in through the little window opened by Mr. Allison; but the effort was in vain. Steadily the light came in, disturbing the owls and bats, and revealing dust, cankering mould, and spider-web obstructions. All on the outside was fair to the world; and as fair, he had believed, within. To be suddenly shown his error, smote him with a painful sense of humiliation.

"What is the highest and noblest attribute of manhood?" Mr. Allison had asked of him during their conversation.

Markland did not answer the question.

"The highest excellence—the greatest glory—the truest honour must be in God," said the old man.

"All will admit that," returned Markland.

"Those, then, who are most like him, are most excellent—most honourable."

"Yes."

"Love," continued Mr. Allison, "is the very essential nature of God—not love of self, but love of creating and blessing others, out of himself. Love of self is a monster; but love of others the essential spirit of true manhood, and therefore its noblest attribute."

Markland bowed his head, convicted in his own heart of having, all his life long, been a self-worshipper; of having turned his eyes away from the true type of all that was noble and excellent, and striven to create something of his own that was excellent and beautiful. But, alas! there was no life in the image; and already its decaying elements were an offence in his nostrils.

"In the human body," said Mr. Allison, "as in the human soul when it came pure from the hands of God, there is a likeness of the Creator. Every organ and member, from the largest to the most hidden and minute, bears this likeness, in its unselfish regard for the good of the whole body. For, as we have seen, each, in its activity, has no respect primarily to its own life. And it is because the human soul has lost this likeness of its loving Creator, that it is so weak, depraved, and unhappy. There must be the restored image, and

21

likeness, before there be the restored Eden."

The noblest type of manhood! Never in all his after life was Edward Markland able to shut out this light of truth from his understanding. It streamed through the little window, shining very dimly at times; but always strong enough to show him that unselfish love was man's highest attribute, and self-love a human monster.

CHAPTER V.

WHILE Mr. Markland was brooding over his own unhappy state, and seeking to shut out the light shining too strongly in upon his real quality of mind, Mrs. Markland was living, in some degree, the very life that seemed so unattractive to him, and receiving her measure of reward. While he wandered, with an unquiet spirit, over his fields, or sat in cool retreats by plashing fountains, his thoughts reaching forward to embrace the coming future, she was active in works of love. Her chief desire was the good of her beloved ones, and she devoted herself to this object with an almost entire forgetfulness of self. Home was therefore the centre of her thoughts and affections, but not the selfish centre: beyond that happy circle often went out her thoughts, laden with kind wishes that died not fruitless.

The family of Mr. Markland consisted of his wife, four children, and a maiden sister—Grace Markland,—the latter by no means one of the worst specimens of her class. With Agnes, in her seventh year, the reader has already a slight acquaintance. Francis, the baby, was two years old, and the pet of every one but Aunt Grace, who never did like children. But he was so sweet a little fellow, that even the stiff maiden would bend toward him now and then, conscious of a warmer heart-beat. George, who boasted of being ten —quite an advanced age, in his estimation—might almost be called a thorn in the flesh to Aunt Grace, whose nice sense of propriety and decorum he daily outraged by rudeness and want of order. George was boy all over, and a strongly-marked specimen of his class—"as like his father, when at his age, as one pea to another," Aunt Grace would say, as certain memories of childhood presented themselves with more than usual vividness. The boy was generally too much absorbed in his own purposes to think about the peculiar claims to respect of age, sex, or condition. Almost from the time he could toddle about the carpeted floor, had Aunt Grace been trying to teach him what she called manners. But he was never an apt scholar in her school. If he mastered the A

B C to-day, most probably on her attempt to advance him to-morrow into his a-b ab's, he had wholly forgotten the previous lesson. Poor Aunt Grace! She saw no hope for the boy. All her labour was lost on him.

Fanny, the oldest child, just completing her seventeenth year, was of fair complexion and delicate frame; strikingly beautiful, and as pure in mind as she was lovely in person. All the higher traits of womanhood that gave such a beauty to the mother's character were as the unfolding bud in her. Every one loved Fanny, not even excepting Aunt Grace, who rarely saw any thing in her niece that violated her strict sense of propriety. Since the removal of the family to Woodbine Lodge, the education of Fanny had been under the direction of a highly accomplished governess. In consequence, she was quite withdrawn from intercourse with young ladies of her own age. If, from this cause, she was ignorant of many things transpiring in city life, the purer atmosphere she daily breathed gave a higher moral tone to her character. In all the sounder accomplishments Fanny would bear favourable comparison with any; and as for grace of person and refinement of manners, these were but the expression of an inward sense of beauty.

As Fanny unfolded toward womanhood, putting forth, like an opening blossom, some newer charms each day, the deep love of her parents began to assume the character of jealous fear. They could not long hide from other's eyes the treasure they possessed, and their hearts grew faint at the thought of having it pass into other hands. But very few years would glide away ere wooers would come, and seek to charm her ears with songs sweeter than ever thrilled them in her own happy home. And there would be a spell upon her spirit, so that she could not help but listen. And, mayhap, the song that charmed her most might come from unworthy lips. Such things had been, alas!

Thus it was with the family of Mr. Markland at the time of our introduction to them. We have not described each individual with minuteness, but sufficiently indicated to give them a place in the reader's mind. The lights and shadows will be more strongly marked hereafter.

The effect of Mr. Allison's conversation was, as has been seen, to leave Markland in a still more dissatisfied state of mind. After various fruitless efforts to get interested in what was around him, and thus compel self-forgetfulness, he thought of some little matter in the city that required his attention, and forthwith ordered the carriage.

"I shall not be home till evening," he said, as he parted with his wife.

During the day, Mrs. Markland paid another visit to the humble home of Mrs. Elder, and ministered as well to her mental as to her bodily wants. She made still closer inquiries about her daughter's family; and especially touching the husband's character for industry, intelligence, and trustworthiness. She had a purpose in this; for the earnest desire expressed by Mrs. Elder to have her daughter with her, had set Mrs. Markland to thinking about the ways and means of effecting the wished-for object. The poor woman was made happier by her visit.

It was near sundown when the carriage was observed approaching through the long, shaded avenue. Mrs. Markland and all the children stood in the porch, to welcome the husband and father, whose absence, though even for the briefest period, left for their hearts a diminished brightness. As the carriage drew nearer, it was seen to contain two persons.

"There is some one with your father," said Mrs. Markland, speaking to Fanny.

"A gentleman—I wonder who it can be?"

"Your Uncle George, probably."

"No; it isn't Uncle George," said Fanny, as the carriage reached the oval in front of the house, and swept around towards the portico. "It's a younger man; and he is dressed in black."

Further conjecture was suspended by the presence of the individual in regard to whom they were in doubt. He was a stranger, and Mr. Markland presented him as Mr. Lyon, son of an old and valued business correspondent, residing in Liverpool. A cordial welcome awaited Mr. Lyon at Woodbine Lodge, as it awaited all who were introduced by the gentlemanly owner. If Mr. Markland thought well enough of any one to present him at home, the home-circle opened smilingly to receive.

The stranger was a young man, somewhere between the ages of twenty-five and thirty; above the medium height; with a well-formed person, well-balanced head, and handsome countenance. His mouth was the least pleasing feature of his face. The lips were full, but too firmly drawn back against his teeth. Eyes dark, large, and slightly prominent, with great depth, but only occasional softness, of expression. His was a face with much in it to attract, and something to repel. A deep, rich voice, finely modulated, completed his personal attractions.

It so happened that Mr. Lyon had arrived from New York that very day, with letters to Mr. Markland. His intention was to remain only until the next morning. The meeting with Mr. Markland was accidental; and it was only after earnest persuasion that the young man deferred his journey southward, and consented to spend a day or two with the retired merchant, in his country home. Mr. Lyon was liberally educated, bad travelled a good deal, and been a close observer and thinker. He was, moreover, well read in human nature. That he charmed the little circle at Woodbine Lodge on the first evening of his visit there, is scarcely a matter of wonder. Nor was he less charmed. Perhaps the only one not altogether pleased was Aunt Grace. By habit a close reader of all who came within range of her observation, she occupied quite as much time in scanning the face of Mr. Lyon, and noting each varying expression of eyes, lips, and voice, as in listening to his entertaining description of things heard and seen.

"I don't just like him." Thus she soliloquized after she had retired to her own room.' "He's deep—any one can see that—deep as the sea. And he has a way of turning his eyes without turning his head that don't please me exactly. Edward is wonderfully taken with him; but he never looks very far below the surface. And Fanny—why the girl seemed perfectly fascinated!"

And Aunt Grace shook her head ominously, as she added—

"He's handsome enough; but beauty's only skin-deep, and he may be as black as Lucifer inside."

A greater part of the next day Mr. Markland and Mr. Lyon spent alone, either in the library or seated in some one of the many shady arbours and cool retreats scattered invitingly over the pleasant estate. The stranger had found the mind of his host hungering for new aliment, and as his own mind was full stored with thought and purpose, he had but to speak to awaken interest. Among other things, he gave Mr. Markland, a minute detail of certain plans for acquiring an immense fortune, in the prosecution of which, in company with some wealthy capitalists, he was now engaged. The result was sure; for every step had been taken with the utmost cautions and every calculation thrice verified.

"And what a dreaming idler I am here!" said Markland, half to himself, in one of the conversational pauses, as there was presented to his mind a vivid contrast of his fruitless inactivity with the vigorous productive industry of others. "I half question, at times, whether, in leaving the busy world, I did not commit a serious error."

"Have you given up all interest in business?" asked Mr. Lyon.

"All."

"Ah!" with slight evidence of surprise. "How do you live?"

"The life of an oyster, I was going to say," replied Markland, with a faint smile.

"I would die if not active. True enjoyment, a wise friend has often said to me, is never found in repose, but in activity. To me a palace would be a prison, if I could find nothing to do; while a prison would be a palace, if mind and hands were fully employed."

"I lack the motive for renewed effort," said Markland. "Wealth beyond my present possession I do not desire. I have more than enough safely invested to give me every comfort and luxury through life."

"But your children?" remarked the guest.

"Will have ample provision."

"There is another motive."

"What?"

"Money is power."

"True."

"And by its proper use a man may elevate himself into almost any position. It is the lever that moves the world."

Markland only shrugged his shoulders slightly.

"Have you no ambition?" inquired the other, in a familiar way.

"Ambition!" The question awakened surprise.

"To stand out prominently in the world's eye, no matter for what, so the distinction be honourable," said Mr. Lyon. "Of the thousands and tens of thousands who toil up the steep and often rugged paths to wealth, and attain the desired eminence, how few are ever heard of beyond the small community in which they live! Some of these, to perpetuate a name, establish at death some showy charity, and thus build for themselves a monument not overshadowed by statelier mausoleums amid the rivalries of a fashionable cemetery. Pah! All this ranges far below my aspiring. I wish to make a name while living. Wealth in itself is only a toy. No true man can find pleasure in its mere glitter for a day. It is only the miser who loves gold for its own sake, and sees nothing beautiful or desirable except the yellow earth he hoards in his coffers. Have you found happiness in the mere possession of wealth?"

"Not in its *mere* possession," was answered.

"Nor even in its lavish expenditure?"

"I have great pleasure in using it for the attainment of my wishes," said Mr. Markland.

"The narrower the bound of our wishes, the quicker comes their consummation, and then all is restlessness again, until we enter upon a new pursuit."

"Truly spoken."

"Is it not wise, then, to give a wide sweep to our aspirations? to lift the ideal of our life to a high position; so that, in its attainment, every latent power may be developed? Depend upon it, Mr. Markland, we may become what we will; and I, for one, mean to become something more than a mere money-getter and money-saver. But first the money-getting, as a means to an end. To that every energy must now be devoted."

Mr. Lyon's purpose was to interest Mr. Markland, and he was entirely successful. He drew for him various attractive pictures, and in the contemplation of each, as it stood vividly before him, the retired merchant saw much to win his ardent admiration. Very gradually, and very adroitly, seeming all the while as if he had not the slightest purpose to interest Mr. Markland in that particular direction, did Mr. Lyon create in his mind a strong confidence in the enlarged schemes for obtaining immense wealth in which he was now engaged. And the tempter was equally successful in his efforts to awaken a desire in Mr. Markland to have his name stand out prominently, as one who had shown remarkable public spirit and great boldness in the prosecution of a difficult enterprise.

One, two, three days went by, and still Mr. Lyon was a lingerer at Woodbine Lodge; and during most of that time he was alone and in earnest conference with Mr. Markland. The evenings were always pleasant seasons in the family circle. Fanny's voice had been well cultivated, and she sung with fine taste; and as Mr. Lyon was also a lover of music, and played and sung exquisitely, the two very naturally spent a portion of their time at the piano. If it crossed the father's mind that an attachment might spring up between them, it did not disturb his feelings.

At the end of a week Mr. Lyon found it necessary to tear himself away from the little paradise into which he had been so unexpectedly introduced. Every day that he lingered there diminished the ardour of his ambition, or robbed of some charm the bright ideal he had worshipped. And so he broke the silken bonds that wove themselves around him, at first light as gossamer, but now strong as twisted cords.

Mr. Markland accompanied him to the city, and did not return home until late in the evening. He was then much occupied with his own thoughts, and entered but little into conversation. Fanny was absent-minded, a fact that did not escape the mother's observation. Aunt Grace noted the change which the stranger's coming and departure had occasioned, and, shaking her wise head, spoke thus within herself—

"He may be very handsome, but he casts a shadow, for all that. I don't see what Edward was thinking about. He'd better let Fanny go right into the world, where she can see dozens of handsome young men, and contrast one with another, than hide her away here, until some attractive young Lucifer comes along—a very Son of the Morning! How can the girl help falling in love, if she sees but one man, and he elegant, accomplished, handsome, and full of winning ways, even though his hidden heart be black with selfishness?"

But Aunt Grace always looked at the shadowy side. Even if the sun shone bright above, she thought of the clouds that were gathering somewhere, and destined ere long to darken the whole horizon.

On the day following, Mr. Markland went again to the city, and was gone until late in the evening. His mind was as much occupied as on the evening previous, and he spent the hours from tea-time until eleven o'clock in the library, writing. If Mrs. Markland did not appear to notice any change in her husband since Mr. Lyon came to Woodbine Lodge, it was not that the change had escaped her. No—she was too deeply interested in all that concerned him to fail in noting every new aspect of thought or feeling. He had said nothing of awakened purpose, quickened into activity by long conferences with his guest, but she saw that such purposes were forming. Of their nature she was in entire ignorance. That they would still further estrange him from Woodbine Lodge, she had too good reason, in a knowledge of his character, to fear. With him, whatever became a pursuit absorbed all others; and he looked to the end with a visions so intent, that all else was seen in obscurity. And so, with a repressed sigh, this gentle, true-hearted, loving woman, whose thought rarely turned in upon herself, awaited patiently the time when her husband would open to her what was in his thoughts. And the time, she knew, was not distant.

CHAPTER VI.

BEFORE Mr. Lyon's visit to Woodbine Lodge, Mr. Markland rarely went to the city. Now, scarcely a day passed that he did not order his carriage immediately after breakfast; and he rarely came back until nightfall. "Some matters of business," he would answer to the questions of his family; but he gave no intimation as to the nature of the business, and evidently did not care to be inquired of too closely.

"What's come over Edward? He isn't the same man that he was a month ago," said Miss Grace, as she stood in the portico, beside Mrs. Markland, one morning, looking after the carriage which was bearing her brother off to the city. There had been a hurried parting with Mr. Markland, who seemed more absorbed than usual in his own thoughts.

Mrs. Markland sighed faintly, but made no answer.

"I wonder what takes him off to town, post-haste, every day?"

"Business, I suppose," was the half-absent remark.

"Business! What kind of business, I'd like to know?"

"Edward has not informed me as to that," quietly answered Mrs. Markland.

"Indeed!" a little querulously. "Why don't you ask him?"

"I am not over-anxious on the subject. If he has any thing to confide to me, he will do it in his own good time."

"Oh! you're too patient." The tone and manner of Miss Grace showed that she, at least, was not overstocked with the virtue.

"Why should I be impatient?"

"Why? Goodness me! Do you suppose that if I had a husband—and it's a blessed thing for me that I haven't—that I'd see him going off, day after day, with lips sealed like an oyster, and remain as patient as a pet lamb tied with a blue ribbon? Oh dear! no! Grace Markland's made of warmer stuff than that. I like people who talk right out. *I* always do. Then you know where to place them. But Edward always had a hidden way about him."

"Oh, no, Grace; I will not agree to that for a moment," said Mrs. Markland.

"Won't you, indeed! I'm his sister, and ought to know something about him."

"And I'm his wife," was the gentle response to this.

"I know you are, and a deal too good for him—the provoking man!" said

Grace, in her off-hand way, drawing her arm within that of Mrs. Markland, to whom she was strongly attached. "And that's what riles me up so."

"Why, you're in a strange humour, Grace! Edward has done nothing at which I can complain."

"He hasn't, indeed?"

"No."

"I'd like to know what he means by posting off to the city every day for a week at a stretch, and never so much as breathing to his wife the purpose of his visits?"

"Business. He said that business required his attention."

"What business?"

"As to that, he did not think it necessary to advise me. Men do not always explain business matters to their wives. One-half would not understand what they were talking about, and the other half would take little interest in the subject."

"A compliment to wives, certainly!" said Grace Markland, with a rather proud toss of her head. "One of your lords of creation would find different stuff in me. But I'm not satisfied with Edward's goings on, if you are, Agnes. It's my opinion that your Mr. Lee Lyon is at the bottom of all this."

A slight shade dimmed the face of Mrs. Markland. She did not reply; but looked, with a more earnest expression, at her sister-in-law.

"Yes—your Mr. Lee Lyon." Grace was warming again. "He's one of your men that cast shadows wherever they go. I felt it the moment his foot crossed our threshold—didn't you?"

Grace gave thought and words to what, with Mrs. Markland, had only been a vague impression. She had felt the shadow of his presence without really perceiving from whence the shadow came. Pausing only a moment for an answer to her query, Grace went on:—

"Mr. Lyon is at the bottom of all this, take my word for it; and if he doesn't get Edward into trouble before he's done with him, my name's not Grace Markland."

"Trouble! What do you mean, Grace?" Another shade of anxiety flitted over the countenance of Mrs. Markland.

"Don't you suppose that Edward's going to town every day has something to do with this Mr. Lyon?"

"Mr. Lyon went South nearly two weeks ago," was answered.

"That doesn't signify. He's a schemer and an adventurer—I could see it in every lineament of his face—and, there's not a shadow of doubt in my mind, has got Edward interested in some of his doings. Why, isn't it as plain as daylight? Were not he and Edward all-absorbed about something while he was here? Didn't he remain a week when he had to be urged, at first, to stay a single day? And hasn't Edward been a different man since he left, from what he was before he came?"

"Your imagination is too active, Grace," Mrs. Markland replied, with a faint smile. "I don't see any necessary connection between Mr. Lyon and the business that requires Edward's attention in the city. The truth is, Edward has grown weary of an idle life, and I shall not at all regret his attention to some pursuit that will occupy his thoughts. No man, with his mental and bodily powers in full vigour, should be inactive."

"That will altogether depend on the direction his mind takes," said Grace.

"Of course. And I do not see any good reason you have for intimating that in the present case the right direction has not been taken." There was just perceptible a touch of indignation in the voice of Mrs. Markland, which, being perceived by Grace, brought the sententious remark,—

"Fore-warned, fore-armed. If my suspicion is baseless, no one is injured."

Just then, Fanny, the oldest daughter, returned from a short walk, and passed her mother and aunt on the portico, without looking up or speaking. There was an air of absent-mindedness about her.

"I don't know what has come over Fanny," said Mrs. Markland. "She isn't at all like herself." And as she uttered these words, not meaning them for other ears than her own, she followed her daughter into the house.

"Don't know what's come over Fanny!" said Aunt Grace to herself, as she moved up and down the vine-wreathed portico—"well, well,—some people *are* blind. This is like laying a block in a man's way, and wondering that he should fall down. Don't know what's come over Fanny? Dear! dear!"

Enough had been said by her sister-in-law to give direction to the vague anxieties awakened in the mind of Mrs. Markland by the recent deportment of her husband. He was not only absent in the city every day, but his mind was so fully occupied when at home, that he took little interest in the family circle. Sometimes he remained alone in the library until a late hour at night; and his sleep, when he did retire, was not sound; a fact but too well known to his wakeful partner.

All through this day there was an unusual pressure on the feelings of Mrs. Markland. When she inquired of herself as to the cause, she tried to be satisfied with assigning it wholly to the remarks of her sister-in-law, and not to any really existing source of anxiety. But in this she was far from being successful; and the weight continued to grow heavier as the hours moved on. Earlier than she had expected its return, the carriage was announced, and Mrs. Markland, with a suddenly-lightened heart, went tripping over the lawn to meet her husband at the outer gate. "Where is Mr. Markland?" she exclaimed, growing slightly pale, on reaching the carriage, and seeing that it was empty.

"Gone to New York," answered the coachman, at the same time handing a letter.

"To New York! When did he go?" Mrs. Markland's thoughts were thrown into sudden confusion.

"He went at five o'clock, on business. Said he must be there to-morrow morning. But he'll tell you all about it in the letter, ma'am."

Recovering herself, Mrs. Markland stepped from the side of the carriage, and as it passed on, she broke the seal of her letter, which she found to contain one for Fanny, directed in a hand with which she was not familiar.

"A letter for you, dear," she said; for Fanny was now by her side.

"Who is it from? Where is father?" asked Fanny in the same breath.

"Your father has gone to New York," said Mrs. Markland, with forced composure.

Fanny needed no reply to the first question; her heart had already given the answer. With a flushed cheek and quickening pulse, she bounded away from her mother's side, and returning into the house, sought the retirement of her own chamber.

"Dear Agnes,"—so ran the note of Mr. Markland to his wife,—"I know that you will be surprised and disappointed at receiving only a letter, instead of your husband. But some matters in New York require my attention, and I go on by the evening train, to return day after to-morrow. I engaged to transact some important business for Mr. Lyon, when he left for the South, and in pursuance of this, I am now going away. In a letter received from Mr. Lyon, to-day, was one for Fanny. I do not know its contents. Use your own discretion about giving it to her. You will find it enclosed. My mind has been so much occupied to-day, that I could not give the subject the serious consideration it requires. I leave it with you, having more faith in your intuitions than in my own judgment. He did not hint, even remotely, at a correspondence with Fanny, when he left; nor has he mentioned the fact of enclosing a letter for her in the one received from him to-day. Thus, delicately, has he left the matter in our hands. Perhaps you had better retain the letter until I return. We can then digest the subject more thoroughly. But, in order to furnish your mind some basis to rest upon, I will say, that during the time Mr. Lyon was here I observed him very closely; and that every thing about him gave me the impression of a pure, high-minded, honourable man. Such is the testimony borne in his favour by letters from men of standing in England, by whom he is trusted with large interests. I do not think an evidence of prepossession for our daughter, on his part, need occasion anxiety, but rather pleasure. Of course, she is too young to leave the home-nest for two or three years yet. But time is pressing, and my mind is in no condition, just now, to think clearly on a subject involving such important results. I think, however, that you had better keep the letter until my return. It will be the most prudent course."

Keep the letter! Its contents were already in the heart of Fanny!

"Where's Edward? What's the matter?" queried Aunt Grace, coming up at this moment, and seeing that all colour had left the cheeks of Mrs. Markland.

Scarcely reflecting on what she did, the latter handed her husband's letter in silence to her sister-in-law, and tottered, rather than walked, to a garden chair near at hand.

"Well, now, here is pretty business, upon my word!" exclaimed Aunt Grace, warmly. "Sending a letter to our Fanny! Who ever heard of such assurance! Oh! I knew that some trouble would come of his visit here. I felt it the moment I set my eyes on him. Keep the letter from Fanny? Of course you will; and when you have a talk with Edward about it, just let me be there; I want my say."

"It is too late," murmured the unhappy mother, in a low, sad voice.

"Too late! How? What do you mean, Agnes?"

"Fanny has the letter already."

"What!" There was a sharp, thrusting rebuke in the voice of Aunt Grace, that seemed like a sword in the heart of Mrs. Markland.

"She stood by me when I opened her father's letter, enclosing the one for her. I did not dream from whence it came, and handed it to her without a thought."

"Agnes! Agnes! What have you done?" exclaimed Aunt Grace, in a troubled voice.

"Nothing for which I need reproach myself," said Mrs. Markland, now

33

grown calmer. "Had the discretion been left with me, I should not have given Fanny the letter until Edward returned. But it passed to her hands through no will of mine. With the Great Controller of events it must now be left."

"Oh dear! Don't talk about the Controller of events in a case of this kind. Wise people control such things through the wisdom given them. I always think of Jupiter and the wagoner, when I hear any one going on this way."

Aunt Grace was excited. She usually was when she thought earnestly. But her warmth of word and manner rarely disturbed Mrs. Markland, who knew her thoroughly, and valued her for her good qualities and strong attachment to the family. No answer was made, and Aunt Grace added, in a slightly changed voice,—

"I don't know that you are so much to blame, Agnes, seeing that Fanny saw the letter, and that you were ignorant of its contents. But Edward might have known that something like this would happen. Why didn't he put the letter into his pocket, and keep it until he came home? He seems to have lost his common sense. And then he must go off into that rigmarole about Mr. Lyon, and try to make him out a saint, as if to encourage you to give his letter to Fanny. I've no patience with him! Mr. Lyon, indeed! If he doesn't have a heart-scald of him before he's done with him, I'm no prophet. Important business for Mr. Lyon! Why didn't Mr. Lyon attend to his own business when he was in New York? Oh! I can see through it all, as clear as daylight. He's got his own ends to gain through Edward, who is blind and weak enough to be led by him."

"Hasty in judgment as ever," said Mrs. Markland, with a subdued, resigned manner, as she arose and commenced moving toward the house, her sister-in-law walking by her side,—"and quick to decide upon character. But neither men nor women are to be read at a glance."

"So much the more reason for holding strangers at arms' length," returned Aunt Grace.

But Mrs. Markland felt in no mood for argument on so fruitless a subject. On entering the house, she passed to her own private apartment, there to commune with herself alone.

CHAPTER VII.

ONLY a few minutes had Mrs. Markland been in her room, when the door

34

opened quietly, and Fanny's light foot-fall was in her ears. She did not look up; but her heart beat with a quicker motion, and her breath was half-suspended.

"Mother!"

She lifted her bowed head, and met the soft, clear eyes of her daughter looking calmly down into her own.

"Fanny, dear!" she said, in half-surprise, as she placed an arm around her, and drew her closely to her side.

An open letter was in Fanny's hand, and she held it toward her mother. There was a warmer hue upon her face, as she said,—

"It is from Mr. Lyon."

"Shall I read it?" inquired Mrs. Markland.

"I have brought it for you to read," was the daughter's answer.

The letter was brief:

"To MISS FANNY MARKLAND:

"As I am now writing to your father, I must fulfil a half promise, made during my sojourn at Woodbine Lodge, to write to you also. Pleasant days were those to me, and they will ever make a green spot in my memory. What a little paradise enshrines you! Art, hand in hand with Nature, have made a world of beauty for you to dwell in. Yet, all is but a type of moral beauty—and its true enjoyment is only for those whose souls are attuned to deeper harmonies.

"Since leaving Woodbine Lodge, my thoughts have acquired a double current. They run backward as well as forward. The true hospitality of your manly-hearted father; the kind welcome to a stranger, given so cordially by your gentle, good mother; and your own graceful courtesy, toward one in whom you had no personal interest, charmed—nay, touched me with a sense of gratitude. To forget all this would be to change my nature. Nor can I shut out the image of Aunt Grace, so reserved but lady-like in her deportment; yet close in observation and quick to read character. I fear I did not make a good impression on her—but she may know me better one of these days. Make to her my very sincere regards.

"And now, what more shall I say? A first letter to a young lady is usually a thing of shreds and patches, made up of sentences that might come in almost any other connection; and mine is no exception to the rule. I do not ask an answer; yet I will say, that I know nothing that would give me more pleasure than such a favour from your hand.

"Remember me in all kindness and esteem to your excellent parents.

"Sincerely yours,
LEE LYON."

The deep breath taken by Mrs. Markland was one of relief. And yet, there was something in the letter that left her mind in uncertainty as to the real intentions of Mr. Lyon. Regret that he should have written at all mingled with certain pleasing emotions awakened by the graceful compliments of their late guest.

"It's a beautiful letter, isn't it, mother?"

"Yes, love," was answered almost without reflection.

Fanny re-folded the letter, with the care of one who was handling something precious.

"Shall I answer it?" she inquired.

"Not now. We must think about that. You are too young to enter into correspondence with a gentleman—especially with one about whom we know so little. Before his brief visit to Woodbine Lodge, we had never so much as heard of Mr. Lyon."

A slight shade of disappointment crossed the bright young face of Fanny Markland—not unobserved by her mother.

"It would seem rude, were I to take no notice of the letter whatever," said she, after reflecting a moment.

"Your father can acknowledge the receipt for you, when he writes to Mr. Lyon."

"But would that do?" asked Fanny, in evident doubt.

"O yes, and is, in my view, the only right course. We know but little, if any thing, about Mr. Lyon. If he should not be a true man, there is no telling how much you might suffer in the estimation of right-minded people, by his representation that you were in correspondence with him. A young girl can never be too guarded, on this point. If Mr. Lyon is a man worthy of your respect, he will be disappointed in you, if he receive an answer to his letter, under your own hand."

"Why, mother? Does he not say that he knows of nothing that would give him more pleasure than to receive an answer from me?" Fanny spoke with animation.

"True, my child, and that part of his letter I like least of all."

"Why so?" inquired the daughter.

"Have you not gathered the answer to your own question from what I have already said? A true man, who had a genuine respect for a young lady, would not desire, on so slight an acquaintance, to draw her into a correspondence; therefore the fact that Mr. Lyon half invites you to a correspondence, causes doubts to arise in my mind. His sending you a letter at all, when he is yet to us almost an entire stranger, I cannot but regard as a breach of the hospitalities

36

extended to him."

"Is not that a harsh judgment?" said Fanny, a warmer hue mantling her face.

"Reflect calmly, my child, and you will not think so."

"Then I ought not to answer this letter?" said Fanny, after musing for some time.

"Let your father, in one of his letters, acknowledge the receipt for you. If Mr. Lyon be a true man, he will respect you the more."

Not entirely satisfied, though she gave no intimation of this, Fanny returned to the seclusion of her own room, to muse on so unexpected a circumstance; and as she mused, the beating of her heart grew quicker. Again she read the letter from Mr. Lyon, and again and again conned it over, until every sentence was imprinted on her memory. She did not reject the view taken by her mother; nay, she even tried to make it her own; but, for all this, not the shadow of a doubt touching Mr. Lyon could find a place in her thoughts. Before her mental vision he stood, the very type of noble manhood.

CHAPTER VIII.

WHAT an error had been committed! How painfully was this realized by Mrs. Markland. How often had she looked forward, with a vague feeling of anxiety, to the time, yet far distant—she had believed—when the heart-strings of her daughter would tremble in musical response to the low-breathed voice of love—and now that time had come. Alas! that it had come so soon—ere thought and perception had gained matured strength and wise discrimination. The voice of the charmer was in her ears, and she was leaning to hearken.

Fanny did not join the family at the tea-table on that evening; and on the next morning, when she met her mother, her face was paler than usual, and her eyes drooped under the earnest gaze that sought to read her very thoughts. It was plain, from her appearance, that her sleep had been neither sound nor refreshing.

Mrs. Markland deemed it wisest to make no allusion to what had occurred on the previous evening. Her views in regard to answering Mr. Lyon's letter had been clearly expressed, and she had no fear that her daughter would act in opposition to them. Most anxiously did she await her husband's return. Thus far in life they had, in all important events, "seen eye to eye," and she had ever reposed full confidence in his judgment. If that confidence wavered in any degree now, it had been disturbed through his seeming entire trust in Mr. Lyon.

Aunt Grace had her share of curiosity, and she was dying, as they say, to know what was in Fanny's letter. The non-appearance of her niece at the tea-table had disappointed her considerably; and it was as much as she could do to keep from going to her room during the evening. Sundry times she tried to discover whether Mrs. Markland had seen the letter or, not, but the efforts were unsuccessful; the mother choosing for the present not to enter into further conversation with her on the subject.

All eye and all ear was Aunt Grace on the next morning, when Fanny made her appearance; but only through the eye was any information gathered, and that of a most unsatisfactory character. The little said by Fanny or her mother, was as a remote as possible from the subject that occupied most nearly their thoughts. Aunt Grace tried in various ways to lead them in the direction she would have them go; but it was all in vain that she asked questions touching the return of her brother, and wondered what could have taken him off to New York in such a hurry; no one made any satisfactory reply. At last, feeling a little chafed, and, at the same time, a little malicious, she said—

"That Mr. Lyon's at the bottom of this business."

The sentence told, as she had expected and intended. Fanny glanced quickly toward her, and a crimson spot burned on her cheek. But no word passed her lips. "So much gained," thought Aunt Grace; and then she said aloud—

"I've no faith in the man myself."

This, she believed, would throw Fanny off of her guard; but she was mistaken. The colour deepened on the young girl's cheeks, but she made no response.

"If he doesn't get Edward into trouble before he's done with him, I'm no prophet," added Aunt Grace, with a dash of vinegar in her tones.

"Why do you say that?" asked Mrs. Markland, who felt constrained to speak.

"I've no opinion of the man, and never had from the beginning, as you are very well aware," answered the sister-in-law.

"Our estimate of character should have a sounder basis than mere opinion,

38

or, to speak more accurately—prejudice," said Mrs. Markland.

"I don't know what eyes were given us for, if we are not to see with them," returned Aunt Grace, dogmatically. "But no wonder so many stumble and fall, when so few use their eyes. There isn't that man living who does not bear, stamped upon his face, the symbols of his character. And plainly enough are these to be seen in the countenance of Mr. Lyon."

"And how do you read them, Aunt Grace?" inquired Fanny, with a manner so passionless, that even the sharp-sighted aunt was deceived in regard to the amount of feeling that lay hidden in her heart.

"How do I read them? I'll tell you. I read them as the index to a whole volume of scheming selfishness. The man is unsound at the core." Aunt Grace was tempted by the unruffled exterior of her niece to speak thus strongly. Her words went deeper than she had expected. Fanny's face crimsoned instantly to the very temples, and an indignant light flashed in her soft blue eyes.

"Objects often take their colour from the medium through which we see them," she said quickly, and in a voice considerably disturbed, looking, as she spoke, steadily and meaningly at her aunt.

"And so you think the hue is in the medium, and not in the object?" said Aunt Grace, her tone a little modified.

"In the present instance, I certainly do," answered Fanny, with some ardour.

"Ah, child! child!" returned her aunt, "this may be quite as true in your case as in mine. Neither of us may see the object in its true colour. You will, at least, admit this to be possible."

"Oh, yes."

"And suppose you see it in a false colour?"

"Well?" Fanny seemed a little bewildered.

"Well? And what then?" Aunt Grace gazed steadily upon the countenance of Fanny, until her eyes drooped to the floor. "To whom is it of most consequence to see aright?"

Sharp-seeing, but not wise Aunt Grace! In the blindness of thy anxiety for Fanny, thou art increasing her peril. What need for thee to assume for the maiden, far too young yet to have the deeper chords of womanhood awakened in her heart to love's music, that the evil or good in the stranger's character might be any thing to her?

"You talk very strangely, Grace," said Mrs. Markland, with just enough of rebuke in her voice to make her sister-in-law conscious that she was going too far. "Perhaps we had better change the subject," she added, after the pause of a few moments.

"As you like," coldly returned Aunt Grace, who soon after left the room, feeling by no means well satisfied with herself or anybody else. Not a word had been said to her touching the contents of Fanny's letter, and in that fact was indicated a want of confidence that considerably annoyed her. She had not, certainly, gone just the right way about inviting confidence; but this defect in her own conduct was not seen very clearly.

A constrained reserve marked the intercourse of mother, daughter, and aunt during the day; and when night came, and the evening circle was formed as usual, how dimly burned the hearth-fire, and how sombre were the shadows cast by its flickering blaze! Early they separated, each with a strange pressure on the feelings, and a deep disquietude of heart.

Most of the succeeding day Fanny kept apart from the family; spending a greater portion of the time alone in her room. Once or twice it crossed the mother's thought, that Fanny might be tempted to answer the letter of Mr. Lyon, notwithstanding her promise not to do so for the present. But she repelled the thought instantly, as unjust to her beautiful, loving, obedient child. Still, Fanny's seclusion of herself weighed on her mind, and led her several times to go into her room. Nothing, either in her manner or employment, gave the least confirmation to the vague fear which had haunted her.

The sun was nearly two hours above the horizon, when Fanny left the house, and bent her steps towards a pleasant grove of trees that stood some distance away. In the midst of the grove, which was not far from the entrance-gate to her father's beautiful grounds, was a summer-house, in Oriental style, close beside an ornamental fountain. This was the favourite resort of the maiden, and thither she now retired, feeling certain of complete seclusion, to lose herself in the bewildering mazes of love's young dream. Before the eyes of her mind, one form stood visible, and that a form of manly grace and beauty,—the very embodiment of all human excellence. The disparaging words of her aunt had, like friction upon a polished surface, only made brighter to her vision the form which the other had sought to blacken. What a new existence seemed opening before her, with new and higher capacities for enjoyment! The half-closed bud had suddenly unfolded itself in the summer air, and every blushing petal thrilled with a more exquisite sense of life.

Every aspect of nature—and all her aspects were beautiful there—had a new charm for the eyes of Fanny Markland. The silvery waters cast upward by the fountain fell back in rainbow showers, ruffling the tiny lake beneath, and filling the air with a low, dreamy murmur. Never had that lovely creation of art, blending with nature, looked so like an ideal thing as now—a very growth of fairy-land. The play of the waters in the air was as the glad motions of a living form.

Around this fountain was a rosary of white and red roses, encircled again by arbor-vitae; and there were statues of choice workmanship, the ideals of modern art, lifting their pure white forms here and there in chastened loveliness. All this was shut in from observation by a stately grove of elms. And here it was that the maiden had come to hide herself from observation, and dream her waking dream of love. What a world of enchantment was dimly opening before her, as her eye ran down the Eden-vistas of the future! Along those aisles of life she saw herself moving, beside a stately one, who leaned toward her, while she clung to him as a vine to its firm support. Even while in the mazes of this delicious dream, a heavy footfall startled her, and she sprang to her feet with a suddenly-stilled pulsation. In the next instant a manly form filled the door of the summer-house, and a manly voice exclaimed:

"Miss Markland! Fanny! do I find you here?"

The colour left the maiden's cheeks for an instant. Then they flushed to deep crimson. But her lips were sealed. Surprise took away, for a time, the power of speech.

"I turned aside," said the intruder, "as I came up the avenue, to have a look at this charming spot, so well remembered; but dreamed not of finding you here."

He had already approached Fanny, and was holding one of her hands tightly in his, while he gazed upon her face with a look of glowing admiration.

"Oh, Mr. Lyon! How you have startled me!" said Fanny, as soon as she could command her voice.

"And how you tremble! There, sit down again, Miss Markland, and calm yourself. Had I known you were here, I should not have approached so abruptly. But how have you been since my brief absence? And how is your good father and mother?"

"Father is in New York," replied Fanny.

"In New York! I feared as much." And a slight shade crossed the face of Mr. Lyon, who spoke as if off of his guard. "When did he go?"

"Yesterday."

41

"Ah! Did he receive a letter from me?"

"Yes, sir." Fanny's eyes drooped under the earnest gaze that was fixed upon her.

"I hoped to have reached here as soon as my letter. This is a little unfortunate." The aspect of Mr. Lyon became grave.

"When will your father return?" he inquired.

"I do not know."

Again Mr. Lyon looked serious and thoughtful. For some moments he remained abstracted; and Fanny experienced a slight feeling of timidity, as she looked upon his shadowed face. Arousing himself, he said:

"This being the case, I shall at once return South."

"Not until to-morrow," said Fanny.

"This very night," answered Mr. Lyon.

"Then let us go to the Lodge at once," and Fanny made a motion to rise. "My mother will be gratified to see you, if it is only for a few moments."

But Mr. Lyon placed a hand upon her arm, and said:

"Stay, Miss Markland—that cannot now be. I must return South without meeting any other member of your family. Did you receive my letter?" he added, abruptly, and with a change of tone and manner.

Fanny answered affirmatively; and his quick eye read her heart in voice and countenance.

"When I wrote, I had no thought of meeting you again so soon. But a few hours after despatching the letter to your father, enclosing yours—a letter on business of importance, to me, at least—I received information that led me to wish an entire change in the programme of operations about to be adopted, through your father's agency. Fearing that a second letter might be delayed in the mails, I deemed it wisest to come on with the greatest speed myself. But I find that I am a day too late. Your father has acted promptly; and what he has done must not be undone. Nay, I do not wish him even to know that any change has been contemplated. Now, Miss Markland," and his voice softened as he bent toward the girlish form at his side, "may one so recently a stranger claim your confidence?"

"From my father and my mother I have no concealments," said Fanny.

"And heaven forbid that I should seek to mar that truly wise confidence," quickly answered Mr. Lyon. "All I ask is, that, for the present, you mention to no one the fact that I have been here. Our meeting in this place is purely accidental—providential, I will rather say. My purpose in coming was, as already explained, to meet your father. He is away, and on business that at once sets aside all necessity for seeing him. It will now be much better that he should not even know of my return from the South—better for me, I mean; for the interests that might suffer are mine alone. But let me explain a little, that you may act understandingly. When I went South, your father very kindly consented to transact certain business left unfinished by me in New York. Letters received on my arrival at Savannah, advised me of the state of the business, and I wrote to your father, in what way to arrange it for me; by the next mail other letters came, showing me different aspect of affairs and rendering a change of plan very desirable. It was to explain this fully to your father, that I came on. But as it is too late, I do not wish him even to know, for the present, that a change was contemplated. I fear it might lessen, for a time, his confidence in my judgment—something I do not fear when he knows me better. Your since, for the present, my dear Miss Markland, will nothing affect your father, who has little or no personal interest in the matter, but may serve me materially. Say, then, that, until you hear from me again, on the subject, you will keep your own counsel."

"You say that my father has no interest in the business, to which you refer?" remarked Fanny. Her mind was bewildered.

"None whatever. He is only, out of a generous good-will, trying to serve the son of an old business friend," replied Mr. Lyon, confidently. "Say, then, Fanny,"—his voice was insinuating, and there was something of the serpent's fascination in his eyes—"that you will, for my sake, remain, for the present, silent on the subject of this return from the South."

As he spoke, he raised one of her hands to his lips, and kissed it. Still more bewildered—nay, charmed—Fanny did not make even a faint struggle to withdraw her hand. In the next moment, his hot lips had touched her pure forehead—and in the next moment, "Farewell!" rung hurriedly in her ears. As the retiring form of the young adventurer stood in the door of the summer-house, there came to her, with a distinct utterance, these confidently spoken words—"I trust you without fear."—And "God bless you!" flung toward her with a heart-impulse, found a deeper place in her soul, from whence, long afterwards, came back their thrilling echoes. By the time the maiden had gathered up her scattered thoughts, she was alone.

CHAPTER IX.

THE maiden's thoughts were yet bewildered, and her heart beating tumultuously, when her quick ears caught the sound of other footsteps than those to whose retreating echoes she had been so intently listening. Hastily retreating into the summer-house, she crouched low upon one of the seats, in order, if possible, to escape observation. But nearer and nearer came the slow, heavy foot-fall of a man, and ere she had time to repress, by a strong effort, the agitation that made itself visible in every feature, Mr. Allison was in her presence. It was impossible for her to restrain an exclamation of surprise, or to drive back the crimson from her flushing face.

"Pardon the intrusion," said the old gentleman, in his usual mild tone. "If I had known that you were here, I would not have disturbed your pleasant reveries."

Some moments elapsed, ere Fanny could venture a reply. She feared to trust her voice, lest more should be betrayed than she wished any one to know. Seeing how much his presence disturbed her, Mr. Allison stepped back a pace or two, saying, as he did so, "I was only passing, my child; and will keep on my way. I regret having startled you by my sudden appearance."

He was about retiring, when Fanny, who felt that her manner must strike Mr. Allison as very singular, made a more earnest effort to regain her self-possession, and said, with a forced smile:

"Don't speak of intrusion; Mr. Allison. Your sudden coming did startle me. But that is past."

Mr. Allison, who had partly turned away, now advanced toward Fanny, and, taking her hand, looked down into her face, from which the crimson flush had not yet retired, with an expression of tender regard.

"Your father is still absent, I believe?" said he.

"Yes, sir."

"He will be home soon."

"We hope so. His visit to New York was unexpected."

"And you therefore feel his absence the more."

"Oh, yes," replied Fanny, now regaining her usual tone of voice and easy address; "and it seems impossible for us to be reconciled to the fact."

"Few men are at home more than your father," remarked Mr. Allison. "His world, it might be said, is included in the circle of his beloved ones."

44

"And I hope it will always be so."

Mr. Allison looked more earnestly into the young maiden's face. He did not clearly understand the meaning of this sentence, for, in the low tones that gave it utterance, there seemed to his ear a prophecy of change. Then he remembered his recent conversation with her father, and light broke in upon his mind. The absence of Mr. Markland had, in all probability, following the restless, dissatisfied state, which all had observed, already awakened the concern of his family, lest it should prove only the beginning of longer periods of absence.

"Business called your father to New York," said Mr. Allison.

"Yes; so he wrote home to mother. He went to the city in the morning, and we expected him back as usual in the evening, but he sent a note by the coachman, saying that letters just received made it necessary for him to go on to New York immediately."

"He is about entering into business again, I presume."

"Oh, I hope not!" replied Fanny.

Mr. Allison remained silent for some moments, and then said—

"I thought your visitor, Mr. Lyon, went South several days ago."

"So he did," answered Fanny, in a quickened tone of voice, and with a manner slightly disturbed.

"Then I was in error," said Mr. Allison, speaking partly to himself. "I thought I passed him in the road, half an hour ago. The resemblance was at least a very close one. You are certain he went South?"

"Oh! yes, sir," replied Fanny, quickly.

Mr. Allison looked intently upon her, until her eyes wavered and fell to the ground. He continued to observe her for some moments, and only withdrew his gaze when he saw that she was about to look up. A faint sigh parted the old man's lips. Ah! if a portion of his wisdom, experience, and knowledge of character, could only be imparted to that pure young spirit, just about venturing forth into a world where mere appearances of truth deceive and fascinate!

"Does Mr. Lyon design returning soon from the South?"

"I heard him say to father that he did not think he would be in this part of the world again for six or eight months."

And again the eyes of Fanny shunned the earnest gaze of Mr. Allison.

"How far South does he go?"

"I am not able to answer you clearly; but I think I heard father say that he would visit Central America."

"Ah! He is something of a traveller, then?"

"Yes, sir; he has travelled a great deal."

"He is an Englishman?"

"Yes, sir. His father is an old business friend of my father's."

"So I understood."

There was a pause, in which Mr. Allison seemed to be thinking intently.

"It is a little singular, certainly," said he, as if speaking only to himself.

"What is singular?" asked Fanny, looking curiously at her companion.

"Why, that I should have been so mistaken. I doubted not, for a moment, that the person I saw was Mr. Lyon."

Fanny did not look up. If she had done so, the gaze fixed upon her would have sent a deeper crimson to her cheek than flushed it a few moments before.

"Have you any skill in reading character, Fanny?" asked Mr. Allison, in a changed and rather animated voice, and with a manner that took away the constraint that had, from the first, oppressed the mind of the young girl.

"No very great skill, I imagine," was the smiling answer.

"It is a rare, but valuable gift," said the old man. "I was about to call it an art; but it is more a gift than an art; for, if not possessed by nature, it is too rarely acquired. Yet, in all pure minds, there is something that we may call analogous—a perception of moral qualities in those who approach us. Have you never felt an instinctive repugnance to a person on first meeting him?"

"Oh, yes."

"And been as strongly attracted in other cases?"

"Often."

"Have you ever compared this impression with your subsequent knowledge of the person's character?"

Fanny thought for a little while, and then said—

"I am not sure that I have, Mr. Allison."

"You have found yourself mistaken in persons after some acquaintance with them?"

"Yes; more than once."

"And I doubt not, that if you had observed the impression these persons made on you when you met them for the first time, you would have found that impression a true index to their character. Scarcely noticing these first impressions, which are instinctive perceptions of moral qualities, we are apt to be deceived by the exterior which almost every one assumes on a first acquaintance; and then, if we are not adepts at reading character, we may be a long time in finding out the real quality. Too often this real character is manifested, after we have formed intimate relations with the person, that may not be dissolved while the heart knows a life-throb. Is that not a serious thought, Fanny?"

"It is, Mr. Allison,—a very serious, and a solemn thought."

"Do you think that you clearly comprehend my meaning?"

"I do not know that I see all you wish me to comprehend," answered Fanny.

"May I attempt to make it clearer?"

"I always listen to you with pleasure and profit, Mr. Allison," said Fanny.

"Did you ever think that your soul had senses as well as your body?" inquired the old man.

"You ask me a strange question. How can a mere spirit—an airy something, so to speak—have senses?"

"Do you never use the words—'I see it clearly'—meaning that you see some form of truth presented to your mind. As, for instance,—if I say, 'To be good is to be happy,' you will answer, 'Oh, yes; I see that clearly.' Your soul, then, has, at least, the sense of sight. And that it has the sense of taste also, will, I think, be clear to you, when you remember bow much you enjoy the reading of a good book, wherein is food for the mind. Healthy food is sometimes presented in so unpalatable a shape, that the taste rejects it; and so it is with truth, which is the mind's food. I instance this, to make it clearer to you. So you see that the soul has at least two senses—sight and taste. That it has feeling needs scarcely an illustration. The mind is hurt quite as easily as the body, and, the path of an injury is usually more permanent. The child who has been punished unjustly feels the injury inflicted on his spirit, days, months, and, it may be, years, after the body has lost the smarting consciousness of stripes. And you know that sharp words pierce the mind with acutest pain. We may speak daggers, as well as use them. Is this at all clear to you, Miss Markland?"

47

"Oh, very clear! How strange that I should never have thought of this myself! Yes—I see, hear, taste, and feel with my mind, as well as with my body."

"Think a little more deeply," said the old man. "If the mind have senses, must it not have a body?"

"A body! You are going too deep for me, Mr. Allison. We say mind and body, to indicate that one is immaterial, and the other substantial."

"May there not be such a thing as a spiritual as well as a material substance?"

"To say spiritual substance, sounds, in my ears, like a contradiction in terms," said Fanny.

"There must be a substance before there can be a permanent impression. The mind receives and retains the most lasting impressions; therefore, it must be an organized substance—but spiritual, not material. You will see this clearer, if you think of the endurance of habit. 'As the twig is bent, the tree's inclined,' is a trite saying that aptly illustrates the subject about which we are now conversing. If the mind were not a substance and a form, how could it receive and retain impressions?"

"True."

"And to advance a step further—if the mind have form, what is that form?"

"The human form, if any," was the answer.

"Yes. And of this truth the minds of all men have a vague perception. A cruel man is called a human monster. In thus speaking, no one thinks of the mere physical body, but of the inward man. About a good man, we say there is something truly human. And believe me, my dear young friend, that our spirits are as really organized substances as our bodies—the difference being, that one is an immaterial and the other a material substance; that we have a spiritual body, with spiritual senses, and all the organs and functions that appertain to the material body, which is only a visible and material outbirth from the spiritual body, and void of any life but what is thence derived."

"I see, vaguely, the truth of what you say," remarked Fanny, "and am bewildered by the light that falls into my mind."

"My purpose in all this," said Mr. Allison, "is to lead you to the perception of a most important fact. Still let your thoughts rest intently on what I am saying. You are aware of the fact, that material substances, as well inorganic as organic, are constantly giving off into the atmosphere minute particles, which we call odors, and which reveal to us their quality. The rose and nightshade, the hawthorn and cicuta fill the air around them with odors which our bodily senses instantly perceive. And it is the same with animals and men. Each has a surrounding material sphere, which is perceived on a near approach, and which indicates the material quality. Now, all things in nature are but effects from interior causes, and correspond to them in every minute particular. What is true of the body will be found true of the mind. Bodily form and sense are but the manifestation, in this outer world, of the body and senses that exist in the inner world. And if around the natural body there exist a sphere by which the natural senses may determine its quality of health or impurity, in like manner is there around the spiritual body a sphere of its quality, that may be discerned by the spiritual senses. And now come back to the philosophy of first impressions, a matter so little understood by the world. These first impressions are rarely at fault, and why? Because the spiritual quality is at once discerned by the spiritual sense. But, as this kind of perception does not fall into the region of thought, it is little heeded by the many. Some, in all times, have observed it more closely than others, and we have proverbs that could only have originated from such observation. We are warned to beware of that man from whose presence a little child shrinks. The reason to me is plain. The innocent spirit of the child is affected by the evil sphere of the man, as its body would be if brought near to a noxious plant that was filling the air with its poisonous vapours. And now, dear Fanny,"—Mr. Allison took the maiden's hand in his, and spoke in a most impressive voice —"think closely and earnestly on what I have said. If I have taxed your mind with graver thoughts than are altogether pleasant, it is because I desire most sincerely to do you good. The world into which you are about stepping, is a false and evil world, and along all its highways and byways are scattered the sad remains of those who have perished ere half their years were numbered; and of the crowd that pressed onward, even to the farthest verge of natural life, how few escape the too common lot of wretchedness! The danger that most threatens you, in the fast-approaching future, is that which threatens every young maiden. Your happiness or misery hangs nicely poised, and if you have not a wise discrimination, the scale may take a wrong preponderance. Alas! if it should be so!"

Mr. Allison paused a moment, and then said:

"Shall I go on?"

"Oh, yes! Speak freely. I am listening to your words as if they came from the lips of my own father."

"An error in marriage is one of life's saddest errors, said Mr. Allison.

"I believe that," was the maiden's calm remark; yet Mr. Allison saw that her eyes grew instantly brighter, and the hue of her cheeks warmer.

"In a *true* marriage, there must be good moral qualities. No pure-minded woman can love a man for an instant after she discovers that he is impure, selfish, and evil. It matters not how high his rank, how brilliant his intellect, how attractive his exterior person, how perfect his accomplishments. In her inmost spirit she will shrink from him, and feel his presence as a sphere of suffocation. Oh! can the thought imagine a sadder lot for a true-hearted woman! And there is no way of escape. Her own hands have wrought the chains that bind her in a most fearful bondage."

Again Mr. Allison paused, and regarded his young companion with a look of intense interest.

"May heaven spare you from such a lot!" he said, in a low, subdued voice.

Fanny made no reply. She sat with her eyes resting on the ground, her lips slightly parted, and her cheeks of a paler hue.

"Can you see any truth in what I have been saying?" asked Mr. Allison, breaking in upon a longer pause than he had meant should follow his last remark.

"Oh, yes, yes; much truth. A new light seems to have broken suddenly into my mind."

"Men bear about them a spiritual as well as a natural sphere of their quality."

"If there is a spiritual form, there must be a spiritual quality," said Fanny, partly speaking to herself, as if seeking more fully to grasp the truth she uttered.

"And spiritual senses, as well, by which qualities may be perceived," added Mr. Allison.

"Yes,—yes." She still seemed lost in her own thoughts.

"As our bodily senses enable us to discern the quality of material objects, and thus to appropriate what is good, and reject what is evil; in like manner will our spiritual senses serve us, and in a much higher degree, if we will but make the effort to use them."

"I see but darkly. Oh! that my vision were clearer!" exclaimed the maiden, while a troubled expression slightly marred her beautiful face.

"Ever, my dear young friend," said Mr. Allison, impressively, "be true to your native instincts. They will quickly warn you, if evil approaches. Oh! heed the warning. Give no favourable regard to the man toward whom you feel an instinctive repulsion at the first meeting. No matter what his station, connections, or personal accomplishments—heed the significant warning. Do not let the fascinations of a brilliant exterior, nor even ardent expressions of regard, make you for a moment forget that, when he first came near you, your spirit shrunk away, as from something that would do it harm. If you observe such a man closely, weigh all that he does and says, when ardent in the pursuit of some desired object, you will not lack for more palpable evidences of his quality than the simple impression which the sphere of his life made at your first meeting. Guarded as men are, who make an exterior different from their real quality, they are never able to assume a perfect disguise—no more than a deformed person can so hide, by dress, the real shape, that the attentive eye cannot discern its lack of symmetry. The eyes of your spirit see truths, as your natural eyes see material objects; and truths are real things. There are true principles, which, if obeyed, lead to what is good; and there are false principles, which, if followed, lead to evil. The one conducts to happiness, the other to inevitable misery. The warning which another sense, corresponding with the perception of odours in the body, gives you of evil in a man, at his first approach, is intended to put you on your guard, and lead to a closer observation of the person. The eyes of your understanding, if kept clear, will soon give you evidence as to his quality that cannot be gainsaid. And, believe me, Fanny, though a slight acquaintance may seem to contradict the instinctive judgment, in nine cases out of ten the warning indication will be verified in the end. Do you understand me?"

"Oh, yes—yes," was the low, but earnest response. Yet the maiden's eyes were not lifted from the ground.

"Will you try and remember what I have said, Fanny?"

"I can never forget it, Mr. Allison—never!" She seemed deeply disturbed.

Both were silent for some time. Mr. Allison then said:

"But the day is waning, my dear young friend. It is time we were both at home."

"True." And Fanny arose and walked by the old man's side, until their ways diverged. Both of their residences were in sight and near at hand.

"Do not think of me, Fanny," said Mr. Allison, when about parting with his companion, "as one who would oppress you with thoughts too serious for your years. I know the dangers that lie in your path of life, and only seek to guard you from evil. Oh! keep your spirit pure, and its vision clear. Remember what I have said, and trust in the unerring instinct given to every innocent heart."

The old man had taken her hand, and was looking tenderly down upon her sweet, young face. Suddenly her eyes were lifted to his. There was a strong light in them.

"God bless you, sir!"

The energy with which these unexpected words were spoken, almost startled Mr. Allison. Ere he had time for a response, Fanny had turned from him, and was bounding away with fleet footsteps toward her home.

CHAPTER X.

EARNESTLY as Fanny Markland strove to maintain a calm exterior before her mother and aunt, the effort availed not; and so, as early in the evening as she could retire from the family, without attracting observation, she did so. And now she found herself in a state of deep disquietude. Far too young was the maiden to occupy, with any degree of calmness, the new position in which she was so unexpectedly placed. The sudden appearance of Mr. Lyon, just when his image was beginning to take the highest place in her mind, and the circumstances attending that appearance, had, without effacing the image, dimmed its brightness. Except for the interview with Mr. Allison, this effect might not have taken place. But his words had penetrated deeply, and awakened mental perceptions that it was now impossible to obscure by any fond reasonings in favour of Mr. Lyon. How well did Fanny now remember the instant repulsion felt towards this man, on their first meeting. She had experienced an instant constriction about the heart, as if threatened with suffocation. The shadow, too, about which Aunt Grace had spoken, had also been perceived by her. But in a little while, under the sunshine of a most fascinating exterior, all these first impressions were lost, and, but for the words of Mr. Allison, would have been regarded as false impressions. Too clearly had the wise old man presented the truth—too clearly had he elevated her thoughts into a region where the mind sees with a steadier vision—to leave her in danger of entering the wrong way, without a distinct perception that it was wrong.

In a single hour, Fanny's mind had gained a degree of maturity, which, under the ordinary progression of her life, would not have come for years. But for this, her young, pure heart would have yielded without a struggle. No voice of warning would have mingled in her ears with the sweet voice of the wooer. No string would have jarred harshly amid the harmonies of her life.

The lover who came to her with so many external blandishments—who attracted her with so powerful a magnetism—would have still looked all perfection in her eyes. Now, the film was removed; and if she could not see all that lay hidden beneath a fair exterior, enough was visible to give the sad conviction that evil might be there.

Yet was Fanny by no means inclined to turn herself away from Mr. Lyon. Too much power over her heart had already been acquired. The ideal of the man had grown too suddenly into a most palpable image of beauty and perfection. Earnestly did her heart plead for him. Sad, even to tears, was it, at the bare thought of giving him up. There was yet burning on her pure forehead the hot kiss he had left there a few hours before—her hand still felt his thrilling touch—his words of love were in her ears—she still heard the impassioned tones in which he had uttered his parting "God bless you!"

Thus it was with the gentle-hearted girl, exposed, far too soon in life, to influences which stronger spirits than hers could hardly have resisted.

Midnight found Mrs. Markland wakeful and thoughtful. She had observed something unusual about Fanny, and noted the fact of her early retirement, that evening, from the family. Naturally enough, she connected this change in her daughter's mind with the letter received from Mr. Lyon, and it showed her but too plainly that the stranger's image was fixing itself surely in the young girl's heart. This conviction gave her pain rather than pleasure. She, too, had felt that quick repulsion towards Mr. Lyon, at their first meeting, to which we have referred; and with her, no after acquaintance ever wholly removed the effect of a first experience like this.

Midnight, as we have said, found her wakeful and thoughtful. The real cause of her husband's absence was unknown to her; but, connecting itself, as it did, with Mr. Lyon,—he had written her that certain business, which he had engaged to transact for Mr. Lyon, required his presence in New York,—and following so soon upon his singularly restless and dissatisfied state of mind, the fact disquieted her. The shadow of an approaching change was dimming the cheerful light of her spirit.

Scarcely a moment since the reception of her husband's letter, enclosing one for Fanny, was the fact that Mr. Lyon had made advances toward her daughter—yet far too young to have her mind bewildered by love's mazy dream—absent from her mind. It haunted even her sleeping hours. And the more she thought of it, the more deeply it disturbed her. As an interesting, and even brilliant, companion, she had enjoyed his society. With more than usual interest had she listened to his varied descriptions of personages, places, and events; and she had felt more than a common admiration for his high mental accomplishments. But, whenever she imagined him the husband of her pure-hearted child, it seemed as if a heavy hand lay upon her bosom, repressing even respiration itself.

Enough was crowding into the mind of this excellent woman to drive slumber from her eyelids. The room adjoining was occupied by Fanny, and, as the communicating door stood open, she was aware that the sleep of her child was not sound. Every now and then she turned restlessly in her bed; and sometimes muttered incoherently. Several times did Mrs. Markland raise herself and lean upon her elbow, in a listening attitude, as words, distinctly spoken, fell from the lips of her daughter. At last the quickly uttered sentence, "Mother! mother! come!" caused her to spring from the bed and hurry to her child.

"What is it, Fanny? What has frightened you?" she said, in a gentle, encouraging voice. But Fanny only muttered something incoherent, in her sleep, and turned her face to the wall.

For several minutes did Mrs. Markland sit upon the bedside, listening, with an oppressed feeling, to the now calm respiration of her child. The dreams which had disturbed her sleep, seemed to have given place to other images. The mother was about returning to her own pillow, when Fanny said, in a voice of sad entreaty—

"Oh! Mr. Lyon! Don't! don't!"

There was a moment or two of breathless stillness, and then, with a sharp cry of fear, the sleeper started up, exclaiming—

"Mother! father! Oh, come to me! Come!"

"Fanny, my child!" was the mother's instant response, and the yet half-dreaming girl fell forward into her arms, which were closed tightly around her. What a strong thrill of terror was in every part of her frame!

"Dear Fanny! What ails you? Don't tremble so! You are safe in my arms. There, love, nothing shall harm you."

"Oh, mother! dear mother! is it you?" half sobbed the not yet fully-awakened girl.

"Yes, love. You are safe with your mother. But what have you been dreaming about?"

"Dreaming!" Fanny raised herself from her mother's bosom, and looked at her with a bewildered air.

"Yes, dear—dreaming. This is your own room, and you are on your own bed. You have only been frightened by a fearful dream."

"Only a dream! How thankful I am! Oh! it was terrible!"

"What was it about, daughter?" asked Mrs. Markland.

Fanny, whose mind was getting clearer and calmer, did not at once reply.

"You mentioned the name of Mr. Lyon," said the mother.

"Did I?" Fanny's voice expressed surprise.

"Yes. Was it of him that you were dreaming?"

"I saw him in my dream," was answered.

"Why were you afraid of him?"

"It was a very strange dream, mother—very strange," said Fanny, evidently not speaking from a free choice.

"I thought I was in our garden among the flowers. And as I stood there, Mr. Lyon came in through the gate and walked up to me. He looked just as he did when he was here; only it seemed that about his face and form there was even a manlier beauty. Taking my hand, he led me to one of the garden chairs, and we sat down side by side. And now I began to see a change in him. His eyes, that were fixed upon mine, grew brighter and deeper, until it seemed as if I could look far down into their burning depths. His breath came hot upon my face. Suddenly, he threw an arm around me, and then I saw myself in the strong folds of a great serpent! I screamed for help, and next found myself in your arms. Oh! it was a strange and a fearful dream!"

"And it may not be all a dream, Fanny," said Mrs. Markland, in a very impressive voice.

"Not all a dream, mother!" Fanny seemed startled at the words.

"No, dear. Dreams are often merely fantastic. But there come visions in sleep, sometimes, that are permitted as warnings, and truly represent things existing in real life."

"I do not understand you, mother."

"There is in the human mind a quality represented by the serpent, and also a quality represented by the dove. When our Saviour said of Herod, 'Go tell that fox,' he meant to designate the man as having the quality of a fox."

"But how does this apply to dreams?" asked Fanny.

"He who sends his angels to watch over and protect us in sleep, may permit them to bring before us, in dreaming images, the embodied form of some predominating quality in those whose association may do us harm. The low, subtle selfishness of the sensual principle will then take its true form of a wily serpent."

Fanny caught her breath once or twice, as these words fell upon her ears, and then said, in a deprecating voice—

"Oh, mother! Don't! don't!" And lifting her head from the bosom of her parent, she turned her face away, and buried it in the pillow. As she did not move for the space of several minutes, Mrs. Markland thought it unwise to intrude other remarks upon her, believing that the distinct image she had already presented would live in her memory and do its work. Soon after, she retired to her own room. Half an hour later, and both were sleeping, in quiet unconsciousness.

CHAPTER XI.

LATE on the following day, Mr. Markland arrived from New York. Eager as all had been for his return, there was something of embarrassment in the meeting. The light-hearted gladness with which every one welcomed him, even after the briefest absence, was not apparent now. In the deep, calm eyes of his wife, as he looked lovingly into them, he saw the shadow of an unquiet spirit. And the tears which no effort of self-control could keep back from Fanny's cheeks, as she caught his hand eagerly, and hid her face on his breast, answered too surely the question he most desired to ask. It was plain to him that Mr. Lyon's letter had found its way into her hands.

"I wish it had not been so!" was the involuntary mental ejaculation. A sigh parted his lips—a sigh that only the quick ears of his wife perceived, and only her heart echoed.

During the short time the family were together that evening, Mr. Markland noticed in Fanny something that gave him concern. Her eyes always fell instantly when he looked at her, and she seemed sedulously to avoid his gaze. If he spoke to her, the colour mounted to her face, and she seemed strangely embarrassed. The fact of her having received a letter from Mr. Lyon, the contents of which he knew, as it came open in one received by himself from that gentleman, was not a sufficient explanation of so entire a change in her deportment.

Mr. Markland sought the earliest opportunity to confer with his wife on the subject of Fanny's altered state of mind, and the causes leading thereto; but the conference did not result in much that was satisfactory to either of them.

"Have you said any thing to her about Mr. Lyon?" asked Mr. Markland.

"Very little," was answered. "She thought it would only be courteous to reply to his letter; but I told her that, if he were a true man, and had a genuine respect for her, he would not wish to draw her into a correspondence on so slight an acquaintance; and that the only right manner of response was through you."

"Through me!"

"Yes. Your acknowledgment, in Fanny's name, when you are writing to Mr. Lyon, will be all that he has a right to expect, and all that our daughter should be permitted to give."

"But if we restrict her to so cold a response, and that by second-hand, may she not be tempted to write to him without our knowledge?"

"No, Edward. I will trust her for that," was the unhesitating answer.

"She is very young," said Mr. Markland, as if speaking to himself.

"Oh, yes!" quickly returned his wife. "Years too young for an experience —or, I might say, a temptation—like this. I cannot but feel that, in writing to our child, Mr. Lyon abused the hospitality we extended to him."

"Is not that a harsh judgment, Agnes?"

"No, Edward. Fanny is but a child, and Mr. Lyon a man of mature experience. He knew that she was too young to be approached as he approached her."

"He left it with us, you know, Agnes; and with a manly delicacy that we ought neither to forget nor fail to appreciate."

The remark silenced, but in no respect changed the views of Mrs. Markland; and the conference on Fanny's state of mind closed without any satisfactory result.

The appearance of his daughter on the next morning caused Mr. Markland to feel a deeper concern. The colour had faded from her cheeks; her eyes were heavy, as if she had been weeping; and if she did not steadily avoid his gaze, she was, he could see, uneasy under it.

As soon as Mr. Markland had finished his light breakfast he ordered the carriage.

"You are not going to the city?" his wife said, with surprise and disappointment in her voice.

"Yes, Agnes, I must be in town to-day. I expect letters on business that will require immediate attention."

"Business, Edward! What business?"

The question appeared slightly to annoy Mr. Markland. But with a forced smile, and in his usual pleasant voice, he answered:

"Oh, nothing of very great importance, but still requiring my presence. Business is business, you know, and ought never to be neglected."

"Will you be home early?"

"Yes."

Mr. Markland walked out into the ample porch, and let his eyes range slowly over the objects that surrounded his dwelling. His wife stood by his side. The absence of a few days, amid other and less attractive scenes, had prepared his mind for a better appreciation of the higher beauties of "Woodbine Lodge." Something of the old feeling came over him; and as he stood silently gazing around, he could not but say, within himself, "If I do not find happiness here, I may look for it through the world in vain."

The carriage was driven round to the door, while he stood there. Fanny came out at the moment, and seeing her father about to step into it, sprang forward, and exclaimed—

"Why, father, you are not going away again?"

"Only to the city, love," he answered, as he turned to receive her kiss.

"To the city again? Why, you are away nearly all the time. Now I wish you wouldn't go so often."

"I will be home early in the afternoon. But come, Fanny, won't you go with me, to spend the day in town? It will be a pleasant change for you."

Fanny shook her head, and answered, "No."

Mr. Markland entered the carriage, waved his hand, and was soon gliding away toward the city. As soon as he was beyond the observation of his family, his whole manner underwent a change. An expression of deep thought settled over his face; and he remained in a state of profound abstraction during his whole ride to the city. On arriving there, he went to the office of an individual well known in the community as possessing ample means, and bearing the reputation of a most liberal, intelligent, and enterprising citizen.

"Good morning, Mr. Brainard," said Markland, with a blending of respect and familiarity in his voice.

"Ah, Mr. Markland!" returned the other, rising, and shaking the hand of his visitor cordially. "When did you get back from New York?"

"Yesterday afternoon. I called after my arrival, but you had left your office."

"Well, what news do you bring home? Is every thing to your mind?"

"Entirely so, Mr. Brainard."

"That's clever—that's right. I was sure you would find it so. Lyon is shrewd and sharp-sighted as an eagle. We have not mistaken our man, depend on it."

"I think not."

"I know we have not," was the confident rejoinder.

"Any further word from him, since I left?"

"I had a letter yesterday. He was about leaving for Mexico."

"Are you speaking of Mr. Lyon, the young Englishman whom I saw in your office frequently, a short time since?" inquired a gentleman who sat reading the morning paper.

"The same," replied Mr. Brainard.

"Did you say he had gone to Mexico?"

"Yes, or was about leaving for that country. So he informed me in a letter I received from him yesterday."

"In a letter?" The man's voice expressed surprise.

"Yes. But why do you seem to question the statement?"

"Because I saw him in the city day before yesterday."

"In the city!"

"Yes, sir. Either him or his ghost."

"Oh! you're mistaken."

"I think not. It is rarely that I'm mistaken in the identity of any one."

"You are, assuredly, too certain in the present instance," said Mr. Markland, turning to the gentleman who had last spoken, "for, it's only a few days since I received letters from him written at Savannah."

Still the man was positive.

"He has a hair-mole on his cheek, I believe."

Mr. Brainard and Mr. Markland looked at each other doubtingly.

"He has," was admitted by the latter.

"But that doesn't make identity," said Mr. Brainard, with an incredulous smile. "I've seen many men, in my day, with moles on their faces."

"True enough," was answered; "but you never saw two Mr. Lyons."

"You are very positive," said Mr. Brainard, growing serious. "Now, as we believe him to be at the South, and you say that he was here on the day before yesterday, the matter assumes rather a perplexing shape. If he really was here, it is of the first importance that we should know it; for we are about trusting important interests to his hands. Where, then, and under what circumstances, did you see him?"

"I saw him twice."

"Where?"

"The first time, I saw him alighting from a carriage, at the City Hotel. He had, apparently, just arrived, as there was a trunk behind the carriage."

"Singular!" remarked Mr. Brainard, with a slightly disturbed manner.

"You are mistaken in the person," said Mr. Markland, positively.

"It may be so," returned the gentleman.

"Where did you next see him?" inquired Mr. Brainard.

"In the neighbourhood of the—Railroad Depot. Being aware that he had spent several days with Mr. Markland, it occurred to me that he was going out to call upon him."

"Very surprising. I don't just comprehend this," said Mr. Markland, with a perplexed manner.

"The question is easily settled," remarked Mr. Brainard. "Sit here a few moments, and I will step around to the City Hotel."

And as he spoke, he arose and went quickly from his office. In about ten minutes he returned.

"Well, what is the result?" was the rather anxious inquiry of Mr. Markland.

"Can't make it out," sententiously answered Mr. Brainard.

"What did you learn?"

"Nothing."

"Of course, Mr. Lyon has not been there?"

"I don't know about that. He certainly was not there as Mr. Lyon."

"Was any one there answering to his description?"

"Yes."

"From the South?"

"Yes. From Richmond—so the register has it; and the name recorded is Melville."

"You asked about him particularly?"

"I did, and the description given, both by the landlord and his clerk, corresponded in a singular manner with the appearance of Mr. Lyon. He arrived by the southern line, and appeared hurried in manner. Almost as soon as his name was registered, he inquired at what hour the cars started on the— road. He went out in an hour after his arrival, and did not return until late in the evening. Yesterday morning he left in the first southern train."

"Well, friends, you see that I was not so very far out of the way," said the individual who had surprised the gentlemen by asserting that Mr. Lyon was in the city only two days before.

"I can't believe that it was Mr. Lyon." Firmly Mr. Markland took this position.

"I would not be sworn to it—but my eyes have certainly played me false, if he were not in the city at the time referred to," said the gentleman; "and let me say to you, that if you have important interests in his hands, which you would regard as likely to suffer were he really in our city at the time alleged, it will be wise for you to look after them a little narrowly, for, if he were not here, then was I never more mistaken in my life."

The man spoke with a seriousness that produced no very pleasing effect upon the minds of his auditors, who were, to say the least, very considerably perplexed by what he alleged.

"The best course, in doubtful cases, is always a prudent one," said Mr. Markland, as soon as the gentleman had retired.

"Unquestionably. And now, what steps shall we take, under this singular aspect of affairs?"

"That requires our first attention. If we could only be certain that Mr. Lyon had returned to the city."

"Ah, yes—if we could only be certain. That he was not here, reason and common sense tell me. Opposed to this is the very positive belief of Mr. Lamar that he saw him on the day before yesterday, twice."

"What had better be done under these circumstances?" queried Mr. Brainard.

"I wish that I could answer that question both to your satisfaction and my own," was the perplexed answer.

"What was done in New York?"

"I had several long conferences with Mr. Fenwick, whom I found a man of extensive views. He is very sanguine, and says that he has already invested some forty thousand dollars."

"Ah! So largely?"

"Yes; and will not hesitate to double the sum, if required."

"His confidence is strong."

"It is—very strong. He thinks that the fewer parties engage in the matter, the better it will be for all, if they can furnish the aggregate capital required."

"Why?"

"The fewer persons interested, the more concert of action there will be, and the larger individual dividend on the business."

"If there should come a dividend," said Mr. Brainard.

"That is certain," replied Mr. Markland, in a very confident manner. "I am quite inclined to the opinion of Mr. Fenwick, that one of the most magnificent fortunes will be built up that the present generation has seen."

"What is his opinion of Mr. Lyon?"

"He expresses the most unbounded confidence. Has known him, and all about him, for over ten years; and says that a man of better capacity, or stricter honour, is not to be found. The parties in London, who have intrusted large interests in his hands, are not the men to confide such interests to any but the tried and proved."

"How much will we be expected to invest at the beginning?"

"Not less than twenty thousand dollars apiece."

"So much?"

"Yes. Only two parties in this city are to be in the Company, and we have the first offer."

"You intend to accept?"

"Of course. In fact, I have accepted. At the same time, I assured Mr. Fenwick that he might depend on you."

"But for this strange story about Mr. Lyon's return to the city—a death's-head at our banquet—there would not be, in my mind, the slightest hesitation."

"It is only a shadow," said Mr. Markland.

"Shadows do not create themselves," replied Mr. Brainard.

"No; but mental shadows do not always indicate the proximity of material substance. If Mr. Lyon wrote to you that he was about starting for Mexico, depend upon it, he is now speeding away in that direction. He is not so sorry a trifler as Mr Lamar's hasty conclusion would indicate."

"A few days for reflection and closer scrutiny will not in the smallest degree affect the general issue, and may develope facts that will show the way clear before us," said Mr. Brainard. "Let us wait until we hear again from Mr. Lyon, before we become involved in large responsibilities."

"I do not see how I can well hold back," replied Mr. Markland. "I have, at least, honourably bound myself to Mr. Fenwick."

"A few days can make no difference, so far as that is concerned," said Mr. Brainard, "and may develope facts of the most serious importance. Suppose it should really prove true that Mr. Lyon returned, in a secret manner, from the South, would you feel yourself under obligation to go forward without the clearest explanation of the fact?"

"No," was the unhesitating answer.

"Very well. Wait for a few days. Time will make all this clearer."

"It will, no doubt, be wisest," said Mr. Markland, in a voice that showed a slight depression of feeling.

"According to Mr. Lamar, if the man he saw was Lyon, he evidently wished to have a private interview with yourself."

"With me?"

"Certainly. Both Mr. Lamar and the hotel-keeper refer to his going to, or being in, the neighbourhood of the cars that run in the direction of 'Woodbine Lodge.' It will be well for you to question the various members of your household. Something may be developed in this way."

"If he had visited Woodbine Lodge, of course I would have known about it," said Mr. Markland, with a slightly touched manner, as if there were something more implied by Mr. Brainard than was clearly apparent.

"No harm can grow out of a few inquiries," was answered. "They may lead to the truth we so much desire to elucidate, and identify the person seen by Mr. Lamar as a very different individual from Mr. Lyon."

Under the existing position of things, no further steps in the very important business they had in progress could be taken that day. After an hour's further conference, the two men parted, under arrangement to meet again in the morning.

CHAPTER XII.

IT was scarcely mid-day when Mr. Markland's carriage drew near to Woodbine Lodge. As he was about entering the gateway to his grounds, he saw Mr. Allison, a short distance beyond, coming down the road. So he waited until the old gentleman came up.

"Home again," said Mr. Allison, in his pleasant, interested way, as he extended his hand. "When did you arrive?"

"Last evening," replied Mr. Markland.

"Been to the city this morning, I suppose."

"Yes. Some matters of business required my attention. The truth is, Mr.

Allison, I grow more and more wearied with my inactive life, and find relief in any new direction of thought."

"You do not design re-entering into business?"

"I have no such present purpose." Mr. Markland stepped from his carriage, as he thus spoke, and told the driver to go forward to the house. "Though it is impossible to say where we may come out when we enter a new path. I am not a man to do things by halves. Whatever I undertake, I am apt to prosecute with considerable activity and concentration of thought."

"So I should suppose. It is best, however, for men of your temperament to act with prudence and wise forethought in the beginning—to look well to the paths they are about entering; for they are very apt to go forward with a blind perseverance that will not look a moment from the end proposed."

"There is truth in your remark, no doubt. But I always try to be sure that I am right before I go ahead. David Crockett's homely motto gives the formula for all high success in life."

"Yes; he spoke wisely. There would be few drones in our hive, if all acted up to his precept."

"Few, indeed. Oh! I get out of all patience sometimes with men in business; they act with such feebleness of nerve—such indecision of purpose. They seem to have no life—none of those clear intuitions that spring from an ardent desire to reach a clearly-seen goal. Without earnestness and concentration, nothing of more than ordinary importance is ever effected. Until a man taxes every faculty of his mind to the utmost, he cannot know the power that is in him."

"Truly said. And I am for every man doing his best; but doing it in the right way. It is deplorable to see the amount of wasted effort there is in the world. The aggregate of misapplied energy is enormous."

"What do you call misapplied energy?" said Markland.

"The energy directed by a wrong purpose."

"Will you define for me a wrong purpose?"

"Yes; a merely selfish purpose is a wrong one."

"All men are selfish," said Mr. Markland.

"In a greater or less degree they are, I know."

"Then all misapply their energies?"

"Yes, all—though not always. But there is a beautiful harmony and precision in the government of the world, that bends man's selfish purposes into serving the common good. Men work for themselves alone, each caring for himself alone; yet Providence so orders and arranges, that the neighbour is more really benefited than the individual worker toiling only for himself. Who is most truly served—the man who makes a garment, or the man who enjoys its warmth? the builder of the house, or the dweller therein? the tiller of the soil, or he who eats the fruit thereof? Yet, how rarely does the skilful artisan, or he who labours in the field, think of, or care for, those who are to enjoy the good things of life he is producing! His thought is on what he is to receive, not on what he is giving; and far too many of those who benefit the world by their labour are made unhappy when they think that others really enjoy what they have produced—if their thought ever reaches that far beyond themselves."

"Man is very selfish, I will admit," said Mr. Markland, thoughtfully.

"It is self-love, my friend," answered the old man, "that gives to most of us our greatest energy in life. We work ardently, taxing all our powers, in the accomplishment of some end. A close self-examination will, in most cases, show us that self is the main-spring of all this activity. Now, I hold, that in just so far as this is the case, our efforts are misapplied."

"But did you not just admit that the world was benefited by all active labour, even if the worker toiled selfishly? How, then, can the labour be misapplied?"

"Can you not see that, if every man worked with the love of benefiting the world in his heart, more good would be effected than if he worked only for himself?"

"Oh, yes."

"And that he would have a double reward, in the natural compensation that labour receives, and in the higher satisfaction of having done good."

"Yes."

"To work for a lower end, then, is to misapply labour, so far as the man is concerned. He robs himself of his own highest reward, while Providence bends the efforts he makes, and causes them to effect good uses to the neighbour he would, in too many cases, rather insure than benefit."

"You have a curious way of looking at things, or, rather, *into* them," said Mr. Markland, forcing a smile. "There is a common saying about taking the conceit out of a man, and I must acknowledge that you can do this as effectually as any one I ever knew."

"When the truth comes to us," said the old gentleman, smiling in return, "it possesses the quality of a mirror, and shows us something of our real state. If we were more earnest to know the truth, so far as it applied to ourselves, we would be wiser, and, it is to be hoped, better. Truth is light, and when it comes to us it reveals our true relation to the world. It gives the ability to define our exact position, and to know surely whether we are in the right or the wrong way. How beautifully has it been called a lamp to our path! And truth possesses another quality—that of water. It cleanses as well as illustrates."

Mr. Markland bent his head in a thoughtful attitude, and walked on in silence. Mr. Allison continued:

"The more of truth we admit into our minds, the higher becomes our discriminating power. It not only gives the ability to know ourselves, but to know others. All our mental faculties come into a more vigorous activity."

"Truth! What is truth?" said Mr. Markland, looking up, and speaking in a tone of earnest inquiry.

"Truth is the mind's light," returned Mr. Allison, "and it comes to us from Him who said 'Let there be light, and there was light,' and who afterward said, 'I am the light of the world.' There is truth, and there is the doctrine of truth—it is by the latter that we are led into a knowledge of truth."

"But how are we to find truth? How are we to become elevated into that region of light in which the mind sees clearly?"

"We must learn the way, before we can go from one place to another."

"Yes."

"If we would find truth, we must first learn the way, or the doctrine of truth; for doctrine, or that which illustrates the mind, is like a natural path or way, along which we walk to the object we desire to reach."

"Still, I do not find the answer to my question. What or where is truth?"

"It often happens that we expect a very different reply to the query we make, from the one which in the end is received—an answer in no way flattering to self-love, or in harmony with our life-purpose. And when I answer you in the words of Him who, spake as never man spoke—'I am the way, the *truth*, and the life,' I cannot expect my words to meet your state of earnest expectation—to be really *light* to your mind."

"No, they are not light—at least, not clear light," said Mr. Markland, in rather a disappointed tone. "If I understand the drift of what you have said, it is that the world has no truth but what stands in some relation to God, who is the source of all truth."

"Just my meaning," replied Mr. Allison.

A pause of some moments followed.

"Then it comes to this," said Mr. Markland, "that only through a religious life can a man hope to arrive at truth."

"Only through a life in just order," was the reply.

"What is a life in just order?"

"A life in harmony with the end of our creation."

"Ah! what a volume of meaning, hidden as well as apparent, does your answer involve! How sadly out of order is the world! how little in harmony with itself! To this every man's history is a living attestation."

"If in the individual man we find perverted order, it cannot, of course, be different with the aggregated man."

"No."

"The out of order means, simply, an action or force in the moral and mental machinery of the world, in a direction opposite to the right movement."

"Yes; that is clear."

"The right movement God gave to the mind of man at the beginning, when he made him in the likeness and image of himself."

"Undoubtedly."

"To be in the image and likeness of God, is, of course, to have qualities like him."

"Yes."

"Love is the essential principle of God—and love seeks the good of another, not its own good. It is, therefore, the nature of God to bless others out of himself; and that he might do this, he created man. Of course, only while man continued in true order could he be happy. The moment he obliterated the likeness and image of his Creator—that is, learned to love himself more than his neighbour—that moment true order was perverted: then he became unhappy. To learn truth is to learn the way of return to true order. And we are not left in any doubt in regard to this truth. It has been written for us on Tables of Stone, by the finger of God himself."

"In the Ten Commandments?"

"Yes. In them we find the sum of all religion. They make the highway along which man may return, without danger of erring, to the order and happiness that were lost far back in the ages now but dimly seen in retrospective vision. No lion is found in this way, nor any ravenous beast; but the redeemed of the Lord may walk there, and return with songs and everlasting joy upon their heads."

"It will be in vain, then, for man to hope for any real good in this life, except he keep the commandments," said Mr. Markland.

"All in vain," was answered. "And his keeping of them must involve something more than a mere literal obedience. He must be in that interior love of what they teach, which makes obedience to the letter spontaneous, and not constrained. The outward act must be the simple effect of a living cause."

"Ah, my friend!" sighed Mr. Markland. "It may be a true saying, but who can hear it?"

"We have wandered far in the wrong direction—are still moving with a swift velocity that cannot be checked without painfully jarring the whole machinery of life; but all this progress is toward misery, not happiness, and, as wise men, it behooves us stop, at no matter what cost of present pain, and begin retracing the steps that have led only to discontent and disappointment. It is all in vain that we fondly imagine that the good we seek lies only a little way in advance—that the Elysian fields will, in the end, be reached. If we are descending instead of ascending, how are we ever to gain the mountain top? If we turn our backs upon the Holy City, and move on with rapid footsteps, is there any hope that we shall ever pass through its gates of pearl or walk its golden streets? To the selfish natural mind, it is a 'hard saying' as you intimate, for obedience to the commandments requires the denial and rejection of self; and such a rejection seems like an extinguishment of the very life. But, if we reject this old, vain life, a new vitality, born of higher and more enduring principles, will at once begin. Remember that we are spiritually organized forms, receptive of life. If the life of selfish and perverted ends becomes inactive, a new, better, and truer life will begin. We must live; for life, inextinguishable life, is the inheritance received from the Creator, who is life eternal in himself. It is with us to determine the quality of life. Live we must, and forever—whether in order or disorder, happiness or misery, is left to our own decision."

"How the thought, as thus presented," said Mr. Markland, very soberly— almost sadly, "thrills me to the very centre of my being! Ah! my excellent friend, what vast interests does this living involve!"

"Vast to each one of us."

"I do not wonder," added Mr. Markland, "that the old hermits and anchorites, oppressed, so to speak, by the greatness of immortal interests over those involved in natural life, separated themselves from the world, that, freed from its allurements, they might lead the life of heaven."

"Their mistake," said Mr. Allison, "was quite as fatal as the mistake of the worldling. Both missed the road to heaven."

"Both?" Mr. Markland looked surprised.

"Yes; for the road to heaven lies through the very centre of the world, and those who seek bypaths will find their termination at an immense distance from the point they had hoped to gain. It is by neighbourly love that we attain to a higher and diviner love. Can this love be born in us, if, instead of living in and for the world's good, we separate ourselves from our kind, and pass the years in fruitless meditation or selfish idleness? No. The active bad man is often more useful to the world than the naturally good or harmless man who is a mere drone. Only the brave soldier receives the laurels of his country's gratitude; the skulking coward is execrated by all."

The only response on the part of Markland was a deep sigh. He saw the truth that would make him free, but did not feel within himself a power sufficient to break the cords that bound him. The two men walked on in silence, until they came near a lovely retreat, half obscured by encircling trees, the scene of Fanny's recent and impassioned interview with Mr. Lyon. The thoughts of Mr. Allison at once reverted to his own meeting with Fanny in the same place, and the disturbed condition of mind in which he found her. The image of Mr. Lyon also presented itself. As the two men paused, at a point where the fountain and some of the fine statues were visible, Mr. Allison said, with an abruptness that gave the pulse of his companion a sudden acceleration—

"Did your English friend, Mr. Lyon, really go South, before you left New York?"

"He did. But why do you make the inquiry?" Mr. Markland turned, and fixed his eyes intently upon the old man's face.

"I was sure that I met him a day or two ago. But I was mistaken, as a man cannot be in two places at once."

"Where did you see the person you took for Mr. Lyon?"

"Not far distant from here?"

"Where?"

"A little way from the railroad station. He was coming in this direction, and, without questioning the man's identity, I naturally supposed that he was on his way to your house."

"Singular! Very singular!" Mr. Markland spoke to himself.

"I met Fanny a little while afterward," continued Mr. Allison, "and I learned from her that Mr. Lyon had actually left the city. No doubt I was mistaken; but the person I saw was remarkably like your friend from England."

"Where did you meet Fanny?" abruptly asked Mr. Markland.

"In the little summer-house, yonder. I stepped aside, as I often do, to enjoy the quiet beauty of the place for a few moments, and found your daughter there alone. She answered, as you have done, my inquiry about Mr. Lyon, that he left for the South a few days before."

"He did. And yet, singularly enough, you are not the only one who has mentioned to me that a person resembling Mr. Lyon was seen after he had left for the South—seen, too, almost on the very day that letters from him arrived by mail. The coincidence is at least remarkable."

"Remarkable enough," answered the old man, "to lead you, at least, to a close scrutiny into the matter."

"I believe it only to be a coincidence," said Mr. Markland, more confidently.

"If the fact of his being here, at the time referred to, would change in any respect your relation to him, then let me advise the most rigid investigation. I cannot get rid of the impression that he really was here—and, let me speak a plainer word—nor that he met your daughter in the summer-house."

Markland started as if an adder had stung him, uttering the word—

"Impossible!"

"Understand me," calmly remarked the old man, "I do not say that it was so. I have no proof to offer. But the impression has haunted me ever since, and I cannot drive it away."

"It is only an impression, then?"

"Nothing more."

"But what, was there in my daughter's conduct that led you to so strange an impression?"

"Her manner was confused; a thing that has never happened at any previous meeting with her. But, then, I came upon her suddenly, as she sat in the summer-house, and gave her, in all probability, a nervous start."

71

"Most likely that is the true interpretation. And I can account for her rather disturbed state of mind on other grounds than a meeting with Mr. Lyon."

"That is good evidence on the other side," returned Mr. Allison, "and I hope you will pardon the freedom I have taken in speaking out what was in my thoughts. In no other way could I express so strongly the high regard I have for both yourself and family, and the interest I feel in your most excellent daughter. The singular likeness to Mr. Lyon in the person I met, and the disturbed state in which Fanny appeared to be, are facts that have kept almost constant possession of my mind, and haunted me ever since. To mention these things to you is but a common duty."

"And you have my thanks," said Mr. Markland, "my earnest thanks."

The two men had moved on, and were now at some distance from the point where the sight of the fountain and summer-house brought a vivid recollection to the mind of Mr. Allison of his interview with Fanny.

"Our ways part here," said the old man.

"Will you not keep on to the house? Your visits always give pleasure," said Mr. Markland.

"No—not at this time. I have some matters at home requiring present attention."

They stood and looked into each other's faces for a few moments, as if both had something yet in their minds unsaid, but not yet in a shape for utterance—then separated with a simple "Good-by."

CHAPTER XIII.

THIS new testimony in regard to the presence of Mr. Lyon in the neighbourhood, at a time when he was believed to be hundreds of miles away, and still receding as rapidly as swift car and steamer could bear him, might well disturb, profoundly, the spirit of Mr. Markland. What could it mean? How vainly he asked himself this question. He was walking onward, with his eyes upon the ground, when approaching feet made him aware of the proximity of some one. Looking up, he saw a man coming down the road from his house, and only a few rods distant from him.

"Mr. Lyon, now!" he exclaimed, in a low, agitated voice. "What does this mean?" he added, as his mind grew bewildered, and his footsteps were stayed.

Another moment, and he saw that he had erred in regard to the man's identity. It wars not Mr. Lyon, but a stranger. Advancing again, they met, and the stranger, pausing, said:

"Mr. Markland, I believe?"

"That is my name, sir," was answered.

"And my name is Willet."

"Ah, yes!" said Mr. Markland extending his hand. "I learned, to-day, in the city, that you had purchased Ashton's fine place. I am happy, sir, to make your acquaintance, and if there is any thing in which I can serve you, do not hesitate to command me."

"Many thanks for your kind offer," returned Mr. Willet. "A stranger who comes to reside in the country has need of friendly consideration; and I stand just in that relation to my new neighbours. To certain extent I am ignorant of the ways and means appertaining to the locality; and can only get enlightened through an intercourse with the older residents. But I have no right to be obtrusive, or to expect too much concession to a mere stranger. Until I am better known, I will only ask the sojourner's kindness—not the confidence one friend gives to another."

There was a charm about the stranger's manner, and a peculiar music in his voice, that won their way into the heart of Mr. Markland.

"Believe me, sir," he replied, "that my tender of friendly offices is no unmeaning courtesy. I comprehend, entirely, your position; for I once held just your relation to the people around me. And now, if there are any questions to which an immediate answer is desired, ask them freely. Will you not return with me to my house?"

"Thank you! Not now. I came over to ask if you knew a man named Burk, who lives in the neighbourhood."

"Yes; very well," answered Mr. Markland.

"Is he a man to be depended upon?"

"He's clever, and a good man about a place; but, I am sorry to say, not always to be depended upon."

"What is the trouble with him?" asked Mr. Willet.

"The trouble with most men who occasionally drink to excess."

"Oh! That's it. You've said enough, sir; he won't suit me. I shall have to be in the city for a time, almost every day, and would not, by any means, feel safe or comfortable in knowing that such a person was in charge of things.

Besides, my mother, who is getting in years, has a particular dread of an intoxicated man, and I would on no account expose her to the danger of being troubled from this cause. My sisters, who have lived all their lives in cities, will be timid in the country, and I therefore particularly desire the right kind of a man on the premises—one who may be looked to as a protector in my absence. You understand, now, what kind of a person I want?"

"Clearly."

"This Burk would not suit."

"I'm afraid not. But for the failing I have mentioned, you could hardly find a more capable, useful, or pleasant man in the neighbourhood; but this mars all."

"It mars all for me, and for reasons I have just mentioned," said Mr. Willet; "so we will have to pass him by. Is there any other available man about here, who would make a trusty overseer?"

"I do not think of one, but will make it my business to inquire," returned Mr. Markland. "How soon will you move out?"

"In about a week. On Monday we shall send a few loads of furniture."

"Cannot you hire Mr. Ashton's gardener? He is trusty in every respect."

"Some one has been ahead of me," replied Mr. Willet. "He is already engaged, and will leave to-morrow."

"I'm sorry for that. Mr. Ashton spoke highly of him."

"His work speaks for him," said Mr. Willet. "The whole place is in beautiful order."

"Yes, it has always been the pride of its owner, and admiration of the neighbourhood. I don't know how Mr. Ashton could make up his mind to part with it."

"I am certainly much obliged to him for yielding it to me," said Mr. Willet. "I regard myself as particularly fortunate. But I will not detain you. If you should think or hear of any one who will suit my purpose, I shall be under particular obligations if you will let me know."

"If I can serve you in the matter, be sure that I will do so," replied Mr. Markland.

Mr. Willet thanked him warmly for the proffered kindness, and then the two men separated, each strongly and favourably impressed by the other.

"That startling mystery is solved," said Mr. Markland, taking a deep breath. "This is the other Dromio. I don't wonder that Mr. Allison and Mr. Lamar were deceived. I was, for a moment. What a likeness he bears to Mr. Lyon! Ah, well!—the matter has worried me, for a short time, dreadfully. I was sure that I knew my man; but this strange affirmation in regard to him threw me into terrible doubts. Thank fortune! the mystery is completely solved. I must go back to the city this very afternoon, and see Brainard. It will not do for him to remain long in doubt. His mind might take a new direction, and become interested in some other enterprise. There is no other man with whom, in so important a business as this, I would care to be associated."

And Mr. Markland, thus communing with himself, moved onward, with light and rapid footsteps, toward his dwelling. A mountain had been lifted from his heart.

CHAPTER XIV.

"YOU had a visitor this afternoon," said Mr. Markland, as he sat conversing with his wife and daughter, soon after his arrival from the city.

"I believe not," returned Mrs. Markland. "Oh, yes. I met a gentleman coming from this direction, and he said that he had been here."

"A gentleman? Who?"

"Our new neighbour, Mr. Willet."

"I did not know that he called."

"He may only have inquired for me at the door," said Mr. Markland. "I wish you had seen him."

"What kind of a man does he appear to be?" asked Mrs. Markland.

"My first impressions are favourable. But there is a singular fact in regard to his appearance in our neighbourhood."

Mrs. Markland and Fanny looked up curiously.

"I have been very much worried, since my return;" and Mr. Markland's eyes rested on his daughter, as he said this. The change that instantly passed over her face a little surprised him. Her eyes fell under his gaze, and the crimson blood rose to her forehead.

"What has worried you?" tenderly inquired Mrs. Markland.

"I met with a strange rumour in the city."

"About what?"

"About Mr. Lyon."

Mrs. Markland's whole manner changed, her usual quiet aspect giving place to strongly manifested interest. Her eyes, as well as those of her husband, turned to-ward Fanny, who, by partial aversion, sought to hide from close observation her suffused countenance.

"What of Mr. Lyon?" asked Mrs. Markland.

"At least two persons have affirmed, quite positively, that they saw Mr. Lyon, as well in the city as in this neighbourhood, on the day before yesterday," said Mr. Markland.

The colour suddenly receded from the face of his wife, who looked half-frightened at so unexpected an announcement. Fanny turned herself further away from observation.

"Saw Mr. Lyon! Can it be possible he did not go South at the time he said that he would leave?" Mrs. Markland's voice was troubled.

"He went, of course," was the cheerful, confident answer of Mr. Markland.

"You are sure of it?"

"Oh, yes!"

"How do you explain the mystery, if it may so be called?"

"After hours of doubt, perplexity, and uneasiness, I met the man himself."

"Not Mr. Lyon?"

Fanny started at her father's announcement, and partly turned toward him a face that was now of a pallid hue.

"No; not Mr. Lyon," said Mr. Markland, in answer to his wife's ejaculation, "but a person so nearly resembling him, that, for a few moments, even I was deceived."

"How singular! Who was the man?"

"Our new neighbour, Mr. Willet."

"Why, Edward! That is remarkable."

"Yes, it is really so. I had just parted from Mr. Allison, who was certain of having seen Mr. Lyon in this neighbourhood, on the day before yesterday, when I met Mr. Willet. I can assure you that I was startled when my eyes first rested upon him. For a few moments, pulsation was suspended. A nearer approach corrected my error; and a brief conversation with our new neighbour, gave me a strong prepossession in his favour."

Before this sentence was completed, Fanny had arisen and gone quietly from the room. For a few moments after her departure, the father's and mother's eyes rested upon the door through which her graceful form had vanished. Then they looked at each other, sighed, and were silent.

The moment Fanny was beyond the observation of her parents, wings seemed added to her feet, and she almost flew to her chamber.

"Bless the child! What's the matter? She looks frightened to death!" exclaimed Aunt Grace, who met her on the way, and she followed her quickly. But, when she tried to open the chamber door, she found it locked within.

"Fanny! Fanny, child!" She rattled at the lock, as she thus called the name of her niece.

But no sound came from within.

"Fanny! Fanny!"

The sound of feet was on the floor.

"Fanny!"

"What is wanted, aunt?" said a low, husky voice, close to the door within. It did not seem like the voice of Fanny.

"I wish to see you for a few moments. Let me in."

"Not now, Aunt Grace. I want to be alone," was answered, in the same altered voice.

"Mercy on us!" sighed Aunt Grace, as she turned, disappointed and troubled, from the door of her niece's chamber. "What is coming over the house? and what ails the child? That dreadful Mr. Lyon is at the bottom of all this. Oh! I wish the ship that brought him over had sunk in the middle of the ocean. I knew he would bring trouble, the moment my eyes rested upon him; and it is here quicker than I expected."

Fanny, oh entering her room, had fallen, half-fainting, across her bed. It required a strong effort to arouse herself and sufficiently command her voice to answer the call of her aunt and refuse to admit her. As soon as the latter had gone away, she staggered back to her bed, and again threw herself upon it, powerless, for the time, in mind as well as body. Never, before, had she concealed anything from her parents—never acted falsely, or with even a shadow of duplicity. Into what a fearful temptation had she suddenly fallen; and what a weight of self-condemnation, mingled with doubt and fear, pressed upon her heart. At the moment when she was about revealing all to her father, and thus ending his doubts, her purpose was checked by the unlooked-for announcement that a person so nearly resembling Mr. Lyon, as even for a moment to deceive her father, was in the neighbourhood, checked the words that were rising to her lips, and sealed them, for the time, in silence. To escape from the presence of her parents was her next impulse, and she obeyed it.

Fully half an hour passed before calmness was restored to the mind of Fanny, and she could think with any degree of clearness. From childhood, up to this period of her life, her mother had been her wise counsellor, her loving friend, her gentle monitor. She had leaned upon her in full confidence—had clung to her in weakness, as the vine to its strong support. And now, when she most needed her counsel, she shrunk from her, and feared to divulge the secret that was burning painfully into her heart. And yet, she did not purpose to keep her secret; for that, her reason and filial love both told her, was wrong; while all the time a low, sweet, almost sad voice, seemed murmuring in her ear—"Go to your mother!"

"I must, I will go to her!" she said, at last, firmly. "A daughter's footsteps must be moving along dangerous ways, if she fears to let her mother know the paths she is treading. Oh, mother!" and she clasped her hands almost wildly against her bosom. "My good, wise, loving mother!—how could I let a stranger come in between us, and tempt my heart from its truth to you for a moment! Yes, yes, you must know all, and this very hour."

Acting from this better state of mind, Fanny unlocked her door, and was passing along one of the passages in the direction of her mother's room, when she met Aunt Grace.

"Oh! child! child! what is the matter with you?" exclaimed the aunt, catching hold of her, and looking intently into her pale face. "Come, now, tell me all about it—that's a dear, good girl."

"Tell you about what, Aunt Grace?" said Fanny, with as much firmness as she could assume, trying, as she spoke, to disengage herself from the firm grasp with which she was held.

"About all this matter that troubles you. Why, dear me! you look just as if you'd come out of a spell of sickness. What is it, dear? Now do tell your aunty, who loves you just as well as if you were her own child. Do, love."

And Aunt Grace tried to draw the head of Fanny close to her bosom. But her niece struggled to be free, answering, as she did so—

"Don't question me now, Aunt Grace, please. Only let me go to mother. I want to see her."

"She is not in her room," said Miss Markland.

"Are you certain?"

"Oh, yes. I have just come from there."

"Where is she, then?"

"In the library, with your father."

Without a word more, Fanny turned from her aunt, and, gliding back to her own chamber, entered, and closed the door.

"Oh, dear, dear, dear! What does ail the child?" almost sobbed Aunt Grace, wringing her hands together, as she stood, with a bewildered air, gazing upon the door through which the form of her niece had just passed. "Something is the matter—something dreadful. And it all comes of Edward's foolish confidence in a stranger, that I could see, with half an eye, was not a man to be trusted."

For some minutes, Miss Markland remained standing as her niece had left her, trying to make up her mind to act in some decided way for the remedy of existing troubles.

"I'll just speak to Edward plainly about this business," she at length said, with considerable warmth of manner. "Shall I stand, with sealed lips, and witness such a sacrifice? No—no—no!"

And with nothing clearly settled or arranged in her thoughts, Aunt Grace started for the library, with the intention of speaking out plainly to her brother. The opportunity for doing so, however, did not occur; for, on entering the library, she found it empty.

CHAPTER XV.

MR. MARKLAND was entirely satisfied. All doubt vanished from his mind. The singular resemblance of their new neighbour to Mr. Lyon cleared up the whole mystery. It was Mr. Willet who had been mistaken for the young Englishman.

"If it were not so late," he said, glancing at the sun, as he stood in the porch, "I would go into the city and see Mr. Brainard. It is unfortunate that any doubtful questions in regard to Mr. Lyon should have intruded themselves upon him, and his mind should be disabused as quickly as possible. It is singular how positive some men are, right or wrong. Now, Lamar was almost ready to be sworn that he saw Mr. Lyon in the city day before yesterday, although he was, at the time, distant from him many hundreds of miles; and, but for my fortunate meeting with Willet this afternoon, his confident assertion of his belief would, in all probability; have caused the most disastrous consequences. From what light causes do most important events sometimes spring!"

On returning to her own apartment, the thoughts of Fanny began to flow in another channel. The interest which the young stranger had awakened in her mind was no fleeting impulse. His image, daguerreotyped on her heart, no light breath could dim. That he was good and honourable, she believed; and, therefore, had faith in him. Yet had his sudden appearance and injunction of silence disturbed her, as we have seen, very deeply. Her guileless heart shrunk from concealment, as if it were something evil. How bewildered were all her perceptions, usually so calm! A sense of relief had been felt, the instant she saw that her father's mind was no longer in doubt on the question of Mr. Lyon's return from the South—relief, that he was deceived in a matter which might involve the most serious consequences. But this feeling did not very long remain; and she became the subject of rapidly alternating states.

Fanny remained alone until the summons to tea startled her from a sad, half-dreaming state of mind.

Not to meet her father and mother at the tea-table would, she saw, attract toward her a closer attention than if she mingled with the family at their evening meal; and so she forced herself away from the congenial seclusion of her own apartment. As she took her place at the table, she was conscious that the eyes of her father and mother, as well as those of Aunt Grace, were fixed scrutinizingly upon her; and she felt the blood growing warmer in her cheeks, and flushing her whole countenance. An unusual restraint marked the intercourse of all during their meal. Two or three times Mr. Markland sought to draw his daughter into a conversation; but she replied to his remarks in the briefest manner, and evidently wished to escape all notice.

"I'm really troubled about Fanny," said Mrs. Markland to her husband, as they sat looking out upon the fading landscape, as the twilight deepened.

"Where is she? I've not had a glimpse of her since tea."

"In her own room, I suppose, where she now spends the greater part of her time. She has become reserved, and her eyes grow moist, and her cheeks flushed, if you speak to her suddenly."

"You must seek her confidence," said Mr. Markland.

"I want that without the apparent seeking," was answered. "She knows me as her truest friend, and I am waiting until she comes to me in the most unreserved freedom."

"But will she come?"

"Oh, yes! yes!"—was the confidently-spoken answer. "Soon her heart will be laid open to me like the pages of a book, so that I can read all that is written there."

"Mr. Lyon awakened a strong interest in her feelings—that is clearly evident."

"Too strong; and I cannot but regard his coming to Woodbine Lodge as a circumstance most likely to shadow all our future."

"I do really believe," said Mr. Markland, affecting a playful mood, "that you have a latent vein of superstition in your character."

"You may think so, Edward," was the seriously-spoken answer; "but I am very sure that the concern now oppressing my heart is far more deeply grounded than your words indicate. Who, beside Mr. Lamar, told you that he saw, or believed that he saw, Mr. Lyon?"

"Mr. Allison."

"Mr. Allison!"

"Yes."

"Where did he see him?"

"He didn't see him at all," confidently answered Mr. Markland. "He saw Mr. Willet."

"He believed that the person he saw was Mr. Lyon."

"So did I, until a nearer approach convinced me that I was in error. If I could be deceived, the fact that Mr. Allison was also deceived is by no means a remarkable circumstance."

"Was it in this neighbourhood that he saw the person he believed to be Mr Lyon?"

"Yes."

Mrs. Markland's eyes fell to the ground, and she sat, for a long time, so entirely abstracted, as almost to lose her consciousness of external things.

"The dew is rather heavy this evening," said her husband, arousing her by the words. She arose, and they went together into the sitting-room, where they found all but Fanny. Soon after, Mr. Markland went to his library, and gave up his thoughts entirely to the new business in which he was engaged with Mr. Lyon. How, golden was the promise that lured him on! He was becoming impatient to tread with swift feet the path to large wealth and honourable distinction that was opening before him. A new life had been born in his mind —it was something akin to ambition. In former times, business was regarded as the means by which a competency might be obtained; and he pursued it with this end. Having secured wealth, he retired from busy life, hoping to find ample enjoyment in the seclusion of an elegant rural home. But, already, restlessness had succeeded to inactivity, and now his mind was gathering up its latent strength for new efforts, in new and broader fields, and under the spur of a more vigorous impulse.

"Edward!" It was the low voice of his wife, and the soft touch of her hand, that startled the dreaming enthusiast from visions of wealth and power that dazzled him with their brilliancy.

"Come, Edward, it is growing late," said his wife.

"How late?" he replied, looking up from the paper he had covered with various memoranda, and clusters of figures.

"It is past eleven o'clock."

"That cannot be, Agnes. It is only a short time since I left the table.

"Full three hours. All have retired and are sleeping. Ah, my husband! I do not like this new direction your thoughts are taking. To me, there is in it a prophecy of evil to us all."

"A mere superstitious impression, Agnes dear: nothing more, you may depend upon it. I am in the vigour of manhood. My mind is yet clear, strong, and suggestive—and my reason, I hope, more closely discriminating, as every man's should be with each added year of his life. Shall I let all these powers slumber in disgraceful inactivity! No, Agnes, it cannot, must not be."

Mr. Markland spoke with a fervid enthusiasm, that silenced his wife— confusing her thoughts, but in no way inspiring her with confidence. Hitherto, he had felt desirous of concealing from her the fact that he was really entering into new business responsibilities; but now, in his confident anticipations of success, he divulged a portion of the enlarged range of operations in which he was to be an active co-worker.

"We have enough, Edward," was the almost mournfully-uttered reply of Mrs. Markland—"why, then, involve yourself in business cares? Large transactions like those bring anxious days and wakeful nights. They are connected with trouble, fatigue, disappointment, and, Edward! *sometimes ruin!*"

Very impressively were the last words spoken; but Mr. Markland answered almost lightly—

"None of your imagined drawbacks have any terror for me, Agnes. As for the ruin, I shall take good care not to invite that by any large risks or imprudent speculations. There are few dangers for wise and prudent men, in any business. It is the blind who fall into the ditch—the reckless who stumble. You may be very certain that your husband will not shut his eyes in walking along new paths, nor attempt the navigation of unaccustomed seas without the most reliable charts."

To this, Mrs. Markland could answer nothing. But his words gave her no stronger confidence in the successful result of his schemes; for well assured was she, in her perceptive Christian philosophy, that man's success in any pursuit was no accidental thing, nor always dependent on his own prudence; the ends he had in view oftener determining the result, than any merit or defect in the means employed. So, the weight of concern which this new direction of her husband's active purpose had laid upon her heart, was in no way lightened by his confident assurances.

CHAPTER XVI.

MR. MARKLAND went to the city early on the next morning. Fanny had not made her appearance when he left. This fact, at any other time, would have excited his attention, and caused an earnest inquiry as to the cause of her absence from the morning meal. But now his thoughts were too intently fixed on other things. He had suddenly become an aeriel castle-builder, and all his mind was absorbed in contemplating the magnificent structures that were rising up at the creative touch of imagination.

Mr. Brainard, upon whom he called immediately upon his arrival in the city, was not so easily satisfied on the subject of Mr. Lyon's alleged return to the city. He happened to know Mr. Willet, and, while he admitted that there was a general resemblance between the two men, did not consider it sufficiently striking to deceive any one as to the identity of either.

"But *I* was deceived," confidently asserted Mr. Markland.

"That is not so remarkable under the circumstances," was answered. "You had Lyon distinctly in your thought, from being most positively assured of his recent presence in your neighbourhood, and when a stranger, bearing some resemblance to him, suddenly came in sight, I do not wonder that you were on the instant deceived. I might have been."

"I am sure of it. The likeness between the two men is remarkable."

"But Willet has no hair mole on his cheek; and to that mark, you will remember, Lamar particularly testified."

"The mark may only have been in his mind, and not on the face of the person he met. Believing it to be Mr. Lyon, he saw the hair mole, as well as the other peculiarities of his countenance."

"No such explanations can satisfy me," replied Mr. Brainard. "I have thought over the matter a great deal since I saw you, and my mind is pretty well made up to withdraw from this whole business while I am at liberty to do so, without pecuniary loss or any compromise of honour."

"And let such a golden opportunity pass?" said Markland, in a voice husky with disappointment.

"If you will," was calmly answered. "I am a firm believer in the 'bird in the hand' doctrine. There are a great many fine singers in the bush, but I want to see them safely caged before I neglect the door that shuts in the bird I possess already."

"But you surely cannot be in earnest about withdrawing from this business," said Markland.

"Very much in earnest. Since yesterday, I have turned the matter over in my mind constantly, and viewed it in many lights and from many positions; and my deliberate convictions are, that it is wisest for me to have nothing whatever to do with these splendid schemes; and if you will be governed by an old stager's advice, resolve to act likewise."

"When my hands are once fairly on the plough," answered Mr. Markland, "I never look back. Before engaging in any new business, I thoroughly examine its promise, and carefully weigh all the probabilities of success or failure. After my decision is made, I never again review the ground over which I travelled in coming to a decision, but pass onward with faith and vigour in the accomplishment of all that I have undertaken. More men are ruined by vacillation than from any other cause."

"My observation brings me to another conclusion," quietly returned Mr. Brainard. The earnest enthusiasm of the one, and the immovable coolness of the other, were finely contrasted.

"And what is that?" inquired Mr. Markland.

"Why, that more men are ruined by a blind perseverance in going the wrong way, than from any other cause. Were we infallible in judgment, it might be well enough to govern ourselves in all important matters on the principle you indicate. But, as we are not, like wise navigators, we should daily make new observations, and daily examine our charts. The smallest deviation from a right line will make an immense error in the course of a long voyage."

"Wise business men are in little danger of making errors," said Markland, confidently.

"A great many sad mistakes are made daily," returned Mr. Brainard.

"Not by wise men."

"If a man's projects succeed," was rejoined, "we applaud his sound business judgment; if they fail, we see the cause of failure so plainly, that we are astonished at his want of forethought in not seeing it at the beginning. But, sir, there's a divinity that shapes our ends, rough hew them as we will. Success or failure, I am well convinced, do not always depend on the man himself."

"Is there no virtue, then, in human prudence?" asked Mr. Markland.

"I am not prepared to say how far we may depend on human prudence," replied the other; "but I know this, that if we fail to use it, we will fail in most of our undertakings. Human prudence must be exercised in all cases; but, too often, we let our confident hopes take the place of prudence, as I think you are doing now."

"But surely, Mr. Brainard," said Markland, in an earnest, appealing way, "you do not intend receding from this business?"

"My mind is fully made up," was answered.

"And so is mine," firmly replied Markland.

"To do what?"

"To take the whole interest myself."

"What?"

"To invest forty thousand dollars, instead of the proposed twenty, at once."

"You show strong faith, certainly."

"My faith, you may be sure, is well grounded. Mr. Fenwick has already put in that sum, and he is not the man to go blindly into any business. Apart from my own clear intuitions, founded on the most careful investigations, I would almost be willing to take risks in any schemes that Mr. Fenwick approved, in the substantial way of investment."

"A very different man am I," said Mr. Brainard. "Twenty years of sharp experience are sufficient to make me chary of substituting others' business judgment for my own."

"Ah, well!" returned Markland, his manner showing him to be disappointed and annoyed. "I cannot but regret your hasty decision in this matter. So far as it concerns myself, even if I saw cause to recede, which I do not, I am too far committed, with both Fenwick and Lyon, to hesitate."

"Every man must decide in such cases for himself," said Brainard. "I always do. If you are fully assured in every particular, and have confidence in your men, your way is of course clear."

"It is clear," was confidently answered, "and I shall walk in it with full assurance of a successful end."

CHAPTER XVII.

IT was some time after her father left for the city, before Fanny came down from her room. She was pale, and looked as if she had passed a sleepless night. Her mother's concerned inquiries were answered evasively, and it was very apparent that she wished to avoid question and observation.

Aunt Grace again sought, in her obtrusive way, to penetrate the mystery of Fanny's changed exterior, but was no more successful than on the preceding evening.

"Don't worry her with so many questions, sister," said Mrs. Markland, aside, to Aunt Grace; "I will know all in good time."

"Your good time may prove a very bad time," was answered, a little sharply.

"What do you mean by that?" asked Mrs. Markland, turning her eyes full upon the face of her companion.

"I mean that in any matter affecting so deeply a girl like Fanny, the mother's time for knowing all about it is now. Something is wrong, you may depend upon it."

At the commencement of this conversation, Fanny retired from the room.

"The child's mind has been disturbed by the unfortunate letter from Mr. Lyon. The something wrong goes not beyond this."

"Unfortunate! You may well say unfortunate. I don't know what has come over Edward. He isn't the same man that he was, before that foreign adventurer darkened our sunny home with his presence. Unfortunate! It is worse than unfortunate! Edward's sending that letter at all was more a crime than a mistake. But as to the wrong in regard to Fanny, I am not so sure that it only consists in a disturbance of her mind."

There was a look of mystery, blended with anxious concern, in the countenance of Aunt Grace, that caused Mrs. Markland to say, quickly—

"Speak out what is in your thoughts, Grace. Have no concealments with me, especially on a subject like this."

"I may be over-suspicious—I may wrong the dear child—but—"

Aunt Grace looked unusually serious.

"But what?" Mrs. Markland had grown instantly pale at the strange words of her husband's sister.

"John, the gardener, says that he saw Mr. Lyon on the day after Edward went to New York."

"Where?"

"Not far from here."

"Deceived, as Edward was. John saw our new neighbour, Mr. Willet."

"Maybe so, and maybe not; and I am strongly inclined to believe in the maybe not. As for that Lyon, I have no faith in him, and never had, as you know, from the beginning. And I shouldn't be at all surprised if he were prowling about here, trying to get stolen interviews with Fanny."

"Grace! How dare you suggest such a thing?" exclaimed Mrs. Markland, with an energy and indignation almost new to her character.

Grace was rather startled by so unexpected a response from her sister-in-law, and for a moment or two looked abashed.

"Better be scared than hurt, you know, Agnes," she replied, coolly, as soon as she had recovered herself.

"Not if scared by mere phantoms of our own diseased imaginations," said Mrs. Markland.

"There is something more solid than a phantom in the present case, I'm afraid. What do you suppose takes Fanny away so often, all by herself, to the Fountain Grove?"

"Grace Markland! What can you mean by such a question?" The mother of Fanny looked frightened.

"I put the question to you for answer," said Grace, coolly. "The time was, and that time is not very distant, when Fanny could scarcely be induced to go a hundred yards from the house, except in company. Now, she wanders away alone, almost daily; and if you observe the direction she takes, you will find that it is toward Fountain Grove. And John says that it was near this place that he met Mr. Lyon."

"Mr. Willet, you mean," said Mrs. Markland, firmly.

"None are so blind as those who will not see," retorted Aunt Grace, in her impulsive way. "If any harm comes to the child, you and Edward will have none but yourselves to blame. Forewarned, forearmed, is a wise saying, by which you seem in no way inclined to profit."

Even while this conversation was in progress, the subject of it had taken herself away to the sweet, retired spot where, since her meeting with Mr. Lyon, she had felt herself drawn daily with an almost irresistible influence. As she passed through the thick, encircling grove that surrounded the open space where the beautiful summer-house stood and the silvery waters sported among the statues, she was startled by a rustling noise, as of some one passing near. She stopped suddenly, her heart beating with a rapid motion, and listened intently. Was she deceived, or did her eyes really get uncertain glimpses of a form hurriedly retiring through the trees? For nearly a minute she stood almost as still as one of the marble figures that surrounded the fountain. Then, with slow, almost stealthy footsteps, she moved onward, glancing, as she did so, from side to side, and noting every object in the range of vision with a sharp scrutiny. On gaining the summer-house, the first object that met her eyes was a folded letter, lying upon the marble table. To spring forward and seize it was the work of an instant. It bore her own name, and in the now familiar hand of Lee Lyon!

A strong agitation seized upon the frame of the young girl, as she caught up the unexpected letter. It was some moments before her trembling fingers could break the seal and unfold the missive. Then her eyes drank in, eagerly, its contents:

"MY EVER DEAR FANNY:—Since our meeting at the fountain, I cannot say to you all that I would say in any letter under care to your father, and so I entrust this to a faithful messenger, who will see that it reaches your hands. I am now far to the South again, in prosecution of most important business, the safe progress of which would be interrupted, and the whole large result endangered, were your father to know of my visit at Woodbine Lodge at a time when he thought me hundreds of miles distant. So, for his sake, as well as my own, be discreet for a brief period. I will not long permit this burden of secrecy to lie upon your dear young heart—oh no! I could not be so unjust to you. Your truest, best, wisest counsellor is your mother, and she should know all that is in your heart. Keep your secret only for a little while, and then I will put you in full liberty to speak of all that has just occurred. None will approve your discretion more than your parents, I know, when all the grave reasons for this concealment are disclosed. Dear Fanny! how ever-present to me you are. It seems, often, as if you were moving by my side. In lonely moments, how like far off, sweet music, comes your voice stealing into my heart. Beloved one!—"

A sudden sound of approaching feet caused Fanny to crumple the letter, scarcely half read, in her hand, and thrust it into her bosom. Turning towards the point from whence the noise came, she perceived the form of her mother, who was only a few paces distant. Mrs. Markland saw the letter in Fanny's hand, and also saw the hasty motion of concealment. When she entered the summer-house where her daughter, who had risen up hurriedly, stood in the attitude of one suddenly alarmed, she marked with deep concern the agitated play of her countenance, and the half-guilty aversion of her eyes.

"My dear child!" she said, in a low, serious voice, as she laid a hand upon her, "what am I to understand by the singular change that has passed over you, and particularly by the strong disturbance of this moment? Why are you here alone? And why are you so startled at your mother's appearance?"

Fanny only bowed her face upon her mother's bosom, and, sobbed violently.

As the wildness of her emotion subsided, Mrs. Markland said:—

"Speak freely to your best friend, my darling child! Hide nothing from one who loves you better than any human heart can love you."

But Fanny answered not, except by a fresh gush of tears.

"Have you nothing to confide to your mother?" inquired Mrs. Markland in as calm a voice as she could assume, after waiting long enough for the heart of her daughter to beat with a more even stroke.

"Nothing," was answered in a voice as calm as that in which the interrogation was asked.

"Nothing, Fanny? Oh, my child! Do not deceive your mother!"

Fanny drew her slight form up into something of a proud attitude, and stood for an instant looking at her mother almost defiantly. But this was only for an instant. For scarcely was the position assumed, ere she had flung herself forward, again sobbing violently, into her arms.

But, for all this breaking down of her feelings, Fanny's lips remained sealed. She was not yet prepared to give up her lover's secret—and did not do so.

CHAPTER XVIII.

ALL doubt in regard to the presence of Mr. Lyon in the neighborhood, as affirmed by Mr. Lamar and others, had, as we have seen, passed from the mind of Markland. He was entirely satisfied that the individual seen by these men was Mr. Willet. But since the refusal of Brainard, regarded as one of the shrewdest men in the city, to enter into a speculation to him so full of promise, he did not feel altogether easy in mind. He had spoken more from impulse than sound judgment, when he declared it to be his purpose to risk forty thousand dollars in the scheme, instead of twenty thousand. A cooler state left room for doubts. What did he really know of Mr. Lyon, on whose discretion, as an agent, so much would depend? The question intruded itself, like an unwelcome guest; and his effort to answer it to his own satisfaction was in vain. Had he been in possession of his daughter's secret, all would have been plain before him. Not for an instant would he have hesitated about keeping faith with a man who could so deceive him.

"I must see Mr. Fenwick again," he said, in his perplexity, after leaving the office of Mr. Brainard.

"Forty thousand dollars is a large sum to invest; and I shall have to sell some of my best property to raise it property yearly increasing in value. Twenty thousand I could have managed by parting with stocks. What folly in Brainard! I'm sadly out with him. Yes, I must see Mr. Fenwick immediately."

In the next train that left for New York, Mr. Markland was a passenger. A hurried note, received by his family that evening, announced the fact of his journey, and threw a deeper shadow on the heart of his troubled wife.

Vainly had Mrs. Markland striven to gain the unreserved confidence of Fanny. The daughter's lips were sealed. Pressing importunity plainly wrought something akin to estrangement; and so, with tears in her eyes and anguish in her heart, the mother turned from her pale-faced child, and left her alone. An hour after being surprised by her mother at the Fountain Grove, Fanny glided into her own room, and turned the key. The letter of Mr. Lyon was still in her bosom, and now, with eager hands, she drew it forth, and read to the end—

—"Beloved one! How often have I blessed the kind Providence that led me into your presence. How strange are these things! For years I have moved amid a blaze of beauty, and coldly turned away from a thousand glittering attractions. But, when my eyes first saw you, there was a pause in my heart's pulsations. I felt that my soul's companion was discovered to me; that, henceforth, my life and yours were to blend. Ah, dear one! wonder not that, from a hasty impulse, I decided to return and see your father. I fear, now, that the cause most strongly influencing me was the desire to look upon your face and feel the thrilling touch of your hand once more. Perhaps it is well he was absent, for I am not so sure that his cooler judgment would have seen sufficient cause for the act. All is going on now just as he, and I, and all concerned, could wish; and not for the world would I have him know, *at present*, our secret. Stolen waters, they say, are sweet. I know not. But that brief, stolen interview at the fountain, was full of sweetness to me. You looked the very Naiad of the place—pure, spiritual, the embodiment of all things lovely. Forgive this warmth of feeling. I would not wound the instinctive delicacy of a heart like yours. Only believe me sincere. Will you not write to me? Direct your letters, under cover, to D. C. L., Baltimore P. O., and they will be immediately forwarded. I will write you weekly. The same hand that conveys this, will see that my letters reach you. Farewell, beloved one!

LEE LYON."

Five times did Fanny attempt to answer this, and as often were her letters destroyed by her own hands. Her sixth, if not more to her own satisfaction, she sealed, and subscribed as directed. It read thus:

"MR. LEE LYON:—MY DEAR SIR—Your unexpected visit, and equally unexpected letter, have bewildered and distressed me. You enjoin a continued silence in regard to your return from the South. Oh, sir! remove that injunction as quickly as possible; for every hour that it remains, increases my unhappiness. You have separated between me and my good mother,—you are holding me back from throwing myself on her bosom, and letting her see every thought of my soul. I cannot very long endure the present. Why not at once write to my father, and explain all to him? He must know that you came back, and the sooner, it seems to me, will be the better. If I do not betray the fact, waking, I shall surely do it in my sleep; for I think of it all the time. Mother surprised me while reading your letter. I am afraid she saw it in my hand. She importuned me to give her my full confidence; and to refuse was one of the hardest trials of my life. I feel that I am changing under this new, painful experience. The ordeal is too fiery. If it continues much longer, I shall cease to be what I was when you were here; and you will find me, on your return, so changed as to be no longer worthy of your love. Oh, sir! pity the child you have awakened from a peaceful, happy dream, into a real life of mingled pain and joy. From the cup you have placed to my lips, I drink with an eager thirst. The draught is delicious to the taste, but it intoxicates—nay, maddens me!

"Write back to me at once, dear Mr. Lyon! I shall count the minutes as hours, until your letter comes. Let the first words be—'Tell all to your mother.' If you cannot write this, we must be as strangers, for I will not bind myself to a man who would make me untrue to my parents. You say that you love me. Love seeks another's happiness. If you really love me, seek my happiness.

FANNY."

Many times did Fanny read over this letter before resolving to send it. Far, very far, was it from satisfying her. She feared that it was too cold—too repellant—too imperative. But it gave the true alternative. She was not yet ready to abandon father and mother for one who had thrown a spell over her heart almost as strong as the enchantment of a sorcerer; and she wished him distinctly to understand this.

Mr. Lyon was in a southern city when this letter came into his hands. He was sitting at a table covered with various documents, to the contents of which he had been giving a long and earnest attention, when a servant brought in a number of letters from the post-office. He selected from the package one post-marked Baltimore, and broke the seal in a hurried and rather nervous manner. As he opened it, an enclosure fell upon the table. It was superscribed with his name, in the delicate hand of a woman. This was Fanny's letter.

A careful observer would have seen more of selfish triumph in the gleam that shot across his face, than true love's warm delight. The glow faded into a look of anxiety as he commenced unfolding the letter, which he read with compressed lips. A long breath, as if a state of suspense were relieved, followed the perusal. Then he sat, for some moments, very still, and lost in thought.

"We'll see about that," he murmured at length, laying the letter of Fanny aside, and taking up sundry other letters which had come by the same mail. For more than an hour these engrossed his attention. Two of them, one from Mr. Markland, were answered during the time.

"Now, sweetheart," he said, almost lightly, as he took Fanny's letter from the table. Every word was read over again, his brows gradually contracting as he proceeded.

"There is some spirit about the girl; more than I had thought. My going back was a foolish blunder. But the best will have to be made of it. Not a whisper must come to Mr. Markland. That is a settled point. But how is the girl to be managed?"

Lyon mused for a long time.

"Dear child!" He now spoke with a tender expression. "I have laid too heavy a weight on your young heart, and I wish it were in my power to remove it; but it is not."

He took a pen, as he said this, and commenced writing an answer to Fanny's letter:—

"DEAREST ONE:—Tell all to your mother; but, in doing so, let it be clearly in your mind that an eternal separation between us must follow as a consequence. I do not say this as a threat—ah, no! Nor are you to understand that I will be offended. No—no—no—nothing of this. I only speak of what must come as the sure result. The moment your father learns that I was at Woodbine Lodge, and had an interview with his daughter, at a time when he thought me far distant, our business and personal relations must cease. He will misjudge me from evidence to his mind powerfully conclusive; and I shall be unable to disabuse him of error, because appearances are against me. But I put you in entire freedom. Go to your mother—confide to her every thing; and, if it be possible, get back the peace of which my coming unhappily robbed you. Think not of any consequences to me—fatal though they should prove. The wide world is before me still.

"And now, dear Fanny! If our ways in life must part, let us hold each other at least in kind remembrance. It will ever grieve me to think that our meeting occasioned a ripple to disturb the tranquil surface of your feelings. I could not help loving you—and for that I am not responsible. Alas! that, in loving, I should bring pain to the heart of the beloved one.

"But why say more? Why trouble your spirit by revealing the disturbance of mine? Heaven bless you and keep you, Fanny; and may your sky be ever bathed in sunshine! I leave my destiny in your hands, and pray for strength to bear the worst.

Adieu.
L. L."

There was a flitting smile on the lips of the young Englishman, as he folded and sealed this letter, and a look of assurance on his face, that little accorded with the words he had just written. Again he took up his pen and wrote—

"MY DEAR D. C. L.:—Faithful as ever you have proved in this affair, which is growing rather too complicated, and beginning to involve too many interests. Miss Markland is fretting sadly under the injunction of secrecy, and says that I must release her from the obligation not to mention my hasty return from the South. And so I have written to her, that she may divulge the fact to her mother. You start, and I hear you say—'Is the man mad?' No, not mad, my friend; or, if mad, with a method in his madness. Fanny will not tell her mother. Trust me for that. The consequences I have clearly set forth—probable ruin to my prospects, and an eternal separation between us. Do you think she will choose this alternative? Not she. 'Imprudent man! To risk so much for a pretty face!' I hear you exclaim. Not all for a pretty face, my grave friend. The alliance, if it can be made, is a good one. Markland, as far as I can learn, is as rich as a Jew; he has a bold, suggestive mind, a large share of enthusiasm, and is, take him all in all, just the man we want actively interested in our scheme. Brainard, he writes me, has backed out. I don't like that; and I like still less the reason assigned for his doing so. 'A foolish report that you were seen in the city some days after your departure for the South, has disturbed his confidence, and he positively refuses to be a partner in the arrangement.' That looks bad; doesn't it? Markland seems not to have the slightest suspicion, and says that he will take the whole forty thousand interest himself, if necessary. He was going, immediately, to New York, to consult with Mr. Fenwick. A good move. Fenwick understands himself thoroughly, and will manage our gentleman.

"Get the enclosed safely into the hands of Fanny, and with as little delay as possible. I am growing rather nervous about the matter. Be very discreet. The slightest error might ruin all. If possible, manage to come in contact with Brainard, and hear how he talks of me, and of our enterprise. You will know how to neutralize any gratuitous assertions he may feel inclined to make. Also get, by some means, access to Mr. Markland. I want your close observation in this quarter. Write me, promptly and fully, and, for the present, direct to me here. I shall proceed no farther for the present.

As ever, yours,
L. L."

CHAPTER XIX.

THE visit to New York, and interview with Mr. Fenwick, fully assured Mr. Markland, and he entered into a formal agreement to invest the sum of forty thousand dollars in the proposed scheme: ten thousand dollars to be paid down at once, and the balance at short dates. He remained away two days, and then returned to make immediate arrangements for producing the money. The ten thousand dollars were raised by the sale of State six per cent. stocks, a transaction that at once reduced his annual income about six hundred dollars. The sum was transmitted to New York.

"Have you reconsidered that matter?" inquired Markland, a few days after his return, on meeting with Mr. Brainard.

"No, but I hope you have," was answered in a serious tone.

"I have been to New York since I saw you."

"Ah! and seen Mr. Fenwick again?"

"Yes."

"Did you mention the report of Lyon's return?"

"I did."

"How did it strike him?"

"As preposterous, of course."

"He did not credit the story?"

"Not he."

"Well, I hope, for your sake, that all will come out right."

"Never fear."

"By-the-way," said Mr. Brainard, "what do you really know about Fenwick? You appear to have the highest confidence in his judgment. Does this come from a personal knowledge of the man, or are you governed in your estimate by common report?"

"He is a man of the first standing in New York. No name, in money circles, bears a higher reputation."

Brainard slightly shrugged his shoulders.

"The common estimate of a man, in any community, is apt to be very near the truth," said Mr. Markland.

"Generally speaking, this is so," was replied. "But every now and then the public mind is startled by exceptions to the rule—and these exceptions have been rather frequent; of late years. As for Fenwick, he stands fair enough, in a general way. If he were to send me an order for five thousand dollars' worth of goods, I would sell him, were I a merchant, without hesitation. But to embark with him in a scheme of so much magnitude is another thing altogether, and I wonder at myself, now, that I was induced to consider the matter at all. Since my withdrawal, and cooler thought on the subject, I congratulate myself, daily, on the escape I have made."

"Escape! From what!" Mr. Markland looked surprised.

"From loss; it may be, ruin."

"You would hardly call the loss of twenty thousand dollars, ruin."

"Do you expect to get off with an investment of only twenty thousand dollars?" asked Mr. Brainard.

"No; for I have agreed to put in forty thousand."

Brainard shook his head ominously, and looked very grave.

"I knew of no other man in the city with whom I cared to be associated; and so, after you declined, took the whole amount that wats to be raised here, myself."

"A hasty and unwise act, believe me, Mr. Markland," said the other. "How soon do you expect returns from this investment?"

"Not for a year, at least."

"Say not for two years."

"Well—admit it. What then?"

"Your annual income is at once diminished in the sum of about twenty-five hundred dollars, the interest on these forty thousand dollars. So, at the end of two years, you are the loser of five thousand dollars by your operation."

"It would be, if the new business paid nothing. But, when it begins to pay, it will be at the rate of one or two hundred per cent. on the amounts paid in."

"May be so."

"Oh! I am sure of it."

"The whole scheme has a fair front, I will admit," answered Brainard. "But I have seen so many days that rose in sunshine go down in storm, that I have ceased to be over confident. If forty thousand were the whole of your investment, you might, for so large a promised return, be justified in taking the risk."

"Mr. Fenwick thinks nothing further will be required," said Markland.

"But don't you remember the letter, in which he stated, distinctly, that several assessments would, in all probability, be made, pro rata, on each partner?"

"Yes; and I called Mr. Fenwick's attention to that statement; for I did not care to go beyond forty thousand."

"What answer did he make?"

"Later intelligence had exhibited affairs in such a state of progress, that it was now certain no further advance of capital would be required."

"I hope not, for your sake," returned Brainard.

"I am sure not," said Markland, confidently, A third party here interrupted the conversation, and the two men separated.

As might be supposed, this interview did not leave the most agreeable impression on the feelings of Markland. The fact that in selling stocks and other property to the amount of forty thousand dollars, and locking up that large sum in an unproductive investment, he would diminish his yearly income over twenty-five hundred dollars, did not present the most agreeable view of the case. He had not thought of this, distinctly, before. A little sobered in mind, he returned homeward during the afternoon. Ten thousand dollars had gone forward to New York; and in the course of next week he must produce a sum of equal magnitude. To do this, would require the sale of a piece of real estate that had, in five years, been doubled in value, and which promised to be worth still more. He felt a particular reluctance to selling this property; and the necessity for doing so worried his mind considerably. "Better let well enough alone." "A bird in the hand is worth two in the bush." One after another, these trite little sayings would come up in his thoughts, unbidden, as if to add to his mental disquietude.

In spite of his efforts to thrust them aside, and to get back his strong confidence in the new business, Mr. Markland's feelings steadily declined towards a state of unpleasant doubt. Reason as he would on the subject, he could not overcome the depression from which he suffered.

"I am almost sorry that I was tempted to embark in this business," he at length said to himself, the admission being extorted by the pressure on his feelings. "If I could, with honour and safety, withdraw, I believe I would be tempted to do so. But that is really not to be thought of now. My hands have grasped the plough, and there must be no wavering or looking back. This is all an unworthy weakness."

Mr. Markland had gained the entrance to Woodbine Lodge, but he was in no state of mind to join his family. So he alighted and sent his carriage forward, intending to linger on his way to the house, in order to regain his lost equilibrium. He had been walking alone for only a few minutes, with his eyes upon the ground, when a crackling noise among the underwood caused him to look up, and turn himself in the direction from which the sound came. In doing so, he caught sight of the figure of a man retiring through the trees, and evidently, from his movements, anxious to avoid observation. Mr. Markland stood still and gazed after him until his figure passed from sight. The impression this incident made upon him was unpleasant. The person of the stranger was so much hidden by trees, that he could make out no resemblance whatever.

It was near that part of Mr. Markland's grounds known as the Fountain Grove, where this occurred, and the man, to all appearance, had been there. The impulse for him to turn aside was, therefore, but natural, and he did so. Passing through a style, and ascending by a few steps to the level of the ornamental grounds surrounding the grove and fountain, the first object that he saw was his daughter Fanny, moving hastily in the direction of the summer-house which has been described. She was only a short distance in advance. Mr. Markland quickened his steps, as a vague feeling of uneasiness came over him. The coincidence of the stranger and his daughter's presence produced a most unpleasant impression.

"Fanny!" he called.

That his daughter heard him, he knew by the start she gave. But instead of looking around, she sprang forward, and hastily entered the summer-house. For a moment or two she was hidden from his view, and in that short period she had snatched a letter from the table, and concealed it in her bosom. Not sufficiently schooled in the art of self-control was Fanny to meet her father with a calm face. Her cheeks were flushed, and her chest rose and fell in hurried respiration, as Mr. Markland entered the summer-house, where she had seated herself.

"You are frightened, my child," said he, fixing his eyes with a look of inquiry on her face. "Didn't you see me, as I turned in from the carriage-way?" he added.

"No, sir," was falteringly answered. "I did not know that you had returned from the city until I heard your voice. It came so unexpectedly that I was startled."

Fanny, as she said this, did not meet her father's gaze, but let her eyes rest upon the ground.

"Are you going to remain here?" asked Mr. Markland.

"I came to spend a little while alone in this sweet place, but I will go back to the house if you wish it," she replied.

"Perhaps you had better do so. I saw a strange man between this and the main road, and he seemed as if he desired to avoid observation."

Fanny started, and looked up, with an expression of fear, into her father's face. The origin of that look Mr. Markland did not rightly conjecture. She arose at once, and said—

"Let us go home."

But few words passed between father and daughter on the way, and their brief intercourse was marked by a singular embarrassment on both sides.

How little suspicion of the real truth was in the mind of Mr. Markland! Nothing was farther from his thoughts than the idea that Fanny had just received a letter from Mr. Lyon, and that the man he had seen was the messenger by whom the missive had been conveyed to the summer-house. A minute earlier, and that letter would have come into his hands. How instantly would a knowledge of its contents have affected all the purposes that were now leading him on with almost the blindness of infatuation. The man he was trusting so implicitly would have instantly stood revealed as a scheming, unprincipled adventurer. In such estimation, at least, he must have been held by Mr. Markland, and his future actions would have been governed by that estimate.

The answer to Fanny's earnest, almost peremptory demand, to be released from the injunction not to tell her parents of Mr. Lyon's return, was in her possession, and the instant she could get away to her own room, she tore the letter open. The reader already knows its contents. The effect upon her was paralyzing. He had said that she was in freedom to speak, but the consequences portrayed were too fearful to contemplate. In freedom? No! Instead of loosing the cords with which he had bound her spirit, he had only drawn them more tightly. She was in freedom to speak, but the very first word she uttered would sound the knell of her young heart's fondest hopes. How, then, could she speak that word? Lyon had not miscalculated the effect of his letter on the inexperienced, fond young girl, around whose innocent heart he had woven a spell of enchantment. Most adroitly had he seemed to leave her free to act from her own desires, while he had made that action next to impossible.

How rapidly, sometimes, does the young mind gain premature strength when subjected to strong trial. Little beyond an artless child was Fanny Markland when she first met the fascinating young stranger; and now she was fast growing into a deep-feeling, strong-thinking woman. Hitherto she had leaned with tender confidence on her parents, and walked the paths lovingly where they led the way. Now she was moving, with unaided footsteps, along a new and rugged road, that led she knew not whither; for clouds and darkness were in the forward distance. At every step, she found a new strength and a new power of endurance growing up in her young spirit. Thought, too, was becoming clearer and stronger. The mature woman had suddenly taken the place of the shrinking girl.

CHAPTER XX.

HALF the night, following the receipt of Mr. Lyon's letter, was spent in writing an answer. Imploringly she besought him to release her, truly, from the obligation to secrecy with which he had bound her. Most touchingly did she picture her state of mind, and the change wrought by it upon her mother. "I cannot bear this much longer," she said. "I am too weak for the burden you have laid upon me. It must be taken away soon, or I will sink under the weight. Oh, sir! if, as you say, you love me, prove that love by restoring me to my parents. Now, though present with them in body, I am removed from them in spirit. My mother's voice has a strange sound in my ears; and when she gazes sadly into my face I can hardly believe that it is my mother who is looking upon me. If she touches me, I start as if guilty of a crime. Oh, sir! to die would be easy for me now. What a sweet relief utter forgetfulness would be."

When Fanny awoke on the next morning, she found her mother standing beside her bed, and gazing down upon her face with a tender, anxious look. Sleep had cleared the daughter's thoughts and tranquilized her feelings. As her mother bent over and kissed her, she threw her arms around her neck and clung to her tightly.

"My dear child!" said Mrs. Markland, in a loving voice.

"Dear, dear mother!" was answered, with a gush of feeling.

"Something is troubling you, Fanny. You are greatly changed. Will you not open your heart to me?"

"Oh, mother!" She sobbed out the words.

"Am I not your truest friend?" said Mrs. Markland, speaking calmly, but very tenderly.

Fanny did not reply.

"Have I ever proved myself unworthy of your confidence?" She spoke as if from wounded feeling.

"Oh, no, no, dearest mother!" exclaimed Fanny. "How can you ask me such a question?"

"You have withdrawn your confidence," was almost coldly said.

"Oh, mother!" And Fanny drew her arms more tightly about her mother's neck, kissing her cheek passionately as she did so.

A little while Mrs. Markland waited, until her daughter's mind grew calmer; then she said—

"You are concealing from me something that troubles you. Whatever doubles you is of sufficient importance to be intrusted to your mother. I am older, have had more experience than you, and am your best friend. Not to confide in me is unjust to yourself, for, in my counsels, more than in those of your own heart, is there safety."

Mrs. Markland paused, and waited for some time, but there was no response from Fanny. She then said—

"You have received a letter from Mr. Lyon."

Fanny started as if a sudden blow had aroused her.

"And concealed the fact from your mother."

No answer; only bitter weeping.

"May I see that letter?" asked the mother, after a short pause. For nearly a minute she waited for a reply. But there was not a word from Fanny, who now lay as still as death. Slowly Mrs. Markland disengaged her arm from her daughter's neck, and raised herself erect. For the space of two or three minutes she sat on the bedside. All this time there was not the slightest movement on the part of Fanny. Then she arose and moved slowly across the room. Her hand was on the door, and the sound of the latch broke the silence of the room. At this instant the unhappy girl started up, and cried, in tones of anguish—

"Oh, my mother! my mother! come back!"

Mrs. Markland returned slowly, and with the air of one who hesitated. Fanny leaned forward against her, and wept freely.

"It is not yet too late, my child, to get back the peace of mind which this concealment has destroyed. Mr. Lyon has written to you?"

"Yes, mother."

"May I see his letter?"

There was no answer.

"Still not willing to trust your best friend," said Mrs. Markland.

"*Can* I trust you?" said Fanny, raising herself up suddenly, and gazing steadily into her mother's face. Mrs. Markland was startled as well by the words of her daughter as by the strange expression of her countenance.

"Trust me? What do you mean by such words?" she answered.

"If I tell you a secret, will you, at least for a little while, keep it in your own heart."

"Keep it from whom?"

"From father."

"You frighten me, my child! What have you to do with a secret that must be kept from your father!"

"I did not desire its custody."

"If it concerns your own or your father's welfare, so much the more is it imperative on you to speak to him freely. No true friend could lay upon you such an obligation, and the quicker you throw it off the better. What is the nature of this secret?"

"I cannot speak unless you promise me."

"Promise what?"

"To conceal from father what I tell you."

"I can make no such promise, Fanny."

"Then I am bound hand and foot," said the poor girl, in a distressed voice.

A long silence followed. Then the mother used argument and persuasion to induce Fanny to unbosom herself. But the effort was fruitless.

"If you promise to keep my secret for a single week, I will speak," said the unhappy girl, at length.

"I promise," was reluctantly answered.

"You know," answered Fanny, "it was rumored that Mr. Lyon had returned from the South while father was in New York." She did not look up at her mother as she said this.

"Yes." Mrs. Markland spoke eagerly.

"It is true that he was here."

"And you saw him?"

"Yes. I was sitting alone in the summer-house, over at the Fountain Grove, on the day after father went to New York, when I was frightened at seeing Mr. Lyon. He inquired anxiously if father were at home, and was much troubled when I told him he had gone to New York. He said that he had written to him to transact certain business; and that after writing he had seen reason to change his views, and fearing that a letter might not reach him in time, had hurried back in order to have a personal interview, but arrived too late. Father had already left for New York. This being so, he started back for the South at once, after binding me to a brief secrecy. He said that the fact of his return, if it became known to father, might be misunderstood by him, and the consequence of such a misapprehension would be serious injury to important interests. So far I have kept this secret, mother, and it has been to me a painful burden. You have promised to keep it for a single week."

"And this is all?" said Mrs. Markland, looking anxiously into her daughter's face.

"No, not all." Fanny spoke firmly. "I have since received two letters from him."

"May I see them?"

Fanny hesitated for some moments, and then going to a drawer, took two letters therefrom, and handed one of them to her mother. Mrs. Markland read it eagerly.

"You answered this?" she said.

"Yes."

"What did you say?"

"I cannot repeat my words. I was half beside myself, and only begged him to let me speak to you freely."

"And his reply?" said Mrs. Markland.

"Read it;" and Fanny gave her the second letter.

"Have you answered this?" inquired Mrs. Markland, after reading it over twice.

Fanny moved across the room again, and taking from the same drawer another letter, folded and sealed, broke the seal, and gave it to her mother.

"My poor, bewildered, unhappy child!" said Mrs. Markland, in a voice unsteady from deep emotion; and she gathered her arms tightly around her. "How little did I dream of the trials through which you were passing. But, now that I know all, let me be your counsellor, your supporter. You will be guided by me?"

"And you will not break your promise?" said Fanny.

"What promise?"

"To keep this from father a single week, or, until I can write to Mr. Lyon, and give him the chance of making the communication himself. This seems to me but just to him, as some interests, unknown to us, are at stake."

"Believe me, my daughter, it will be wisest to let your father know this at once."

"A week can make but little difference," urged Fanny.

"Consequences to your father, of the utmost importance, may be at stake. He is, I fear, involving himself with this man."

"Mr. Lyon is true and honourable," said Fanny. "He committed an error, that is all. Let him at least have the privilege of making his own explanations. I will add to my letter that only for a week longer can I keep his secret, and, to make an immediate revelation imperative on him, will say that you know all, and will reveal all at the end of that time, if he does not."

No considerations that Mrs. Markland could urge had any effect to change the purpose of Fanny in this matter.

"I must hold you to your promise," was the brief, final answer to every argument set forth by her mother.

How far she might hold that promise sacred was a subject of long and grave debate in the mind of Mrs. Markland. But we will not here anticipate her decision.

CHAPTER XXI.

OVER ten days had elapsed since Mr. Lyon answered the letter of Fanny Markland, and he was still awaiting a reply.

"This is a risky sort of business," so his friend had written him. "I succeeded in getting your letter into the young lady's hands, but not without danger of discovery. For whole hours I loitered in the grounds of Mr. Markland, and was going to leave for the city without accomplishing my errand, when I saw Fanny coming in the direction of the summer-house. After the letter was deposited in the place agreed upon, and I was making my way off, I almost stumbled over her father, who had just returned from the city. He saw me, though, of course, he did not know me, nor suspect my errand. But my evident desire to avoid observation must have excited some vague suspicions in his mind; for, on reaching a point from which I could observe without being observed, I saw that he was gazing intently in the direction I had taken. Then he stepped aside from the road, and walked towards the grove. But Fanny was a little in advance of him, and secured the letter. I waited to see him join her, and then hurried off.

"I tell you again, Lee, this is a risky business. Two days have passed, and yet there is no answer. I've seen Markland in the city once since that time. He looked unusually sober, I thought. Perhaps it was only imagination. You can think so if you please. Take my advice, and make no further advances in this direction. There is too much danger of discovery. Markland has paid over ten thousand dollars to Fenwick, and is to produce as much more this week. He goes in, you know, for forty thousand. The balance ought to be had from him as soon as possible. Write to Fenwick to get it without delay. That is my advice. If you get his treasure, you will have his heart. Nothing like a money interest to hold a man.

"What I fear is, that the girl has told him all. You were crazy to say that she could do so if it pleased her. Well, well! We shall soon see where this wind will drift us. You shall hear from me the moment I know any thing certain."

Lyon was much disturbed by this letter. He at once wrote to Mr. Fenwick, suggesting the propriety of getting the whole of Mr. Markland's investment as early as possible.

"I hear," he said, "that he is somewhat inclined to vacillate. That, after making up his mind to do a thing, and even after initiative steps are taken, he is apt to pause, look back, and reconsider. This, of course, will not suit us. The best way to manage him will be to get his money in our boat, and then we are sure of him. He is very wealthy, and can be of great use in the prosecution of our schemes."

Two or three days more elapsed, and Lyon was getting nervously anxious, when a letter from Fanny reached him. It was brief, but of serious import.

"I have revealed all to my mother," it began, "and my heart feels lighter. She promises to keep our secret one week, and no longer. Then all will be revealed to father. I gained this much time in order that you might have an opportunity to write and tell him every thing yourself. This, it seems to me, will be the best way. No time is to be lost. The week will expire quite as soon as your letter can reach him. So pray, Mr. Lyon, write at once. I shall scarcely sleep until all is over."

With an angry imprecation, Lyon dashed this letter on the floor. "Mad girl!" he said; "did I not warn her fully of the consequences? Write to her father? What shall I write? Tell him that I have deceived him! That when he thought me far away I was sitting beside his daughter, and tempting her to act towards him with concealment, if not duplicity! Madness! folly!"

"I was a fool," he communed with himself in a calmer mood, "to put so much in jeopardy for a woman! Nay, a girl—a mere child. But what is to be done? Three days only intervene between this time and the period at which our secret will be made known; so, whatever is to be done must be determined quickly. Shall I treat the matter with Markland seriously, or lightly? Not seriously, for that will surely cause him to do the same. Lightly, of course; for the manner in which I speak of it will have its influence. But first, I must manage to get him off to New York, and in the hands of Fenwick. The larger his actual investment in this business, the more easily the matter will be settled."

So he drew a sheet of paper before him, and wrote:

"MY DEAR MR. MARKLAND:—I have had so much important correspondence with Mr. Fenwick, our managing agent in New York, consequent on letters from London and Liverpool by last steamer, that I have been unable to proceed further than this point, but shall leave to-morrow. Mr. Fenwick has some very important information to communicate, and if he has not found time to write you, I would advise your going on to New York immediately. At best, hurried business letters give but imperfect notions of things. An hour's interview with Mr. Fenwick will enable you to comprehend the present state of affairs more perfectly than the perusal of a volume of letters. Some new aspects have presented themselves that I particularly wish you to consider. Mr. Fenwick has great confidence in your judgment, and would, I know, like to confer with you.

"Do not fail to bring me to the remembrance of Mrs. Markland and Fanny.

Ever yours,
LEE LYON."

"This for to-day's mail," said he, is he folded the letter. "If it does the work it is designed to accomplish, time, at least, will be gained. Now for the harder task."

Three times he tried to address Mr. Markland again, and as often tore up his letter. A fourth trial brought something nearer the mark.

"I'm afraid," he wrote, "a certain hasty act of mine, of which I ought before to have advised you, may slightly disturb your feelings. Yet don't let it have that effect, for there is no occasion whatever. Soon after leaving for the South, I wrote you to go to New York. The next mail brought me letters that rendered such a visit unnecessary, and fearing a communication by mail might not reach you promptly, I returned rapidly, and hastened to Woodbine Lodge to see you. Approaching your dwelling, I met Fanny, and learned from her that you had left for New York. Foolishly, as I now see it, I desired your daughter to keep the fact a secret for a short period, fearing lest you might not clearly comprehend my reason for returning. I wished to explain the matter myself. This trifling affair, it seems, has made Fanny very unhappy. I am really sorry. But it is over now, and I trust her spirits will rise again. You understand me fully, and can easily see why I might naturally fall into this trifling error.

"I wrote you yesterday, and hope you acted upon my suggestion. I proceed South in an hour. Every thing looks bright."

CHAPTER XXII.

"IT must be done this evening, Fanny," said Mrs. Markland, firmly. "The week has expired."

"Wait until to-morrow, dear mother," was urged in a manner that was almost imploring.

"My promise was for one week. Even against my own clear convictions of right, have I kept it. This evening, your father must know all."

Fanny buried her face, in her hands and wept violently. The trial and conflict of that week were, to Mrs. Markland, the severest, perhaps, of her whole life. Never before had her mind been in so confused a state; never had the way of duty seemed so difficult to find. A promise she felt to be a sacred thing; and this feeling had constrained her, even in the face of most powerful considerations, to remain true to her word. But now, she no longer doubted or hesitated; and she was counting the hours that must elapse before her husband's return from the city, eager to unburden her heart to him.

"There is hardly time," said Fanny, "for a letter to arrive from Mr. Lyon."

"I cannot help it, my child. Any further delay on my part would be criminal. Evil, past all remedy, may have already been done."

"I only asked for time, that Mr. Lyon might have an opportunity to write to father, and explain every thing himself."

"Probably your father has heard from him to-day. If so, well; but, if not, I shall certainly bring the matter to his knowledge."

There was something so decisive about Mrs. Markland, that Fanny ceased all further attempts to influence her, and passively awaited the issue.

The sun had only a few degrees to make ere passing from sight behind the western mountains. It was the usual time for Mr. Markland's return from the city, and most anxiously was his appearing looked for. But the sun went down, and the twilight threw its veil over wood and valley, and still his coming was delayed. He had gone in by railroad, and not by private conveyance as usual. The latest train had swept shrieking past, full half an hour, when Mrs. Markland turned sadly from the portico, in which she had for a long time been stationed, saying to Grace, who had been watching by her side—

"This is very strange! What can keep Edward? Can it be possible that he has remained in the city all night? I'm very much troubled. He may be sick."

"More likely," answered Grace, in a fault-finding way, "he's gone *trapseing* off to New York again, after that Englishman's business. I wish he would mind his own affairs."

"He would not have done this without sending us word," replied Mrs. Markland.

"Oh! I'm not so sure of that. I'm prepared for any thing."

"But it's not like Edward. You know that he is particularly considerate about such things."

"He used to be. But Edward Markland of last year is not the Edward Markland of to-day, as you know right well," returned the sister-in-law.

"I wish you wouldn't speak in that way about Edward any more, Grace. It is very unpleasant to me."

"The more so, because it is the truth," replied Grace Markland. "Edward, I'll warrant you, is now sweeping off towards New York. See if I'm not right."

"No, there he is now!" exclaimed Mrs. Markland, stepping back from the door she was about to enter, as the sound of approaching feet arrested her ear.

The two women looked eagerly through the dusky air. A man's form was visible. It came nearer.

"Edward!" was just passing joyfully from the lips of Mrs. Markland, when the word was suppressed.

"Good-evening, ladies," said a strange voice, as a man whom neither of them recognised paused within a few steps of where they stood.

"Mr. Willet is my name," he added.

"Oh! Mr. Willet, our new neighbour," said Mrs. Markland, with a forced composure of manner. "Walk in, if you please. We were on the lookout for Mr. Markland. He has not yet arrived from the city, and we are beginning to feel anxious about him."

"I am here to relieve that anxiety," replied the visitor in a cheerful voice, as he stepped on the portico. "Mr. Markland has made me the bearer of a message to his family."

"Where is he? What has detained him in the city?" inquired Mrs. Markland, in tones expressing her grief and disappointment.

"He has gone to New York," replied Mr. Willet.

"To New York!"

"Yes. He desired me to say to you, that letters received by the afternoon's mail brought information that made his presence in New York of importance. He had no time, before the cars started, to write, and I, therefore, bring you his verbal message."

It had been the intention of Mr. Willet to accept any courteous invitation extended by the family to pass a part of the evening with them; but, seeing how troubled Mrs. Markland was at the absence of her husband, he thought it better to decline entering the house, and wait for a better opportunity to make their more intimate acquaintance. So he bade her a good evening, after answering what further inquiries she wished to make, and returned to his own home.

Aunt Grace was unusually excited by the information received through their neighbour, and fretted and talked in her excited way for some time; but nothing that she said elicited any reply from Mrs. Markland, who seemed half stupefied, and sat through the evening in a state of deep abstraction, answering only in brief sentences any remarks addressed to her. It seemed to her as if her feet had wandered somehow into the mazes of a labyrinth, from which at each effort to get free she was only the more inextricably involved. Her perceptions had lost their clearness, and, still worse, her confidence in them was diminishing. Heretofore she had reposed all trust in her husband's rational intelligence; and her woman's nature had leaned upon him and clung to him as the vine to the oak. As his judgment determined, her intuitions had approved. Alas for her that this was no longer! Hitherto she had walked by his side with a clear light upon their path. She was ready to walk on still, and to walk bravely so far as herself was concerned, even though her straining eyes could not penetrate the cloudy veil that made all before her darkness and mystery.

Fanny, who had looked forward with a vague fear to her father's return on that evening, felt relieved on hearing that he had gone to New York, for that would give sufficient time for him to receive a letter from Mr. Lyon.

Thus it was with the family of Mr. Markland on this particular occasion. A crisis, looked for with trembling anxiety, seemed just at, hand; and yet it was still deferred—leaving, at least in one bosom, a heart-sickness that made life itself almost a burden.

CHAPTER XXIII.

THE close of the next day did not bring Mr. Markland, but only a hurried letter, saying that important business would probably keep him in New York a day or two longer. A postscript to the letter read thus:

"Mr. Elbridge will send you a deed of some warehouse property that I have sold. Sign and return it by the bearer."

If Mr. Markland had only said where a letter would reach him in New York, his wife would have lost no time in writing fully on the subject of Mr. Lyon's conduct toward Fanny. But, as there was great uncertainty about this, she felt that she could only await his return. And now she blamed herself deeply for having kept her word to Fanny. It was one of those cases, she saw, in which more evil was likely to flow from keeping a blind, almost extorted promise, than from breaking it.

"I ought to have seen my duty clearer," she said, in self-condemnation. "What blindness has possessed me!" And so she fretted herself, and admitted into her once calm, trusting spirit, a flood of self-reproaches and disquietude.

Fanny, now that the so anxiously dreaded period had gone by, and there was hope that her father would learn all from Mr. Lyon before he returned home, relapsed into a more passive state of mind. She had suffered much beyond her natural powers of endurance, in the last few days. A kind of reaction now followed, and she experienced a feeling of indifference as to results and consequences, that was a necessary relief to the over-strained condition of mind which had for some time existed.

On the day following, another letter was received from Mr. Markland.

"You must not expect me until the last of this week," he said. "Business matters of great importance will keep me here until that time. I have a letter from Mr. Lyon which I do not much like. It seems that he was at Woodbine Lodge, and saw Fanny, while I was away in New York. I have talked with a Mr. Fenwick here, a gentleman who knows all about him and his business, and he assures me that the reasons which Mr. Lyon gave for returning as he did from the South are valid. What troubles me most is that Fanny should have concealed it from both you and her father. We will talk this matter over fully on my return. If I had known it earlier, it might have led to an entire change of plans for the future. But it is too late now.

"I wrote you yesterday that I wished you to sign a deed which Mr. Elbridge would send out. He will send two more, which I would also like you to sign. I am making some investments here of great prospective value."

Mrs. Markland read this letter over and over again, and sat and thought about its contents until her mind grew so bewildered that it seemed as if reason were about to depart. If it was suggested that she ought not to sign the deeds that were to be presented for her signature, the suggestion was not for a single moment entertained; but rather flung aside with something of indignation.

A day or two after Mr. Willet called with the message from Mr. Markland, he went over again to Woodbine Lodge. It was late in the afternoon, and Fanny was sitting in the portico that looked from the western front of the dwelling, with her thoughts so far away from the actual things around her that she did not notice the approach of any one, until Mr. Willet, whom she had never met, was only a few yards distant; then she looked up, and as her eyes rested upon him, she started to her feet and struck her hands together, uttering an involuntary exclamation of surprise. The name of Mr. Lyon was half uttered, when she saw her mistake, and made a strong effort to compose her suddenly disturbed manner.

"Mrs. Markland is at home, I presume," said the visitor, in a respectful manner, as he paused a few paces distant from Fanny, and observed, with some surprise, the agitation his appearance had occasioned.

"She is. Will you walk in, sir?" The voice of Fanny trembled, though she strove hard to speak calmly and with apparent self-possession.

"My name is Mr. Willet."

"Oh! our new neighbour." And Fanny forced a smile, while she extended her hand, as she added:

"Walk in, sir. My mother will be gratified to see you."

"Has your father returned from New York?" inquired Mr. Willet, as he stood looking down upon the face of Miss Markland, with a feeling of admiration for its beauty and innocence.

"Not yet. Mother does not look for him until the last of this week."

"He did not expect to be gone over a single day, when he left?"

"No, sir. But business has detained him. Will you not walk in, Mr. Willet?" The earnestness with which he was looking into her face was disconcerting Fanny. So she stepped toward the door, and led the way into the house.

"Mr. Willet," said Fanny, introducing her visitor, as they entered the sitting-room.

Mrs. Markland extended her hand and gave their new neighbour a cordial reception. Aunt Grace bowed formally, and fixed her keen eyes upon him with searching glances. While the former was thinking how best to entertain their visitor, the latter was scrutinizing his every look, tone, word, and movement. At first, the impression made upon her was not altogether favourable; but gradually, as she noted every particular of his conversation, as well as the various changes of his voice and countenance, her feelings toward him underwent a change; and when he at length addressed a few words to her, she replied, with unusual blandness of manner.

"How are your mother and sisters?" inquired Mrs. Markland, soon after Mr. Willet came in. "I have not yet called over to see them, but shall do so to-morrow."

"They are well, and will be exceedingly gratified to receive a visit from you," replied Mr. Willet.

"How are they pleased with the country?"

"That question they would find it difficult yet to answer. There is much pleasant novelty, and much real enjoyment of nature's varied beauties. A sense of freedom and a quietude of spirit, born of the stillness that, to people just from the noisy town, seems brooding over all things. Some of the wants, created by our too artificial mode of living in cities, are occasionally felt; but, on the whole, we are gainers, so far, by our experiment."

"Your sisters, I am sure, must enjoy the beauty with which you are surrounded. There is not a lovelier place than the one you have selected in the whole neighbourhood."

"Always excepting Woodbine Lodge," returned the visitor, with a courteous bow. "Yes," he added, "Sweetbrier is a charming spot, and its beauty grows upon you daily. My sister Flora, just about your own age," and Mr. Willet turned toward Fanny, "is particularly desirous to make your acquaintance. You must call over with your mother. I am sure you will like each other. Flora, if a brother may venture to herald a sister's praise, is a dear, good girl. She has heard a friend speak of you, and bears already, toward you, a feeling of warmer tone than mere friendship."

Mr. Willet fixed his eyes so earnestly on the countenance of Fanny, that she partly averted her face to conceal the warm flush that came to her cheeks.

"I shall be happy to make her acquaintance," she replied. "Our circle of friends cannot be so large here as in the city; but we may find compensation in closer attachments."

"I will say to my mother and sisters, that they may expect to see you to-morrow," And Mr. Willet looked from face to face.

"Yes; we will ride over to-morrow," said Mrs. Markland.

"And you, also, Miss Markland." The courteous manner in which this was said quite won the heart of Aunt Grace, and she replied that she would give herself that pleasure.

Mr. Willet sat for an hour, during which time he conversed in the most agreeable and intelligent manner; and, on retiring, left behind him a very favourable impression.

"I like that man," said Aunt Grace, with an emphasis that caused Mrs. Markland to look toward her and smile.

"That's a little remarkable. You are not very apt to like men at first sight."

"I like him, for he's a true man and a gentleman," returned Aunt Grace. "And true men, I think, are scarce articles."

"Ever hasty in your conclusions, whether favourable or unfavourable," said Mrs. Markland.

"And rarely in error. You may add that," replied the sister-in-law, confidently. "When Mr. Lyon darkened our doors,"—Fanny was passing from the room, and Aunt Grace spoke in a guarded voice—"I said he would leave a shadow behind him, and so he has. Was my judgment hasty, so far as he was concerned? I think you will hardly say so. But, my word for it, the presence of Mr. Willet will ever bring a gleam of sunshine. I am glad he has come into our neighbourhood. If his mother and sisters are like him, they are a company of choice spirits."

113

CHAPTER XXIV.

TO the opinion of her sister-in-law, Mrs. Markland made no dissent. She was, also, favourably impressed with Mr. Willet, and looked forward with pleasure to making the acquaintance of his mother and sisters.

On the following morning the carriage was ordered, and about eleven o'clock Mrs. Markland, Aunt Grace, and Fanny, were driven over to "Sweetbrier," the fanciful name which Mr. Ashton, the former owner, had given to the beautiful seat, now the property of Mr. Willet.

The day was cloudless, the air cool and transparent, the sky of the deepest cerulean. These mirrored themselves in the spirits of our little party. Mrs. Markland looked calm and cheerful; Fanny's thoughts were drawn out of herself, and her heart responded to the visible beauty around her. Even Aunt Grace talked of the sky, the trees, and the flowers, and saw a new charm in every thing.

"I presume we shall not meet Mr. Willet," she remarked, as the carriage drove within the elegant grounds of their neighbour.

"He probably goes to the city every day," said Mrs. Markland. "I believe he is engaged in business."

"Yes; I think I heard Edward say that he was."

"Our visit might be a pleasant one in some respects," observed Mrs. Markland, "if he were at home. To him, we are not entire strangers."

"I see him in the portico," said Fanny, leaning toward the carriage window. They were now in sight of the house.

"Yes, there he is," added Aunt Grace, in a pleased tone of voice.

In a few minutes the carriage drew up at the beautiful mansion, in the portico of which were Mr. Willet and his mother and sisters, waiting to receive them. The welcome was most cordial, and the ladies soon felt at home with each other.

Flora, the youngest sister of Mr. Willet, was a lovely girl about Fanny's age. It did not take them long to know and appreciate each other. The mind of Flora was naturally stronger than that of Fanny, partaking slightly of the masculine type; but only sufficient to give it firmness and self-reliance. Her school education had progressed farther, and she had read, and thought, and seen more of the world than Fanny. Yet the world had left no stain upon her garments, for, in entering it, she had been lovingly guarded. To her brother she looked up with much of a child's unwavering confidence. He was a few years her senior, and she could not remember the time when she had not regarded him as a man whose counsels were full of wisdom.

"Where have you been for the last hour?" Mr. Willet inquired of the young maidens, as they entered, arm-in-arm, their light forms gently inclined to each other.

"Wandering over your beautiful grounds," replied Fanny.

"I hardly thought you would see them as beautiful," said Mr. Willet.

"Do you think that I have no eye for the beautiful?" returned Fanny, with a smile.

"Not so," quickly answered Mr. Willet. "Woodbine Lodge is so near perfection that you must see defects in Sweetbrier."

"I never saw half the beauty in nature that has been revealed to my eyes this morning," said Fanny. "It seemed as if I had come upon enchanted ground. Ah, sir, your sister has opened a new book for me to read in—the book of nature."

Mr. Willet glanced, half-inquiringly, toward Flora.

"Fanny speaks with enthusiasm," said the sister.

"What have you been talking about? What new leaf has Flora turned for you, Miss Markland?"

"A leaf on which there is much written that I already yearn to understand. All things visible, your sister said to me, are but the bodying forth in nature of things invisible, yet in harmony with immutable laws of order."

"Reason will tell you that this is true," remarked Mr. Willet.

"Yes; I see that it must be so. Yet what a world of new ideas it opens to the mind! The flower I hold in my hand, Flora says, is but the outbirth, or bodily form, of a spiritual flower. How strange the thought!"

"Did she not speak truly?" asked Mr. Willet, in a low, earnest voice.

"What is that?" inquired Mrs. Markland, who was not sure that she had heard her daughter correctly.

"Flora say that this flower is only the bodily form of a spiritual flower; and that, without the latter, the former would have no existence."

Mrs. Markland let her eyes fall to the floor, and mused for some moments.

"A new thought to me," she at length said, looking up. "Where did you find it, Flora?"

"I have believed this ever since I could remember any thing," replied Flora.

"You have?"

"Yes, ma'am. It was among the first lessons that I learned from my mother."

"Then you believe that every flower has a spirit," said Mrs. Markland.

"Every flower has life," was calmly answered.

"True."

"And every different flower a different life. How different, may be seen when we think of the flower which graces the deadly nightshade, and of that which comes the fragrant herald of the juicy orange. We call this life the spiritual flower."

"A spiritual flower! Singular thought!" Mrs. Markland mused for some time.

"There is a spiritual world," said Mr. Willet, in his gentle, yet earnest way.

"Oh, yes. We all believe that." Mrs. Markland fixed her eyes on the face of Mr. Willet with a look of interest.

"What do we mean by a world?"

Mrs. Markland felt a rush of new ideas, though seen but dimly, crowding into her mind.

"We cannot think of a world," said Mr. Willet, "except as filled with objects, whether that world be spiritual or natural. The poet, in singing of the heavenly land, fails not to mention its fields of 'living green,' and 'rivers of delight.' And what are fields without grass, and flowers, and tender herb? If, then, there be flowers in the spiritual world, they must be spiritual flowers."

"And that is what Flora meant?" said Mrs. Markland.

"Nothing more," said Flora; "unless I add, that all flowers in the natural world derive their life from flowers in the spiritual world; as all other objects in nature have a like correspondent origin."

"This comes to me as an entirely new idea," said Mrs. Markland, in a thoughtful way. "Yet how beautiful! It seems to bring my feet to the verge of a new world, and my hand trembles with an impulse to stretch itself forth and lift the vail."

"Do not repress the impulse," said Mrs. Willet, laying a hand gently upon one of Mrs. Markland's.

"Ah! But I grope in the dark."

"We see but dimly here, for we live in the outward world, and only faint yet truthful images of the inner world are revealed to us. No effort of the mind is so difficult as that of lifting itself above the natural and the visible into the spiritual and invisible—invisible, I mean, to the bodily eyes. So bound down by mere sensual things are all our ideas, that it is impossible, when the effort is first made, to see any thing clear in spiritual light. Yet soon, if the effort be made, will the straining vision have faint glimpses of a world whose rare beauties have never been seen by natural eyes. There is the natural, and there is the spiritual; but they are so distinct from each other, that the one by sublimation, increase, or decrease, never becomes the other. Yet are they most intimately connected; so intimately that, without the latter, the former could have no existence. The relation is, in fact, that of cause and effect."

"I fear this subject is too grave a one for our visitors," said Mr. Willet, as his mother ceased speaking.

"It may be," remarked the lady, with a gentle smile that softened her features and gave them a touch of heavenly beauty. "And Mrs. Markland will forgive its intrusion upon her. We must not expect that others will always be attracted by themes in which we feel a special interest."

"You could not interest me more," said Mrs. Markland. "I am listening with the deepest attention."

"Have you ever thought much of the relation between your soul and body; or, as I would say, between your spiritual body and your natural body?" asked Mrs. Willet.

"Often; but with a vagueness that left the mind wearied and dissatisfied."

"I had a long talk with Mr. Allison on that subject," said Fanny.

"Ah!" Mrs. Willet looked toward Fanny with a brightening face. "And what did he say?"

"Oh! a great deal—more than I can remember."

"You can recollect something?"

"Oh yes. He said that our spiritual bodies were as perfectly organized as our material bodies, and that they could see, and hear, and feel."

"He said truly. That our spirits have vision every one admits, when he uses the words, on presenting some idea or principle to another—'Can't you see it?' The architect sees the palace or temple before he embodies it in marble, and thus makes it visible to natural eyes. So does the painter see his picture; and the sculptor his statue in the unhewn stone. You see the form of your absent father with a distinctness of vision that makes every feature visible; but not with the eyes of your body."

"No, not with my bodily eyes," said Fanny. "I have thought a great deal about this since I talked with Mr. Allison; and the more I think of it, the more clearly do I perceive that we have spiritual bodies as well as natural bodies."

"And the inevitable conclusion is, that the spiritual body must live, breathe, and act in a world above or within the natural world, where all things are adapted to its functions and quality."

"In this world are the spiritual flowers we were speaking about?" said Mrs. Markland, smiling.

"Yes, ma'am; in this world of *causes*, where originate all *effects* seen in the world of nature," answered Mrs. Willet;—"the world from which flowers as well as men are born."

"I am bewildered," said Mrs. Markland, "by these suggestions. That a volume of truth lies hidden from common eyes in this direction, I can well believe. As yet my vision is too feeble to penetrate the vail."

"If you look steadily in this direction, your eyes will, in time, get accustomed to the light, and gradually see clearer and clearer," said Mrs. Willet.

CHAPTER XXV.

SOME incidents interrupted the conversation at this point, and when it flowed on again, it was in a slightly varied channel, and gradually changed from the abstract into matters of more personal interest.

"What a mystery is life!" exclaimed Mrs. Markland, the words following an observation that fell from the lips of Mr. Willet.

"Is it a mystery to you?" was asked, with something of surprise in the questioner's tone.

"There are times," replied Mrs. Markland, "when I can see a harmony, an order, a beauty in every thing; but my vision does not always remain clear. Ah! if we could ever be content to do our duty in the present, and leave results to Him who cares for us with an infinite love!"

"A love," added Mrs. Willet, "that acts by infinite wisdom. Can we not trust these fully? Infinite love and infinite wisdom?"

"Yes!—yes!—reason makes unhesitating response. But when dark days come, how the poor heart sinks! Our faith is strong when the sky is bright. We can trust the love and wisdom of our Maker when broad gleams of sunshine lie all along our pathway."

"True; and therefore the dark days come to us as much in mercy as the bright ones, for they show us that our confidence in Heaven is not a living faith. 'There grows much bread in the winter night,' is a proverb full of a beautiful significance. Wheat, or bread, is, in the outer world of nature, what good is in the inner world of spirit. And as well in the winter night of trial and adversity is bread grown, as in the winter of external nature. The bright wine of truth we crush from purple clusters in genial autumn; but bread grows even while the vine slumbers."

"I know," said Mrs. Markland, "that, in the language of another, 'sweet are the uses of adversity.' I know it to be true, that good gains strength and roots itself deeply in the winter of affliction and adversity, that it may grow up stronger, and produce a better harvest in the end. As an abstract truth, how clear this is! But, at the first chilling blast, how the spirit sinks; and when the sky grows dull and leaden, how the heart shivers!"

"It is because we rest in mere natural and external things as the highest good."

"Yes—how often do we hear that remarked! It is the preacher's theme on each recurring Sabbath," said Mrs. Markland, in an abstracted way. "How often have words of similar import passed my own lips, when I spoke as a mentor, and vainly thought my own heart was not wedded to the world and the good things it offers for our enjoyment!"

"If we are so wedded," said Mrs. Willet, in her earnest, gentle way, "is not that a loving Providence which helps us to a knowledge of the truth, even though the lesson prove a hard one to learn—nay, even if it be acquired under the rod of a stern master?"

"Oh, yes, yes!" said Mrs. Markland, unhesitatingly.

"It is undoubtedly true," said Mrs. Willet, "that all things of natural life are arranged, under Providence, with a special view to the formation and development within us of spiritual life, or the orderly and true lives of our spirits. We are not born into this world merely to eat, drink, and enjoy sensual and corporeal pleasures alone. This is clear to any mind on the slightest reflection. The pleasures of a refined taste, as that of music and art, are of a higher and more enduring character than these; and of science and knowledge, still more enduring. Yet not for these, as the highest development of our lives, were we born. Taste, science, knowledge, even intelligence, to which science and knowledge open the door, leave us still short of our high destiny. The Temple of Wisdom is yet to be penetrated."

"Science, knowledge, intelligence, wisdom!" said Mrs. Markland, speaking slowly and thoughtfully. "What a beautiful and orderly series! First we must learn the dead formulas."

"Yes, the lifeless scientifics, if they may so be called, must first be grounded in the memory. Arrangement and discrimination follow. One fact or truth is compared with another, and the mind thus comes to know, or has knowledge. Mere facts in the mind are lifeless without thought. Thought broods over dead science in the external memory, and knowledge is born."

"How clear! How beautiful!" ejaculated Mrs. Markland.

"But knowledge is little more than a collection of materials, well arranged; intelligence builds the house."

"And wisdom is the inhabitant," said Mrs. Markland, whose quick perceptions were running in advance.

"Yes—all that preceded was for the sake of the inhabitant. Science is first; then knowledge, then intelligence—but all is for the sake of wisdom."

"Wisdom—wisdom." Mrs. Markland mused again.

"What is wisdom?"

"Angelic life," said Mrs. Willet. "One who has thought and written much on heavenly themes, says, 'Intelligence and wisdom make an angel.'"

Mrs. Markland sighed, but did not answer. Some flitting thought seemed momentarily to have shadowed her spirit.

"To be truly wise is to be truly good," said Mrs. Willet. "We think of angels as the wisest and best of beings, do we not?"

"Oh, yes."

"The highest life, then, toward which we can aspire, is angelic life. Their life is a life of goodness, bodying itself in wisdom."

"How far below angelic life is the natural life that we are leading here!" said Mrs. Markland.

"And therefore is it that a new life is prescribed,—a life that begins in learning heavenly truths first, as mere external formulas of religion. These are to be elevated into knowledge, intelligence, and afterward wisdom. And it is because we are so unwilling to lead this heavenly life that our way in the world is often made rough and thorny, and our sky dark with cloud and tempest."

Mr. Willet now interrupted the conversation by a remark that turned the thoughts of all from a subject which he felt to be too grave for the occasion, and soon succeeded in restoring a brighter hue to the mind of Mrs. Markland. Soon after, the visitors returned home, all parties feeling happier for the new acquaintance which had been formed, and holding in their hearts a cheerful promise of many pleasant interchanges of thought and feeling.

Many things said by Mr. Willet, and by his mother and sisters, made a strong impression on the mind of Mrs. Markland and her daughter. They perceived some things in a new and clearer light that had been to them vailed in obscurity before.

"Flora is a lovely girl," said Fanny, "and so wise beyond her years. Many times I found myself looking into her face and wondering not to see the matron there. We are fortunate in such neighbours."

"Very fortunate, I think," replied her mother. "I regard them as having minds of a superior order."

"Flora is certainly a superior girl. And she seems to me as good as she is wise. Her thought appears ever lifting itself upward, and there is a world of new ideas in her mind. I never heard any one talk just as she does."

"What struck me in every member of the family," said Mrs. Markland, "was a profound religious trust; a full confidence in that Infinite Wisdom which cannot err, nor be unkind. Ah! my daughter, to possess that were worth more than all this world can offer."

A servant who had been despatched for letters, brought, late in the day, one for Mrs. Markland from her husband, and one for Fanny from Mr. Lyon. This was the first communication the latter had sent to Fanny direct by post. The maiden turned pale as she received the letter, and saw, by the superscription, from whom it came. Almost crushing it in her hand, she hurried away, and when alone, broke the seal, and with unsteady hands unfolded it, yet scarcely daring to let her eyes rest upon the first words:—

"MY EVER DEAR FANNY."—[How her heart leaped as she read these words!]
—"I write to you direct by post, for there remains no longer any reason why our correspondence should be a concealed one. I have also written to your father, and shall await his response with the deepest anxiety. Let his decision in the matter be what it may, I shall forever bear your image in my heart as a most sacred possession. Will you not write immediately? Conceal nothing of the effect produced on your father's mind. Send your letter as addressed before, and it will be

forwarded to my hands. May heaven bless you, dear Fanny! In haste, suspense, and deep anxiety.

LEE LYON."

Mrs. Markland's letter from her husband was very brief, and rather vague as to his purposes:

"I will be home, if possible, this week; but may be kept here, by important business, over Sunday. If so, I will write again. Every thing is progressing to my fullest satisfaction. Little danger, I think, of my dying from *ennui* in the next twelve months. Head and hands will both be pretty well occupied for that period, if not longer. There is too much vitality about me for the life of a drone. I was growing restless and unhappy from sheer idleness and want of purpose. How does our dear Fanny seem? I feel no little concern about her. Mr. Lyon makes no direct proposition for her hand, but it is evidently his purpose to do so. I wish I knew him better, and that I had, just now, a freer mind to consider the subject. Weigh it well in your thoughts, Agnes; and by all means observe Fanny very closely. Dear child! She is far too young for this experience. Ah, me! The more I think of this matter, the more I feel troubled.

"But good-by, for a little while. I am writing in haste, and cannot say half that is in my thoughts."

CHAPTER XXVI.

IT was not until the middle of the succeeding week that Mr. Markland returned from New York. He had a look of care that did not escape the observation of his wife. To her inquiries as to the cause of his prolonged absence, he replied vaguely, yet with reference to some business of vast magnitude, in which he had become interested. Two days passed without allusion, on either side, to the subject of their daughter's relation to Mr. Lyon, and then, to some question of Mrs. Markland, her husband replied in so absent a way, that she did not press the matter on his attention. Fanny was reserved and embarrassed in the presence of her father, and evidently avoided him.

More than a week went by in this unsatisfactory manner, when, on returning one day from the city, Mr. Markland showed an unusual elation of

spirits. As soon as there was an opportunity to be alone with his wife, he said
—

"I may have to be absent several weeks."

"Why so?" she asked, quickly, as a shadow fell over her face.

"Business," was briefly answered.

Mrs. Markland sighed, and her eyes fell to the floor.

"I have been a drone in the world's busy hive long enough, Agnes; and now I must go to work again, and that in right good earnest. The business that took me to New York is growing daily in importance, and will require my best thought and effort. The more thoroughly I comprehend it, the more clearly do I see its vast capabilities. I have already embarked considerable money in the enterprise, and shall probably see it to my interest to embark more. To do this, without becoming an active worker and director, would neither be wise nor like your husband, who is not a man to trust himself on the ocean of business without studying well the charts, and, at times, taking fast hold upon the rudder."

"You might have been so happy here, Edward," said Mrs. Markland, looking into his face and smiling feebly.

"A happy idler? Impossible!"

"You have been no idler, my husband, since our retirement from the city. Look around, and say whose intelligence, whose taste, are visible wherever the eye falls?"

"A poor, vain life, for a man of thought and energy, has been mine, Agnes, during the last few years. The world has claims on me beyond that of mere landscape-gardening! In a cultivation of the beautiful alone no man of vigorous mind can or ought to rest satisfied. There is a goal beyond, and it is already dimly revealed, in the far distance, to my straining vision."

"I greatly fear, Edward," replied his wife, speaking in her gentle, yet impressive way, "that when the goal you now appear so eager to reach, is gained, you will see still another beyond."

"It may be so, Agnes," was answered, in a slightly depressed voice; "yet the impulse to bear onward to the goal now in view is not the less ardent for the suggestion. I can no more pause than the avalanche once in motion. I must onward in the race I have entered."

"To gain what, Edward?"

"I shall gain large wealth."

"Have we not all things here that heart can desire, my husband?"

"No, Agnes," was replied with emphasis.

"What is lacking?"

"Contentment."

"Edward!" There came a quick flush to the brow of Mrs. Markland.

"I cannot help the fact, Agnes," said Mr. Markland. "For months I have suffered from a growing dissatisfaction with the fruitless life I am leading."

"And yet with what a fond desire we looked forward to the time when we could call a spot like this our own! The world had for us no more tempting offer."

"While struggling up from the valley, we cannot know how wide the landscape will spread beneath our enchanted vision. We fix our eyes on the point to be gained. That reached, we are, for a time, content with our elevation. But just enough of valley and mountain, stretching far off in the dim distance, is revealed, to quicken our desire for a more extended vision, and soon, with renewed strength, we lift our gaze upward, and the word 'excelsior!' comes almost unbidden to our lips. There is a higher and a highest place to be gained, and I feel, Agnes, that there will be no rest for my feet until I reach the highest."

"Pray heaven your too eager feet stumble not!" almost sobbed Mrs. Markland, with something of a prophetic impulse.

The tone and manner of his wife, more than her words, disturbed Mr. Markland.

"Why should the fact of my re-entering business so trouble you?" he asked. "An active, useful life is man's truest life, and the only one in which he can hope for contentment."

Mrs. Markland did not answer, but partly turned her face away to conceal its expression.

"Are you not a little superstitious?" inquired her husband.

"I believe not," was answered with forced calmness. "But I may be very selfish."

"Selfish, Agnes! Why do you say that?"

"I cannot bear the thought of giving you up to the busy world again," she answered, tenderly, leaning her head against him. "Nor will it be done without struggle and pain on my part. When we looked forward to the life we have been leading for the last few years, I felt that I could ask of the world nothing of external good beyond; I have yet asked nothing. Here I have found my earthly paradise. But if banishment must come, I will try to go forth patiently, even though I cannot shut the fountain of tears. There is another Eden."

Mr. Markland was about replying, when his sister entered the room, and he remained silent.

CHAPTER XXVII.

THE conversation was resumed after they were again alone.

"Grace frets herself continually about Fanny," said Mrs. Markland, as her sister-in-law, after remaining for a short time, arose and left the room.

"She is always troubling herself about something," answered Mr. Markland, impatiently.

"Like many others, she generally looks at the shadowed side. But Fanny is so changed, that not to feel concern on her account would show a strange indifference."

Mr. Markland sighed involuntarily, but made no answer. He, too, felt troubled whenever his thoughts turned to his daughter. Yet had he become so absorbed in the new business that demanded his attention, and in the brilliant results which dazzled him, that to think, to any satisfactory conclusion, on the subject of Fanny's relation to Mr. Lyon, had been impossible; and this was the reason why he rather avoided than sought a conference with his wife. She now pressed the matter on his attention so closely, that he could not waive its consideration.

"Mr. Lyon's purposes are not to be mistaken," said Mrs. Markland.

"In what respect?" was evasively inquired.

"In respect to Fanny."

"I think not," was the brief response.

"Has he written you formally on the subject?"

"No."

"His conduct, then, to speak in the mildest terms, is very singular."

"His relation to Fanny has been an exceedingly embarrassing one," said

Mr. Markland. "There has been no opportunity for him to speak out freely."

"That disability no longer exists."

"True, and I shall expect from him an early and significant communication."

"Let us look this matter directly in the face, Edward," said Mrs. Markland, in a sober voice. "Suppose he ask for the hand of our daughter."

"A thing not at all unlikely to happen," answered her husband.

"What then?"

"I fear you are prejudiced against Mr. Lyon," said Markland, a little coldly.

"I love my child!" was the simple, touching answer.

"Well?"

"I am a woman," she further said, "and know the wants of a woman's heart. I am a wife, and have been too tenderly loved and cared for, not to desire a like happy condition for my child." And she leaned against her husband, and gazed into his face with a countenance full of thankful love.

"Mr. Lyon is a man of honour," said Mr. Markland. "Has he a tender, loving heart? Can he appreciate a woman?"

"If Fanny loves him—"

"Oh, Edward! Edward!" returned his wife, interrupting him. "She is only a child, and yet incapable of genuine love. The bewildering passion this man has inspired in her heart is born of impulse, and the fires that feed it are consuming her. As for me—and I speak the words thoughtfully and sadly—I would rather stretch forth my hand to drop flowers on her coffin than deck her for such a bridal."

"Why do you speak so strongly, Agnes? You know nothing against Mr. Lyon. He may be all you could desire in the husband of your child."

"A mother's instincts, believe me, Edward, are rarely at fault here."

Mr. Markland was oppressed by the subject, and could not readily frame an answer that he felt would be satisfactory to his wife. After a pause, he said:

"There will be time enough to form a correct judgment."

"But let us look the matter in the face now, Edward," urged his wife. "Suppose, as I just suggested, he ask for the hand of our daughter,—a thing, as you admit, likely to happen. What answer shall we make? Are you prepared to give a decisive reply?"

"Not on the instant. I should wish time for consideration."

"How long?"

"You press the subject very closely, Agnes."

"I cannot help doing so. It is the one that involves most of good or evil in the time to come. All others are, for the present, dwarfed by it into insignificance. A human soul has been committed to our care, capable of the highest enjoyments or the deepest misery. An error on our part may prove fatal to that soul. Think of this, Edward! What are wealth, honour, eminence, in comparison with the destiny of a single human soul? If you should achieve the brilliant results that now dazzle your eyes, and in pursuit of which you are venturing so much, would there be any thing in all you gained to compensate for the destruction of our daughter's happiness?"

"But why connect things that have no relation, Agnes? What has the enterprise I am now prosecuting to do with this matter of our daughter?"

"Much, every way. Does it not so absorb your mind that you cannot think clearly on any other subject? And does not your business connection with Mr. Lyon bias your feelings unduly in his favour?"

Mr. Markland shook his head.

"But think more earnestly, Edward. Review what this man has done. Was it honourable for him so to abuse our hospitality as to draw our child into a secret correspondence? Surely something must warp your mind in his favour, or you would feel a quick indignation against him. He cannot be a true man, and this conviction every thing in regard to him confirms. Believe me, Edward, it was a dark day in the calendar of our lives when the home circle at Woodbine Lodge opened to receive him."

"I trust to see the day," answered Mr. Markland, "when you will look back to this hour and smile at the vague fears that haunted your imagination."

"Fears? They have already embodied themselves in realities," was the emphatic answer. "The evil is upon us, Edward. We have failed to guard the door of our castle, and the enemy has come in. Ah, my husband! if you could see with my eyes, there would stand before you a frightful apparition."

"And what shape would it assume?" asked Mr. Markland, affecting to treat lightly the fears of his wife.

"That of a beautiful girl, with white, sunken cheeks, and hollow, weeping eyes."

An instant paleness overspread the face of Mr. Markland.

"Look there!" said Mrs. Markland, suddenly, drawing the attention of her husband to a picture on the wall. The eyes of Mr. Markland fell instantly on a portrait of Fanny. It was one of those wonders of art that transform dead colours into seeming life, and, while giving to every lineament a faultless reproduction, heightens the charm of each. How sweetly smiled down upon Mr. Markland the beautiful lips! How tender were the loving eyes, that fixed themselves upon him and held him almost spell-bound!

"Dear child!" he murmured, in a softened voice, and his eyes grew so dim that the picture faded before him.

"As given to us!" said Mrs. Markland, almost solemnly.

A dead silence followed.

"But are we faithful to the trust? Have we guarded this treasure of uncounted value? Alas! alas! Already the warm cheeks are fading; the eyes are blinded with tears. I look anxiously down the vista of years, and shudder. Can the shadowy form I see be that of our child?"

"Oh, Agnes! Agnes!" exclaimed Mr. Markland, lifting his hands, and partly averting his face, as if to avoid the sight of some fearful image.

There was another hushed silence. It was broken by Mrs. Markland, who grasped the hand of her husband, and said, in a low, impressive voice—

"Fanny is yet with us—yet in the sheltered fold of home, though her eyes have wandered beyond its happy boundaries and her ears are hearkening to a voice that is now calling her from the distance. Yet, under our loving guardianship, may we not do much to save her from consequences my fearful heart has prophesied?"

"What can we do?" Mr. Markland spoke with the air of one bewildered.

"Guard her from all further approaches of this man; at least, until we know him better. There is a power of attraction about him that few so young and untaught in the world's strange lessons as our child, can resist."

"He attracts strongly, I know," said Mr. Markland, in an absent way.

"And therefore the greater our child's danger, if he be of evil heart."

"You, wrong him, believe me, Agnes, by even this intimation. I will vouch for him as a man of high and honourable principles." Mr. Markland spoke with some warmth of manner.

"Oh, Edward! Edward!" exclaimed his wife, in a distressed voice. "What has so blinded you to the real quality of this man? 'By their fruit ye shall know them.' And is not the first fruit, we have plucked from this tree, bitter to the taste?"

"You are excited and bewildered in thought, Agnes," said Mr. Markland, in a soothing voice. "Let us waive this subject for the present, until both of us can refer to it with a more even heart-beat."

Mrs. Markland caught her breath, as if the air had suddenly grown stifling.

"Will they ever beat more evenly?" she murmured, in a sad voice.

"Why, Agnes! Into what a strange mood you have fallen! You are not like yourself."

"And I am not, to my own consciousness. For weeks it has seemed to me as if I were in a troubled dream."

"The glad waking will soon come, I trust," said Mr. Markland, with forced cheerfulness of manner.

"I pray that it may be so," was answered, in a solemn voice.

There was silence for some moments, and then the other's full heart overflowed. Mr. Markland soothed her, with tender, hopeful words, calling her fears idle, and seeking, by many forms of speech, to scatter the doubts and fears which, like thick clouds, had encompassed her spirit.

CHAPTER XXVIII.

FROM that period, Mr. Markland not only avoided all conference with his wife touching their daughter's relation to Mr. Lyon, but became so deeply absorbed in business matters, that he gave little earnest thought to the subject. As the new interests in which he was involved grew into larger and larger importance, all things else dwindled comparatively.

At the end of six months he was so changed that, even to his own family, he was scarcely like the same individual. All the time he appeared thinking intensely. As to "Woodbine Lodge," its beauties no longer fell into thought or perception. The charming landscape spread itself wooingly before him, but he saw nothing of its varied attractions. Far away, fixing his inward gaze with the fascination of a serpent's eye, was the grand result of his new enterprise, and all else was obscured by the brightness of a vortex toward which he was moving in swiftly-closing circles. Already two-thirds of his handsome fortune was embarked in this new scheme, that was still growing in magnitude, and still, like the horse-leech, crying "Give! give!" All that now remained was "Woodbine Lodge," valued at over twenty-five thousand dollars. This property he determined to leave untouched. But new calls for funds were constantly being made by Mr. Fenwick, backed by the most flattering reports from Mr. Lyon and his associates in Central America, and at last the question of selling or heavily mortgaging the "Lodge" had to be considered. The latter alternative was adopted, and the sum of fifteen thousand dollars raised, and thrown, with a kind of desperation, into the whirlpool which had already swallowed up nearly the whole of his fortune.

With this sum in his hands, Mr. Markland went to New York. He found the Company's agent, Mr. Fenwick, as full of encouraging words and sanguine anticipations as ever.

"The prize is just within our grasp," said he, in answer to some close inquiries of Markland. "There has been a most vigorous prosecution of the works, and a more rapid absorption of capital, in consequence, than was anticipated; but, as you have clearly seen, this is far better than the snail-like progress at which affairs were moving when Mr. Lyon reached the ground. Results which will now crown our efforts in a few months, would scarcely have been reached in as many years."

"How soon may we reasonably hope for returns?" asked Mr. Markland, with more concern in his voice than he meant to express.

"In a few months," was answered.

"In two, three, or four months?"

"It is difficult to fix an exact period," said Mr. Fenwick, evasively. "You know how far the works have progressed, and what they were doing at the latest dates."

"There ought to be handsome returns in less than six months."

"And will be, no doubt," replied the agent.

"There *must* be," said Mr. Markland, betraying some excitement.

Mr. Fenwick looked at him earnestly, and with a slight manifestation of surprise.

"The assessments have been larger and more frequent than was anticipated. I did not intend embarking more than twenty thousand dollars in the beginning, and already some sixty thousand have been absorbed."

"To return you that sum, twice told, in less than a year, besides giving you a position of power and influence that the richest capitalist in New York might envy."

And, enlarging on this theme, Fenwick, as on former occasions, presented to the imagination of Mr. Markland such a brilliant series of achievements, that the latter was elevated into the old state of confidence, and saw the golden harvest he was to reap already bending to the sickle.

Twice had Markland proposed to visit the scene of the Company's operations, and as often had Mr. Fenwick diverted his thoughts from that direction. He again declared his purpose to go out at an early date.

"We cannot spare you from our councils at home," said Mr. Fenwick, pleasantly, yet with evident earnestness.

"Oh, yes, you can," was promptly answered. "I do not find myself of as much use as I desire to be. The direction at this point is in good enough hands, and can do without my presence. It is at the chief point of operations that I may be of most use, and thither I shall proceed."

"We will talk more about that another time," said Mr. Fenwick. "Now we must discuss the question of ways and means. There will yet be many thousand dollars to provide."

"Beyond my present investment, *I* can advance nothing," said Mr. Markland, seriously.

"It will not be necessary," replied Mr. Fenwick. "The credit of the Company—that is, of those in this and other cities, including yourself, who belong to the Company, and have the chief management of its affairs—is good for all we shall need."

"I am rather disappointed," said Markland, "at the small advances made, so far, from the other side of the Atlantic. They ought to have been far heavier. We have borne more than our share of the burden."

"So I have written, and expect good remittances by next steamers."

"How much?"

"Forty or fifty thousand dollars at least."

"Suppose the money does not come?"

"I will suppose nothing of the kind. It must and will come."

"You and I have both lived long enough in the world," said Markland, "to know that our wills cannot always produce in others the actions we desire."

"True enough. But there are wills on the other side of the Atlantic as well as here, and wills acting in concert with ours. Have no concern on this head; the English advances will be along in good season. In the mean time, if more money is wanted, our credit is good to almost any amount."

This proposition in regard to credit was no mere temporary expedient, thought of at the time, to meet an unexpected contingency. It had been all clearly arranged in the minds of Fenwick and other ruling spirits in New York, and Markland was not permitted to leave before his name, coupled with that of "some of the best names in the city," was on promissory notes for almost fabulous amounts.

Taking into account the former business experience of Mr. Markland, his present reckless investments and still more reckless signing of obligations for large sums, show how utterly blind his perceptions and unsettled his judgment had become. The waters he had so successfully navigated before were none of them strange waters. He had been over them with chart, compass, and pilot, many times before he adventured for himself. But now, with a richly freighted argosy, he was on an unknown sea. Pleasantly the summer breeze had wafted him onward for a season. Spice-islands were passed, and golden shores revealed themselves invitingly in the distance. The haven was almost gained, when along the far horizon dusky vapours gathered and hid the pleasant land. Darker they grew, and higher they arose, until at length the whole sky was draped, and neither sun nor stars looked down from its leaden depths. Yet with a desperate courage he kept steadily onward, for the record of observations since the voyage began was too imperfect to serve as a guide to return. Behind was certain destruction; while beyond the dark obscurity, the golden land of promise smiled ever in the glittering sunshine.

CHAPTER XXIX.

MR. MARKLAND'S determination to visit the scene of the Company's operations was no suddenly-formed impulse; and the manifest desire that he should not do so, exhibited by Mr. Fenwick, in no way lessened his purpose to get upon the ground as early as possible, and see for himself how matters were progressing. His whole fortune was locked up in this new enterprise, and his compeers were strangers, or acquaintances of a recent date. To have acted with so much blindness was unlike Markland; but it was like him to wish to know all about any business in which he was engaged. This knowledge he had failed to obtain in New York. There his imagination was constantly dazzled, and while he remained there, uncounted, treasure seemed just ready to fall at his feet. The lamp of Aladdin was almost within his grasp. But, on leaving Fenwick and his sanguine associates, a large portion of his enthusiasm died out, and his mind reached forth into the obscurity around him and sought for the old landmarks.

On returning home from this visit to New York, Mr. Markland found his mind oppressed with doubts and questions, that could neither be removed nor answered satisfactorily. His entire fortune, acquired through years of patient labour, was beyond his reach, and might never come back into his possession, however desperately he grasped after it. And "Woodbine Lodge,"—its beauty suddenly restored to eyes from which scales had fallen—held now only by an uncertain tenure, a breath might sweep from his hand.

Suddenly, Markland was awakened, as if from a dream, and realized the actual of his position. It was a fearful waking to him, and caused every nerve in his being to thrill with pain. On the brink of a gulf he found himself standing, and as he gazed down into its fearful obscurity, he shuddered and grew sick. And now, having taken the alarm, his thoughts became active in a new direction, and penetrated beneath surfaces which hitherto had blinded his eyes by their golden lustre. Facts and statements which before had appeared favourable and coherent now presented irreconcilable discrepancies, and he wondered at the mental blindness which had prevented his seeing things in their present aspects.

It was not possible for a man of Mr. Markland's peculiar temperament and business experience to sit down idly, and, with folded hands, await the issue of this great venture. Now that his fears were aroused, he could not stop short of a thorough examination of affairs, and that, too, at the chief point of operations, which lay thousands of miles distant.

Letters from Mr. Lyon awaited his return from New York. They said little of matters about which he now most desired specific information, while they seemed to communicate a great many important facts in regard to the splendid enterprise in which they were engaged. Altogether, they left no satisfactory impression on his mind. One of them, bearing a later date than the rest, disturbed him deeply. It was the first, for some months, in which allusion was made to his daughter. The closing paragraph of this letter ran thus:—

"I have not found time, amid this pressure of business, to write a word to your daughter for some weeks. Say to her that I ever bear her in respectful remembrance, and shall refer to the days spent at Woodbine Lodge as among the brightest of my life."

There had been no formal application for the hand of his daughter up to this time; yet had it not crossed the thought of Markland that any other result would follow; for the relation into which Lyon had voluntarily brought himself left no room for honourable retreat. His letters to Fanny more than bound him to a pledge of his hand. They were only such as one bearing the tenderest affection might write.

Many weeks had elapsed since Fanny received a letter, and she was beginning to droop under the long suspense. None came for her now, and here was the cold, brief reference to one whose heart was throbbing toward him, full of love.

Markland was stung by this evasive reference to his daughter, for its meaning he clearly understood. Not that he had set his heart on an alliance of Fanny with this man, but, having come to look upon such an event as almost certain, and regarding all obstacles in the way as lying on his side of the question, pride was severely shocked by so unexpected a show of indifference. And its exhibition was the more annoying, manifested, as it was, just at the moment when he had become most painfully aware that all his worldly possessions were beyond his control, and might pass from his reach forever.

"Can there be such baseness in the man?" he exclaimed, mentally, with bitterness, as the thought flitted through his mind that Lyon had deliberately inveigled him, and, having been an instrument of his ruin, now turned from him with cold indifference.

"Impossible!" he replied, aloud, to the frightful conjecture. "I will not cherish the thought for a single moment."

But a suggestion like this, once made to a man in his circumstances, is not to be cast out of the mind by a simple act of rejection. It becomes a living thing, and manifests its perpetual presence. Turn his thought from it as he would, back to that point it came, and the oftener this occurred, the more corroborating suggestions arrayed themselves by its side.

Mr. Markland was alone in the library, with Mr. Lyon's hastily read letters before him, and yet pondering, with an unquiet spirit, the varied relations in which he had become placed, when the door was quietly pushed open, and he heard light footsteps crossing the room. Turning, he met the anxious face of his daughter, who, no longer able to bear the suspense that was torturing her, had overcome all shrinking maiden delicacy, and now came to ask if, enclosed in either of his letters, was one for her. She advanced close to where he was sitting, and, as he looked at her with a close observation, he saw that her countenance was almost colourless, her lips rigid, and her heart beating with an oppressed motion, as if half the blood in her body had flowed back upon it.

"Fanny, dear!" said Mr. Markland, grasping her hand tightly. As he did so, she leaned heavily against him, while her eyes ran eagerly over the table.

Two or three times she tried to speak, but was unable to articulate.

"What can I say to you, love?" Her father spoke in a low, sad, tender voice, that to her was prophetic of the worst.

"Is there a letter for me?" she asked, in a husky whisper.

"No, dear."

He felt her whole frame quiver as if shocked.

"You have heard from Mr. Lyon?" She asked this after the lapse of a few moments, raising herself up as she spoke, and assuming a calmness of exterior that was little in accord with the tumult within.

"Yes. I have three letters of different dates."

"And none for me?"

"None."

"Has he not mentioned my name?"

A moment Mr. Markland hesitated, and then answered—

"Yes."

He saw a slight, quick flush mantle her face, that grew instantly pale again.

"Will you read to me what he says?"

"If you wish me to do so." Mr. Markland said this almost mechanically.

"Read it." And as her father took from the table a letter, Fanny grasped his arm tightly, and then stood with the immovable rigidity of a statue. She had already prophesied the worst. The cold, and, to her, cruel words, were like chilling ice-drops on her heart. She listened to the end, and then, with a low cry, fell against her father, happily unconscious of further suffering. To her these brief sentences told the story of unrequited love. How tenderly, how ardently he had written a few months gone by! and now, after a long silence, he makes to her a mere incidental allusion, and asks a "respectful remembrance!" She had heard the knell of all her dearest hopes. Her love had become almost her life, and to trample thus upon it was like extinguishing her life.

"Fanny! Love! Dear Fanny!" But the distressed father called to her in vain, and in vain lifted her nerveless body erect. The oppressed heart was stilled.

A cry of alarm quickly summoned the family, and for a short time a scene of wild terror ensued; for, in the white face of the fainting girl, all saw the image of death. A servant was hurriedly despatched for their physician, and the body removed to one of the chambers.

But motion soon came back, feebly, to the heart; the lungs drew in the vital air, and the circle of life was restored. When the physician arrived, nature had done all for her that could be done. The sickness of her spirit was beyond the reach of any remedy he might prescribe.

CHAPTER XXX.

THE shock received by Fanny left her in a feeble state of mind as well as body. For two or three days she wept almost constantly. Then a leaden calmness, bordering on stupor, ensued, that, even more than her tears, distressed her parents.

Meantime, the anxieties of Mr. Markland, in regard to the business in which he had ventured more than all his possessions, were hourly increasing. Now that suspicion had been admitted into his thought, circumstances which had before given him encouragement bore a doubtful aspect. He was astonished at his own blindness, and frightened at the position in which he found himself placed. Altogether dissatisfied with the kind and amount of information to be gained in New York, his resolution to go South was strengthened daily. Finally, he announced to his family that he must leave them, to be gone at least two or three months. The intelligence came with a shock that partially aroused Fanny from the lethargic state into which she had fallen. Mrs. Markland made only a feeble, tearful opposition. Upon her mind had settled a brooding apprehension of trouble in the future, and every changing aspect in the progression of events but confirmed her fears.

That her husband's mind had become deeply disturbed Mrs. Markland saw but too clearly; and that this disturbance increased daily, she also saw. Of the causes she had no definite information; but it was not difficult to infer that they involved serious disappointments in regard to the brilliant schemes which had so captivated his imagination. If these disappointments had thrown him back upon his home, better satisfied with the real good in possession, she would not very much have regretted them. But, on learning his purpose to go far South, and even thousands of miles beyond the boundaries of his own country, she became oppressed with a painful anxiety, which was heightened, rather than allayed, by his vague replies to all her earnest inquiries in regard to the state of affairs that rendered this long journey imperative.

"Interests of great magnitude," he would say, "require that all who are engaged in them should be minutely conversant with their state of progress. I have long enough taken the statements of parties at a distance: now I must see and know for myself."

How little there was in all this to allay anxiety, or reconcile the heart to a long separation from its life-partner, is clear to every one. Mrs. Markland saw that her husband wished to conceal from her the exact position of his affairs, and this but gave her startled imagination power to conjure up the most frightful images. Fears for the safety of her husband during a long journey in a distant country, where few traces of civilization could yet be found, were far more active than concern for the result of his business. Of that she knew but little; and, so far as its success or failure had power to affect her, experienced but little anxiety. On this account, her trouble was all for him.

Time progressed until the period of Markland's departure was near at hand. He had watched, painfully, the slow progress of change in Fanny's state of mind. There was yet no satisfactory aspect. The fact of his near departure had ruffled the surface of her feelings, and given a hectic warmth to her cheeks and a tearful brightness to her eyes. Most earnestly had she entreated him, over and over again, not to leave them.

"Home will no longer be like home, dear father, when you are far absent," she said to him, pleadingly, a few days before the appointed time for departure had come. "Do not go away."

"It is no desire to leave home that prompts the journey, Fanny, love," he answered, drawing his arm around her and pressing her closely to his side. "At the call of duty, none of us should hesitate to obey."

"Duty, father?" Fanny did not comprehend the meaning of his words.

"It is the duty of all men to thoroughly comprehend what they are doing, and to see that their business is well conducted at every point."

"I did not before understand that you had business in that distant country," said Fanny.

"I am largely interested there," replied Mr. Markland, speaking as though the admission to her was half-extorted.

"Not with Mr. Lyon, I hope?" said Fanny, quickly and earnestly. It was the first time she had mentioned his name since the day his cold allusion to her had nearly palsied her heart.

"Why not with Mr. Lyon, my child? Do you know any thing in regard to him that would make such a connection perilous to my interest?" Mr.

Markland looked earnestly into the face of his daughter. Her eyes did not fall from his, but grew brighter, and her person became more erect. There was something of indignant surprise in the expression of her countenance.

"Do you know any thing in regard to him that would make the connection perilous to my interest?" repeated Mr. Markland.

"Will that man be true to the father, who is false to his child?" said Fanny, in a deep, hoarse voice.

He looked long and silently into her face, his mind bewildered by the searching interrogatory.

"False to you, Fanny!" he at length said, in a confused way. "Has he been false to you?"

"Oh, father! father! And is it from you this question comes?" exclaimed Fanny, clasping her hands together and then pressing them tightly against her bosom.

"He spoke of you in his letter with great kindness," said Mr. Markland. "I know that he has been deeply absorbed in a perplexing business; and this may be the reason why he has not written."

"Father,"—Fanny's words were uttered slowly and impressively—"if you are in any manner involved in business with Mr. Lyon—if you have any thing at stake through confidence in him—get free from the connection as early as possible. He is no true man. With the fascinating qualities of the serpent, he has also the power to sting."

"I fear, my daughter," said Mr. Markland, "that too great a revulsion has taken place in your feelings toward him; that wounded pride is becoming unduly active."

"Pride!" ejaculated Fanny—and her face, that had flushed, grew pale again —"pride! Oh, father! how sadly you misjudge your child! No—no. I was for months in the blinding mazes of a delicious dream; but I am awake now— fully awake, and older—how much older it makes me shudder to think—than I was when lulled into slumber by melodies so new, and wild, and sweet, that it seemed as if I had entered another state of existence. Yes, father, I am awake now; startled suddenly from visions of joy and beauty into icy realities, like thousands of other dreamers around me. Pride? Oh, my father!"

And Fanny laid her head down upon the breast of her parent, and wept bitterly.

Mr. Markland was at a loss what answer to make. So entire a change in the feelings of his daughter toward Mr. Lyon was unsuspected, and he scarcely knew how to explain the fact. Fascinated as she had been, he had looked for nothing else but a clinging to his image even in coldness and neglect. That she would seek to obliterate that image from her heart, as an evil thing, was something he had not for an instant expected. He did not know how, treasured up in tenderest infancy, through sunny childhood, and in sweetly dawning maidenhood, innocence and truth had formed for her a talisman by which the qualities of others might be tested. At the first approach of Mr. Lyon this had given instinctive warning; but his personal attractions were so great, and her father's approving confidence of the man so strong, that the inward monitor was unheeded. But, after a long silence following a series of impassioned letters, to find herself alluded to in this cold and distant way revealed a state of feeling in the man she loved so wildly, that proved him false beyond all question. Like one standing on a mountain-top, who suddenly finds the ground giving way beneath his feet, she felt herself sweeping down through a fearfully intervening space, and fell, with scarcely a pulse of life remaining, on the rocky ground beneath. She caught at no object in her quick descent, for none tempted her hand. It was one swift plunge, and the shock was over.

"No, father," she said, in a calmer voice, lifting her face from his bosom —"it is not pride, nor womanly indignation at a deep wrong. I speak of him as he is now known to me. Oh, beware of him! Let not his shadow fall darker on our household."

The effect of this conversation in no way quieted the apprehensions of Mr. Markland, but made his anxieties the deeper. That Lyon had been false to his child was clear even to him; and the searching questions of Fanny he could not banish from his thoughts.

"All things confirm the necessity of my journey," he said, when alone, and in close debate with himself on the subject. "I fear that I am in the toils of a serpent, and that escape, even with life, is doubtful. By what a strange infatuation I have been governed! Alas! into what a fearful jeopardy have I brought the tangible good things given me by a kind Providence, by grasping at what dazzled my eyes as of supremely greater value! Have I not been lured by a shadow, forgetful of the substance in possession?"

CHAPTER XXXI.

"I SHOULD have been contented amid so much beauty, and with even more than my share of earthly blessings." Thus Mr. Markland communed with himself, walking about alone, near the close of the day preceding that on which his appointed journey was to begin. "Am I not acting over again that old folly of the substance and shadow? Verily, I believe it is so. Ah! will we ever be satisfied with any achievement in this life? To-morrow I leave all by which I am here surrounded, and more, a thousand-fold more—my heart's beloved ones; and for what? To seek the fortune I was mad enough to cast from me into a great whirlpool, believing that it would be thrown up at my feet again, with every disk of gold changed into a sparkling diamond. I have waited eagerly on the shore for the returning tide, but yet there is no reflux, and now my last hope rests on the diver's strength and doubtful fortune. I must make the fearful plunge."

A cold shudder ran through the frame of Mr. Markland, as he realized, too distinctly, the image he had conjured up. A feeling of weakness and irresolution succeeded.

"Ah!" he murmured to himself, "if all had not been so blindly cast upon this venture, I might be willing to wait the issue, providing for the worst by a new disposition of affairs, and by new efforts here. But I was too eager, too hopeful, too insanely confident. Every thing is now beyond my reach."

This was the state of his mind when Mr. Allison, whom he had not met in a familiar manner for several weeks, joined him, saying, as he came up with extended hand, and fine face, bright with the generous interest in others that always burned in his heart—

"What is this I hear, Mr. Markland? Is it true that you are going away, to be absent for some months? Mr. Willet was telling me about it this morning."

"It is too true," replied Mr. Markland, assuming a cheerful air, yet betraying much of the troubled feeling that oppressed him. "The calls of business cannot always be disregarded."

"No—but, if I understand aright, you contemplate going a long distance South—somewhere into Central America."

"Such is my destination. Having been induced to invest money in a promising enterprise in that far-off region, it is no more than right to look after my interests there."

"With so much to hold your thoughts and interests here," said Mr. Allison, "I can hardly understand why you should let them wander off so far from home."

"And I can hardly understand it myself," returned Mr. Markland, in a lower tone of voice, as if the admission were made reluctantly. "But so it is. I am but a man, and man is always dissatisfied with his actual, and always looking forward to some good time coming. Ah, sir, this faculty of imagination that we possess is one of the curses entailed by the fall. It is forever leading us off from a true enjoyment of what we have. It has no faith in to-day—no love for the good and beautiful that really exists."

"I can show you a person whose imagination plays no truant pranks like this," replied Mr. Allison. "And this shall be at least one exception to your rule."

"Name that person," was the half-incredulous response.

"Your excellent wife," said Mr. Allison.

For some moments Mr. Markland stood with his eyes cast down; then, lifting them to the face of the old man, he said:

"The reference is true. But, if she be not the only exception, the number who, like her, can find the best reward in the present, are, alas! but few."

"If not found in the present, Mr. Markland, will it ever be found? Think!"

"Never!" There was an utterance of grief in the deep tone that thus responded-for conviction had come like a quick flash upon his heart.

"But who finds it, Mr. Allison?" he said, shortly after, speaking with stern energy. "Who comprehends the present and the actual? who loves it sufficiently? Ah, sir! is the present ever what a fond, cheating imagination prefigured it?"

"And knowing this so well," returned the old man, "was it wise for you to build so largely on the future as you seem to have done?"

"No, it was not wise." The answer came with a bitter emphasis.

"We seek to escape the restlessness of unsatisfied desire," said Mr. Allison, "by giving it more stimulating food, instead of firmly repressing its morbid activities. Think you not that there is something false in the life we are leading here, when we consider how few and brief are the days in which we experience a feeling of rest and satisfaction? And if our life be false—or, in other words, our life-purposes—what hope for us is there in any change of pursuit or any change of scene?"

"None—none," replied Mr. Markland.

"We may look for the good time coming, but look in vain. Its morning will never break over the distant mountain-tops to which our eyes are turned."

"Life is a mockery, a cheating dream!" said Mr. Markland, bitterly.

"Not so, my friend," was the calmly spoken answer.

"Not so. Our life here is the beginning of an immortal life. But, to be a happy life, it must be a true one. All its activities must have an orderly pulsation."

Mr. Markland slowly raised a hand, and, pressing it strongly against his forehead, stood motionless for some moments, his mind deeply abstracted.

"My thoughts flow back, Mr. Allison," he said, at length, speaking in a subdued tone, "to a period many months gone by, and revives a conversation held with you, almost in this very place. What you then said made a strong impression on my mind. I saw, in clear light, how vain were all efforts to secure happiness in this world, if made selfishly, and thus in a direction contrary to true order. The great social man I recognised as no mere idealism, but as a verity. I saw myself a member of this body, and felt deeply the truth then uttered by you, that just in proportion as each member thinks of and works for himself alone will that individual be working in selfish disorder, and, like the member of the human body that takes more than its share of blood, must certainly suffer the pain of inflammation. The truth then presented to my mind was like a flood of light; but I did not love the truth, and shut my eyes to the light that revealed more than I wished to know. Ah, sir! if I could have accepted all you then advanced—if I could have overcome the false principle of self-seeking then so clearly shown to be the curse of life —I would not have involved myself in business that must now separate me for months from my home and family."

"And should you achieve all that was anticipated in the beginning," said Mr. Allison, "I doubt if you will find pleasure enough in the realization to compensate for this hour of pain, to say nothing of what you are destined to suffer during the months of separation that are before you."

"Your doubts are my own," replied Markland, musingly. "But,"—and he spoke in a quicker and lighter tone,—"this is all folly! I must go forward, now, to the end. Why, then, yield to unmanly weakness?"

"True, sir," returned the old man. "No matter how difficult the way in which our feet must walk, the path must be trodden bravely."

"I shall learn some lessons of wisdom by this experience," said Mr. Markland, "that will go with me through life. But, I fear, they will be all too dearly purchased."

"Wisdom," was the answer, "is a thing of priceless value."

"It is sometimes too dearly bought, for all that."

"Never," replied the old man,—"never. Wisdom is the soul's true riches; and there is no worldly possession that compares with it in value. If you acquire wisdom by any experience, no matter how severe it may prove, you are largely the gainer. And here is the compensation in every affliction, in every disappointment, and in every misfortune. We may gather pearls of wisdom from amid the ashes and cinders of our lost hopes, after the fires have consumed them."

Mr. Markland sighed deeply, but did not answer. There was a dark sky above and around him; yet gleams of light skirted a cloud here and there, telling him that the great sun was shining serenely beyond. He felt weak, sad, and almost hopeless, as he parted from Mr. Allison, who promised often to visit his family during his absence; and in his weakness, he lifted his heart involuntarily upward, and asked direction and strength from Him whom he had forgotten in the days when all was light around him, and, in the pride and strength of conscious manhood, he had felt that he possessed all power to effect the purposes of his own will.

CHAPTER XXXII.

AFTER a night that was sleepless to at least three members of the family the morning of the day on which Mr. Markland was to start on his journey came. Tearful eyes were around him. Even to the last, Fanny begged him not to leave them, and almost clung to him at the moment of parting. Finally, the separation was accomplished, and, shrinking back in the carriage that conveyed him to the city, Mr. Markland gave himself up to sad reveries. As his thoughts reached forward to the point of his destination, and he tried to arrange in his mind all the information he had relating to the business in which he was now embarked, he saw more clearly than ever the feeble hold upon his fortune that remained to him. Less confident, too, was he of the good result of his journey. Now that he was fairly on the way, doubt began to enter his mind.

This was Mr. Markland's state of feelings on reaching the city. His first act was to drive to the post-office, to get any letters that might have arrived for him. He received only one, and that was from New York. The contents were of a startling character. Mr. Fenwick wrote:

"Come on immediately. Your presence is desired by all the members of the Company here. We have news of an unexpected and far from pleasant character."

This was all; but it came with a painful shock upon the feelings of Mr. Markland. Its very vagueness made it the more frightful to him; and his heart imagined the worst.

Without communicating with his family, who supposed him on his journey southward, Mr. Markland took the first train for New York, and in a few hours arrived in that city, and called at the office of Mr. Fenwick. A single glance at the agent's countenance told him that much was wrong. A look of trouble shadowed it, and only a feeble smile parted his lips as he came forward to meet him.

"What news have you?" eagerly inquired Mr. Markland.

"Bad news, I am sorry to say," was answered.

"What is its nature?" The face of Mr. Markland was of an ashen hue, and his lips quivered.

"I fear we have been mistaken in our man," said Mr. Fenwick.

"In Lyon?"

"Yes. His last letters are of a very unsatisfactory character, and little in agreement with previous communications. We have, besides, direct information from a partly on the ground, that tends to confirm our worst fears."

"Worst fears of what?" asked Markland, still strongly agitated.

"Unfair—nay, treacherous—dealing."

"Treachery!"

"That word but feebly expresses all we apprehend."

"It involves fearful meaning in the present case," said Markland, in a hoarse voice.

"Fearful enough," said Fenwick, gloomily.

"I was just on the eve of starting for the ground of the Company's operations, when your letter reached me this morning. An hour later, and I would have been on my journey southward," said Mr. Markland.

"It is well that I wrote, promptly," remarked Fenwick. "You were, at least, saved a long and fruitless journey."

"It will yet have to be taken, I fear," said Markland.

Fenwick shook his head ominously, and muttered, half to himself—"Vain —vain!"

"Will you state clearly, yet in brief, the nature of the information you have received from Mr. Lyon?" said Markland. "I comprehend nothing yet."

"His last communication," was answered, "gives a hurried, rather confused account of the sudden flooding of the main shaft, in sinking which a large part of the capital invested has been expended, and the hopeless abandonment of the work in that direction."

"Do you believe this statement?" asked Mr. Markland.

"I have another letter from one of the party on the ground, bearing the same date."

"What does he say?"

"But little of the flooded shaft. Such an occurrence had, however, taken place, and the writer seemed to think it might require a steam-engine and pump to keep it clear, involving a delay of several months. The amount of water which came in was sufficient to cause a suspension of work, which he thought might be only temporary; but he could not speak with certainty in regard to that. But the most serious part of his communication is this:"

Mr. Fenwick took a letter from his desk, and read:—

"The worst feature of the case is the lack of funds. The Government officials have demanded the immediate payment of the second, third, and fourth instalments due on the Company's grant of land, and have announced their purpose to seize upon all the effects here, and declare a forfeiture, unless these dues are forthcoming at the end of the present month. Mr. Lyon is greatly troubled, but mysterious. He has not, from the first day of his arrival out up to the present moment, admitted any one fully into his counsels. I know he has been seriously hampered for lack of funds, but was not aware, until now, that the second and third instalments of purchase-money remained unpaid; and my knowledge of this, and the impending danger from the Government, was only acquired through accident. No doubt Mr. Lyon has fully advised you of all the facts in the case; still, I feel it to be my duty also to refer to the subject."

"Good heavens!" exclaimed Mr. Markland, as Fenwick paused, and lifted his eyes from the letter. "The second, third, and fourth instalments not paid! What can it mean? Was not the money forwarded to Mr. Lyon?"

"He took out funds to meet the second and third regular payments; and the money for the fourth went forward in good time. There is something wrong."

"Wrong!" Mr. Markland was on his feet, and pacing the floor in an agitated manner. "Something wrong! There exists, I fear, somewhere in this business a conspiracy to swindle."

And as he said this, he fixed his eyes intently on the countenance of Mr. Fenwick.

"The agent with whom we intrusted so much has, I fear, abused our confidence," said Mr. Fenwick, speaking calmly, and returning the steady gaze of Markland.

"Who is the person who gives this information about the unpaid instalments?" asked the latter.

"A man in whose word every reliance may be placed."

"You know him personally?"

"Yes."

"Is his position on the ground such as to bring him within the reach of information like that which he assumes to give?"

"Yes."

"Is he a man of intelligence?"

"He is."

"And one of cool judgment?"

"Yes; and this is why the information he gives is of such serious import. He would never communicate such information on mere rumour or inference. He knows the facts, or he would not have averred to their existence."

"Has there been a meeting of the Board?" inquired Markland.

"There was a hurried meeting yesterday afternoon; and we shall convene again at six this evening."

"What was done?"

"Nothing. Consternation at the intelligence seized upon every one. There were regrets, anxieties, and denunciations, but no action."

"What is the general view in regard to Lyon?"

"Some refuse to admit the implied charge that lies against him; while others take the worst for granted, and denounce him in unmeasured terms."

"What is your opinion?" asked Markland.

"Knowing the man from whom information comes, I am led to fear the worst. Still, there may have been some mistake—some misapprehension on his part."

"The meeting takes place at six o'clock?" said Markland, after remaining a short time silent.

"Yes."

"Will you propose any thing?"

"I wish, first, to hear the views of others. Prompt action of some kind is certainly required."

"If Lyon be actually the villain he now seems, he will put himself entirely beyond our reach on the first intimation of danger," said Markland.

"So I have reasoned. Our only hope, therefore, is to get possession of his person. But how is this to be accomplished?"

"Give immediate notice to the—Government, that he is in possession of the funds due them by the Company, and they will not fail to secure his person," said Markland.

"A good suggestion," replied Fenwick. And he sat in a thoughtful attitude for some moments. "Yes, that is a good suggestion," he repeated. "We must send a shrewd, confidential agent at once to L—, and give information of the exact position of affairs."

"What is the date of the last communication from Lyon?" asked Markland.

"He wrote on the tenth."

"Of last month?"

"Yes."

"And the—Government threatened to enter upon and seize our property on the first of the present month?"

"True—true; and the worst may have already happened," said Fenwick. "Still, an agent must go out, and vigorous efforts be made to save our property."

"It will scarcely be worth saving, if in the condition represented, and all our funds dissipated."

Fenwick sighed. There was something in that sigh, as it reached the ears of Markland, which seemed like a mockery of trouble. He raised his glance quickly to the agent's face, and searched it over with the sharp eye of suspicion. Fenwick bore this scrutiny without the faltering of a muscle. If he comprehended its meaning, his consciousness thereof was in no way revealed.

"The Board will meet here at six o'clock this evening," said he, quietly. "In the mean time, you had better digest the information we have, and come prepared to aid us with your better judgment. The crisis is one that demands calm, earnest thought and decisive action."

"I will be here," replied Markland, rising. Then, with a formal bow, he left the agent's office.

CHAPTER XXXIII.

THE time until six o'clock, the meeting-hour of the Board, was not spent by Mr. Markland in solitary thought. He visited, during that period, three of the principal men interested in the business, and gleaned from them their views in regard to the late startling intelligence. Most of them seemed utterly confounded, and no two had arrived at the same conclusion as to what was best to be done. Nearly all were inclined to credit fully the report of Lyon's having failed to pay the last three instalments on the Company's land, and they denounced him bitterly. These conferences had the effect of extinguishing all hope in the breast of Mr. Markland. Even if the half of what he feared were true, he was hopelessly ruined.

At the hour of meeting, Markland assembled with the New York members of the Company, and two from Boston, who had been summoned on the day previous by telegraph. The last communications received by Mr. Fenwick were again read, and the intelligence they brought discussed with more of passion than judgment. Some proposed deferring all action until further news came; while others were for sending out an agent, with full powers, immediately. To this latter view the majority inclined. "If it be true," suggested Markland, "that the—Government has threatened to seize upon our property if the three instalments were not paid on the first of the present month, every thing may now be in its hands."

"Lyon would hardly let it come to that," said another, "He has in his possession the means of preventing such a catastrophe, by paying over one of the instalments, and thus gaining time."

"Time for what?" was asked. "If he mean to enrich himself at our expense, he can do it best now. He is too shrewd not to understand that; if a question of his integrity arises, his further power to reach our funds is gone."

"But he does not know that we have information of the unpaid instalments."

"And that information may come from one who has an interest in ruining him," said another.

"You may think so, gentlemen," said Mr. Fenwick, coolly, "but I will stake my life on the unwavering faith of my correspondent in all he alleges. Moreover, he is not the man to make a communication of such serious import lightly. He knows the facts, or he would not affirm them. My advice is to send out an agent immediately."

"For what purpose?" was inquired.

"To ascertain the true position of affairs; and if our property have really been seized by the—Government, to take steps for its release."

"More funds will be required," said one of the Company.

"We cannot, of course, send out an agent empty-handed," was replied.

"Depletion must stop, so far as I am concerned," was the firm response of one individual. "I will throw no more good money after bad. If you send out an agent, gentlemen, don't call on me to bear a part of the expense."

"You are not, surely, prepared to abandon every thing at this point," said another.

"I am prepared to wait for further news, before I let one more dollar leave my pocket; and I will wait," was answered.

"And so will I," added another.

Two parties were gradually formed; one in favour of sending out an agent forthwith, and the other decided in their purpose not to risk another dollar until more certain information was received. This was the aspect of affairs when the Board adjourned to meet again on the next evening.

The result of this conference tended in no degree to calm the fears of Mr. Markland. How gladly would he now give up all interest in the splendid enterprise which had so captivated his imagination, if he could do so at the expense of one-half of his fortune!

"If I could save only a small part of the wreck!" he said to himself, as he paced the floor of his room at the hotel. It was far past the hour of midnight, but no sleep weighed upon his eyelids. "Even sufficient," he added, in a sad voice, "to keep in possession our beautiful home. As for myself, I can go back into busy life again. I am yet in the prime of manhood, and can tread safely and successfully the old and yet unforgotten ways to prosperity. Toil will be nothing to me, so the home-nest remain undisturbed, and my beloved ones suffer not through my blindness and folly."

A new thought came into his mind. His investments in the enterprise, now in such jeopardy, reached the sum of nearly one hundred thousand dollars. The greater part of this had been actually paid in. His notes and endorsements made up the balance.

"I will sell out for twenty-five cents in the dollar," said he.

There was a feeble ray of light in his mind, as the thought of selling out his entire interest in the business, at a most desperate sacrifice, grew more and more distinct. One or two members of the Board of Direction had, during the evening's discussion, expressed strong doubts as to the truth of the charge brought against Mr. Lyon. The flooding of the shaft was not, they thought, unlikely, and it might, seriously delay operations; but they were unwilling to believe affairs to be in the hopeless condition some were disposed to think. Here was a straw at which the drowning man caught. He would call upon one of these individuals in the morning, and offer his whole interest at a tempting reduction. Relieved at this thought, Mr. Markland could retire for the night; and he even slept soundly. On awaking in the morning, the conclusion of the previous night was reviewed. There were some natural regrets at the thought of giving up, by a single act, three-fourths of his whole fortune; but, like the mariner whose ship was sinking, there was no time to hesitate on the question of sacrificing the rich cargo.

"Yes—yes," he said within himself, "I will be content with certainty. Suspense like the present is not to be endured."

And so he made preparations to call upon a certain broker in Wall street, who had expressed most confidence in Lyon, and offer to sell him out his whole interest. He had taken breakfast, and was about leaving the hotel, when, in passing the reading-room, it occurred to him to glance over the morning papers. So he stepped in for that purpose.

Almost the first thing that arrested his attention was the announcement of an arrival, and news from Central America. "BURSTING OF A MAGNIFICENT BUBBLE—FLIGHT OF A DEFAULTING AGENT."— were the next words that startled him. He read on:

"The Government of—has seized upon all that immense tract of land, reported to be so rich in mineral wealth, which was granted some two years ago to the—Company. A confidential agent of this company, to whom, it is reported, immense sums of money were intrusted, and who failed to pay over the amounts due on the purchase, has disappeared, and, it is thought, passed over to the Pacific. He is believed to have defrauded the company out of nearly half a million of dollars."

"So dies a splendid scheme," was the editorial remark in the New York paper. "Certain parties in this city are largely interested in the Company, and have made investments of several hundred thousand dollars. More than one of these, it is thought, will be ruined by the catastrophe. Another lesson to the too eager and over-credulous money-seeker! They will not receive a very large share of public sympathy."

Mr. Markland read to the end, and then staggered back into a chair, where he remained for many minutes, before he had the will or strength to rise. He then went forth hastily, and repaired to the office of Mr. Fenwick. Several members of the Company, who had seen the announcement in the morning papers, were there, some pale with consternation, and some strongly excited. The agent had not yet arrived. The clerk in the office could answer no questions satisfactorily. He had not seen Mr. Fenwick since the evening previous.

"Have his letters yet arrived?" was inquired by one.

"He always takes them from the post-office himself," answered the clerk.

"What is his usual hour for coming to his office in the morning?"

"He is generally here by this time—often much earlier."

These interrogations, addressed to the clerk by one of those present, excited doubts and questions in the minds of others.

"It is rather singular that he should be absent at this particular time," said Markland, giving indirect expression to his own intruding suspicions.

"It is very singular," said another. "He is the medium of information from the theatre of our operations, and, above all things, should not be out of the way now."

"Where does he live?" was inquired of the clerk.

"At No.—, Fourteenth street."

"Will you get into a stage and ride up there?"

"If you desire it, gentlemen," replied the young man; "though it is hardly probable that I will find him there at this hour. If you wait a little while longer, he will no doubt be in."

The door opened, and two more of the parties interested in this bursting bubble arrived.

"Where is Fenwick?" was eagerly asked.

"Not to be found," answered one, abruptly, and with a broader meaning in his tones than any words had yet expressed.

"He hasn't disappeared, also!"

Fearful eyes looked into blank faces at this exclamation.

"Gentlemen," said the clerk, with considerable firmness of manner, "language like this must not be used here. It impeaches the character of a man whose life has thus far been above reproach. Whatever is said here, remember, is said in his ears, and he will soon be among you to make his own response."

The manner in which this was uttered repressed, for a time, further remarks reflecting on the integrity of the agent. But, after the lapse of nearly an hour, his continued absence was again referred to, and in more decided language than before.

"Will you do us one favour?" said Mr. Markland, on whose mind suspense was sitting like a nightmare. He spoke to the clerk, who, by this time, was himself growing restless.

"Any thing you desire, if it is in my power," was answered.

"Will you go down to the post-office, and inquire if Mr. Fenwick has received his letters this morning?"

"Certainly, I will." And the clerk went on the errand without a moment's delay.

"Mr. Fenwick received his letters over two hours ago," said the young man, on his return. He looked disappointed and perplexed.

"And you know nothing of him?" was said.

"Nothing, gentlemen, I do assure you. His absence is to me altogether inexplicable."

"Where's Fenwick?" was now asked, in an imperative voice, by a new comer.

"Not been seen this morning," replied Markland.

"Another act in this tragedy! Gone, I suppose, to join his accomplice on the Pacific coast, and share his plunder," said the man, passionately.

"You are using very strong language, sir!" suggested one.

"Not stronger than the case justifies. For my own assurance, I sent out a secret agent, and I have my first letter from him this morning. He arrived just in time to see our splendid schemes dissolve in smoke. Lyon is a swindler, Fenwick an accomplice, and we a parcel of easy fools. The published intelligence we have to-day is no darker than the truth. The bubble burst by the unexpected seizure of our lands, implements, and improvements, by the— Government. It contained nothing but air! Fenwick and Lyon had just played one of their reserved cards—it had something to do with the flooding of a shaft, which would delay results, and require more capital—when the impatient grantors of the land foreclosed every thing. From the hour this catastrophe became certain, Lyon was no more seen. He was fully prepared for the emergency."

In confirmation of this, letters giving the minutest particulars were shown, thus corroborating the worst, and extinguishing the feeblest rays of hope.

All was too true. The brilliant bubble had indeed burst, and not the shadow of a substance remained. When satisfied of this beyond all doubt, Markland, on whose mind suffering had produced a temporary stupor, sought his room at the hotel, and remained there for several days, so hopeless, weak, and undecided, that he seemed almost on the verge of mental imbecility. How could he return home and communicate the dreadful intelligence to his family? How could he say to them, that, for his transgressions, they must go forth from their beautiful Eden?

"No—no!" he exclaimed, wringing his hands in anguish. "I can never tell them this! I can never look into their faces! Never! never!"

The moment had come, and the tempter was at his ear. There was, first, the remote suggestion of self-banishment in some distant land, where the rebuking presence of his injured family could never haunt him. But he felt that a life in this world, apart from them, would be worse than death.

"I am mocked! I am cursed!" he exclaimed, bitterly.

The tempter was stealthily doing his work.

"Oh! what a vain struggle is this life! What a fitful fever! Would that it were over, and I at rest!"

The tempter was leading his thoughts at will.

"How can I meet my wronged family? How can I look my friends in the face? I shall be to the world only a thing of pity or reproach. Can I bear this?

No—no—I cannot—I cannot!"

Magnified by the tempter, the consequence looked appalling. He felt that he had not strength to meet it—that all of manhood would be crushed out of him.

"What then?" He spoke the words almost aloud, and held his breath, as if for answer.

"A moment, and all will be over!"

It was the voice of the tempter.

Markland buried his face in his hands, and sat for a long time as motionless as if sleep had obscured his senses; and all that time a fearful debate was going on in his mind. At last he rose up, changed in feeling as well as in aspect. His resolution was taken, and a deep, almost leaden, calmness pervaded his spirit. He had resolved on self-destruction!

With a strange coolness, the self-doomed man now proceeded to select the agent of death. He procured a work on poisons, and studied the effects of different substances, choosing, finally, that which did the fatal work most quickly and with the slightest pain. This substance was then procured. But he could not turn forever from those nearest and dearest, without a parting word.

The day had run almost to a close in these fearful struggles and fatal preparations; and the twilight was falling, when, exhausted and in tears, the wretched man folded, with trembling hands, a letter he had penned to his wife. This done, he threw himself, weak as a child, upon the bed, and, ere conscious that sleep was stealing upon him, fell off into slumber.

Sleep! It is the great restorer. For a brief season the order of life is changed, and the involuntary powers of the mind bear rule in place of the voluntary. The actual, with all its pains and pleasures, is for the time annihilated. The pressure of thought and the fever of emotion are both removed, and the over-taxed spirit is at rest. Into his most loving guardianship the great Creator of man, who gave him reason and volition, and the freedom to guide himself, takes his creature, and, while the image of death is upon him, gathers about him the Everlasting Arms. He suspends, for a time, the diseased voluntary life, that he may, through the involuntary, restore a degree of health, and put the creature he has formed for happiness in a new condition of mental and moral freedom.

Blessed sleep! Who has not felt and acknowledged thy sweet influences? Who has not wondered at thy power in the tranquil waking, after a night that closed around the spirit in what seemed the darkness of coming despair?

Markland slept; and in his sleep, guided by angels, there came to him the spirits of his wife and children, clothed in the beauty of innocence. How lovingly they gathered around him! how sweet were their words in his ears! how exquisite the thrill awakened by each tender kiss! Now he was with them in their luxurious home; and now they were wandering, in charmed intercourse, amid its beautiful surroundings. Change after change went on; new scenes and new characters appeared, and yet the life seemed orderly and natural. Suddenly there came a warning of danger. The sky grew fearfully dark; fierce lightning burned through the air, and the giant tempest swept down upon the earth with resistless fury. Next a flood was upon them. And now he was seized with the instinct of self-preservation, and in a moment had deserted his helpless family, and was fleeing, alone to a place of safety. From thence he saw wife and children borne off by the rush of waters, their white, imploring faces turned to him, and their hands stretched out for succour. Then all his love returned; self was forgotten; he would have died to save them. But it was too late! Even while he looked, they were engulfed and lost.

From such a dream Markland was awakened into conscious life. The shadowy twilight had been succeeded by darkness. He started up, confused and affrighted. Some moments passed before his bewildered thoughts were able to comprehend his real position; and when he did so, he fell back, with a groan, horror-stricken, upon the bed. The white faces and imploring hands of his wife and children were still vividly before him.

"Poor, weak, coward heart!" he at last murmured to himself. "An evil spirit was thy counsellor. I knew not that so mean and base a purpose could find admittance there. What! Beggar and disgrace my wife and children, and then, like a skulking coward, leave them to bear the evil I had not the courage to face! Edward Markland! Can this, indeed, be true of thee?"

And the excited man sprang from the bed. A feeble light came in through the window-panes above the door, and made things dimly visible. He moved about, for a time, with an uncertain air, and then rung for a light. The first object that met his eyes, when the servant brought in a lamp, was a small, unopened package, lying on the table. He knew its contents. What a strong shudder ran through his frame! Seizing it the instant the attendant left the room, he flung it through the open window. Then, sinking on his knees, he thanked God fervently for a timely deliverance.

The fierce struggle with pride was now over. Weak, humbled, and softened in feeling almost to tears, Markland sat alone, through the remainder of that evening, with his thoughts reaching forward into the future, and seeking to discover the paths in which his feet must walk. For himself he cared not now. Ah! if the cherished ones could be saved from the consequences of his folly!

If he alone were destined to move in rough and thorny ways! But there was for them no escape. The paths in which he moved they must move. The cup he had made bitter for himself would be bitter for them also.

Wretched man! Into what a great deep of misery had he plunged himself!

CHAPTER XXXIV.

IT was near the close of the fifth day since Mr. Markland left his home to commence a long journey southward; and yet, no word had come back from him. He had promised to write from Baltimore, and from other points on his route, and sufficient time had elapsed for at least two letters to arrive. A servant, who had been sent to the city post-office, had returned without bringing any word from the absent one; and Mrs. Markland, with Fanny by her side, was sitting near a window sad and silent.

Just one year has passed since their introduction to the reader. But what a change one year has wrought! The heart's bright sunshine rested then on every object. Woodbine Lodge was then a paradise. Now, there is scarcely a ray of this warm sunshine. Yet there had been no bereavement—no affliction; nothing that we refer to a mysterious Providence. No,—but the tempter was admitted. He came with specious words and deceiving pretences. He vailed the present good, and magnified the worth of things possessing no power to satisfy the heart. Too surely has he succeeded in the accomplishment of his evil work.

At the time of the reader's introduction to Woodbine Lodge, a bright day was going down in beauty; and there was not a pulse in nature that did not beat in unison with the hearts of its happy denizens. A summer day was again drawing to its close, but sobbing itself away in tears. And they were in tears also, whose spirits, but a single year gone by, reflected only the light and beauty of nature.

By the window sat the mother and daughter, with oppressed hearts, looking out upon the leaden sky and the misty gusts that swept across the gloomy landscape. Sad and silent, we have said, they were. Now and then they gazed into each other's faces, and the lips quivered as if words were on them. But each spirit held back the fear by which it was burdened—and the eyes turned wearily again from the open window.

At last, Fanny's heavy heart could bear in silence the pressure no longer.

Hiding her face in her mother's lap, she sobbed out violently. Repressing her own struggling emotions, Mrs. Markland spoke soothing, hopeful words; and even while she sought to strengthen her daughter's heart, her own took courage.

"My dear child," she said, in a voice made even by depressing its tone, "do you not remember that beautiful thought expressed by Mrs. Willet yesterday? 'Death,' said she, 'signifies life; for in every death there is resurrection into a higher and purer life. This is as true,' she remarked, 'of our affections, which are but activities of the life, as of the natural life itself.'"

The sobs of the unhappy girl died away. Her mother continued, in a low, earnest voice, speaking to her own heart as well as to that of her child, for it, too, needed strength and comfort.

"How often have we been told, in our Sabbath instructions, that natural affections cannot be taken to heaven; that they must die, in order that spiritual affections may be born."

Fanny raised herself up, and said, with slight warmth of manner—

"Is not my love for you a natural affection for my natural mother? And must that die before I can enter heaven?"

"May it not be changed into a love of what is good in your mother, instead of remaining only a love of her person?"

"Dear mother!" almost sobbed again the unhappy child,—clasping eagerly the neck of her parent,—"it is such a love now! Oh! if I were as good, and patient, and self-denying as you are!"

"All our natural affections," resumed Mrs. Markland, after a few moments were given to self-control, "have simple regard to ourselves; and their indulgence never brings the promised happiness. This is why a wise and good Creator permits our natural desires to be so often thwarted. In this there is mercy, and not unkindness; for the fruition of these desires would often be most exquisite misery."

"Hark!" exclaimed Fanny, starting up at this moment, and leaning close to the window. The sound that had fallen upon her ear had also reached the ears of the mother.

"Oh! it's father!" fell almost wildly from the daughter's lips, and she sprang out into the hall, and forth to meet him in the drenching rain. Mrs. Markland could not rise, but sat, nerveless, until the husband entered the room.

"Oh, Edward! Edward!" she then exclaimed, rising, and staggering forward to meet him. "Thank our kind Father in heaven that you are with us again!" And her head sunk upon his bosom, and she felt his embracing arms drawn tightly around her. How exquisitely happy she was for the moment! But she was aroused by the exclamation of Fanny:—

"Oh, father! How pale you look!"

Mrs. Markland raised herself quickly, and gazed into her husband's face. What a fearful change was there! He was pale and haggard; and in his bloodshot eyes she read a volume of wretchedness.

"Oh, Edward! what has happened?" she asked, eagerly and tenderly.

"More than I dare tell you!" he replied, in a voice full of despair.

"Perhaps I can divine the worst."

Markland had turned his face partly away, that he might conceal its expression. But the unexpected tone in which this sentence was uttered caused him to look back quickly. There was no foreboding fear in the countenance of his wife. She had spoken firmly—almost cheerfully.

"The worst? Dear Agnes!" he said, with deep anguish in his voice. "It has not entered into your imagination to conceive the worst!"

"All is lost!" she answered, calmly.

"All," he replied, "but honour, and a heart yet brave enough and strong enough to battle with the world for the sake of its beloved ones."

Mrs. Markland hid her face on the breast of her husband, and stood, for some minutes, silent. Fanny approached her father, and laid her head against him.

"All this does not appal me," said Mrs. Markland, and she looked up and smiled faintly through tears that could not be repressed.

"Oh, Agnes! Agnes! can you bear the thought of being driven out from this Eden?"

"Its beauty has already faded," was the quiet answer. "If it is ours no longer, we must seek another home. And home, you know, dear Edward, is where the heart is, and the loved ones dwell."

But not so calmly could Fanny bear this announcement. She had tried hard, for her father's sake, to repress her feelings; but now they gave way into hysterical weeping. Far beyond his words her thoughts leaped, and already bitter self-reproaches had begun. Had she at once informed him of Mr. Lyon's return, singular interview, and injunction of secrecy, all these appalling consequences might have been saved. In an instant this flashed upon her mind, and the conviction overwhelmed her.

"My poor child," said Mr. Markland, sadly, yet with great tenderness, —"would to heaven I could save you from the evil that lies before us! But I am powerless in the hands of a stern necessity."

"Oh, father!" sobbed the weeping girl, "if I could bear this change alone, I would be happy."

"Let us all bear it cheerfully together," said Mrs. Markland, in a quiet voice, and with restored calmness of spirit. "Heaven, as Mrs. Willet says, with so much truth, is not without, but within us. The elements of happiness lie not in external, but in internal things. I do not think, Edward, even with all we had of good in possession, you have been happy for the past year. The unsatisfied spirit turned itself away from all that was beautiful in nature—from all it had sought for as the means of contentment, and sighed for new possessions. And these would also have lost their charms, had you gained them, and your restless heart still sighed after an ideal good. It may be—nay, it must be—in mercy, that our heavenly Father permitted this natural evil to fall upon us. The night that approaches will prove, I doubt not, the winter night in which much bread will grow."

"Comforter!" He spoke the word with emotion.

"And should I not be?" was the almost cheerful answer. "Those who cannot help should at least speak words of comfort."

"Words! They are more than words that you have spoken. They have in them a substance and a life. But, Fanny, dear child!" he said, turning to his still grieving daughter—"your tears distress me. They pain more deeply than rebuking sentences. My folly"—

"Father!" exclaimed Fanny—"it is I—not you—that must bear reproach. A word might have saved all. Weak, erring child that I was! Oh! that fatal secret which almost crushed my heart with its burden! Why did I not listen to the voice of conscience and duty?"

"Let the dead past rest," said Mr. Markland. "Your error was light, in comparison with mine. Had I guarded the approaches to the pleasant land, where innocence and peace had their dwelling-place, the subtle tempter could never have entered. To mourn over the past but weakens the spirit."

But of all that passed between these principal members of a family upon whom misfortune had come like a flood, we cannot make a record. The father's return soon became known to the rest, and the children's gladness fell, like a sunny vail, over the sterner features of the scene.

CHAPTER XXXV.

THE disaster was complete. Not a single dollar of all Markland had cast so blindly into the whirling vortex ever came back to him. Fenwick disappeared from New York, leaving behind conclusive evidence of a dark complicity with the specious Englishman, whose integrity had melted away, like snow in the sunshine, beneath the fire of a strong temptation. Honourably connected at home, shrewd, intelligent, and enterprising, he had been chosen as the executive agent of a company prepared to make large investments in a scheme that promised large results. He was deputed to bring the business before a few capitalists on this side of the Atlantic, and with what success has been seen. His recreancy to the trust reposed in him was the ruin of many.

How shall we describe the scenes that followed, too quickly, the announcement by Mr. Markland that Woodbine Lodge was no longer to remain in his possession? No member of the family could meet the stern necessity without pain. The calmest of all the troubled household was Mrs. Markland. Fanny, whom the event had awakened from a partial stupor, gradually declined into her former state. She moved about more like an automaton than a living figure; entering into all the duties and activities appertaining to the approaching change, yet seeming entirely indifferent to all external things. She was living and suffering in the inner world, more than in the outer. With the crushing out of a wild, absorbing love, had died all interest in life. She was in the external world, but, so far as any interest in passing events was concerned, not of it. Sad, young heart. A most cruel experience was thine!

When the disastrous intelligence was made known to Aunt Grace, that rather peculiar and excitable personage did not fail to say that it was nothing more than she had expected; that she had seen the storm coming, long and long ago, and had long and long ago lifted, without avail, a voice of warning. As for Mr. Lyon, he received a double share of execration—ending with the oft-repeated remark, that she had felt his shadow when he first came among them, and that she knew he must be a bad man. The ebullition subsided, in due time, and then the really good-hearted spinster gave her whole thought and active energy to the new work that was before them.

After the fierce conflict endured by Mr. Markland, ending wellnigh fatally, a calmness of spirit succeeded. With him, the worst was over; and now, he bowed himself, almost humbly, amid the ruins of his shattered fortunes, and, with a heavy heart, began to reconstruct a home, into which his beloved ones might find shelter. Any time within the preceding five or six years, an intimation on his part that he wished to enter business again would have opened the most advantageous connections. It was different now. There had been a season of overtrading. Large balances in England and France were draining the Atlantic cities of specie, and short crops made it impossible for western and southern merchants to meet their heavy payments at the east. Money ruled high, in consequence; weak houses were giving way, and a general uneasiness was beginning to prevail. But, even if these causes had not operated against the prospects of Mr. Markland, his changed circumstances would have been a sufficient bar to an advantageous business connection. He was no longer a capitalist; and the fact that he had recklessly invested his money in what was now pronounced one of the wildest schemes, was looked upon as conclusive evidence against his discretion and sound judgment. The trite saying, that the world judges of men by success or failure, was fully illustrated in his case. Once, he was referred to as the shrewdest of business men; now, he was held up to ambitious young tradesmen as a warning wreck, stranded amid the breakers.

How painfully was Mr. Markland reminded, at almost every turn, of the changed relations he bore to the world! He had not doubted his ability to form a good business connection with some house of standing, or with some young capitalist, ready to place money against his experience and trade. But in this he was doomed to disappointment. His friends spoke discouragingly; and everywhere he met but a cold response to his views. Meantime, one creditor of the Company, in New York, who held a matured piece of paper on which Mr. Markland's name was inscribed, commenced a suit against him. To prevent this creditor getting all that remained of his wasted estate, an assignment for the benefit of all was made, and preparations at once commenced for removing from Woodbine Lodge.

A few days after this arrangement, Mr. Willet, whose family had gathered closer around their neighbours the moment the fact of their misfortune was known, came over to see Mr. Markland and have some talk with him about his future prospects. A brief conversation which had taken place on the day previous opened the way for him to do so without seeming to intrude. The impossibility of getting into business at the present time was admitted, on both sides, fully. Mr. Willet then said—

"If the place of salesman in a large jobbing-house would meet your views, I believe I can manage it for you."

"I am in no situation," replied Mr. Markland, "to make my own terms with the world. Standing at the foot of the ladder, I must accept the first means of ascent that offers."

"You will, then, take the place?"

"Yes, if the offer is made."

"The salary is not as large as I could wish," said Mr. Willet.

"How much?"

"Twelve hundred dollars."

"Get it for me, Mr. Willet, and I will be deeply grateful. That sum will save my children from immediate want."

"I wish it were more, for your sake," replied the kind neighbour. "But I trust it will be the beginning of better things. You will, at least, gain a footing on the first round of the ladder."

"But the advantage is only in prospect," said Mr. Markland. "The place is not yet mine."

"You have the refusal," was the pleased answer. "I had you in my mind when I heard of the vacancy, and mentioned your name. The principal of the firm said, without a word of hesitation, that if you were available, you would just suit him."

"I shall not soon forget your real kindness," responded Markland, grasping the hand of Mr. Willet. "You have proved, indeed, though an acquaintance of recent date, a true friend. Ah, sir! my heart had begun to despond. So many cold looks, changed tones, and discouraging words! I was not prepared for them. When a man is no longer able to stand alone, how few there are to reach out an arm to give him support!"

"It is the way of the world," replied Mr. Willet; "and if we give it credit for more virtue than it possesses, a sad disappointment awaits us. But there are higher and better principles of action than such as govern the world. They bring a higher and better reward."

"May the better reward be yours," said Mr. Markland, fervently. His heart was touched by this real but unobtrusive kindness.

"When do you purpose leaving here?" next inquired Mr. Willet.

"As early as I can make arrangements for removing my family," was answered.

"Where do you think of going?"

"Into the city."

"Would you not prefer remaining in this pleasant neighbourhood? I do not see how my mother and sisters are going to give you all up. Mrs. Markland has already won her way into all their affections, and they have mourned over your misfortunes as deeply, I believe, as if they had been our own. Pardon the freedom of speech which is only a warm heart-utterance, when I say that there is a beauty in the character of Mrs. Markland that has charmed us all; and we cannot think of losing her society. Walker told me to-day that his wife was dissatisfied with a country life, and that he was going to sell his pleasant cottage. I offered him his price, and the title-deeds will be executed to-morrow. Will you do me the favour to become my tenant? The rent is two hundred and fifty dollars."

Mr. Willet spoke very earnestly. It was some moments before there was any reply. Then Mr. Markland raised his eyes from the floor, and said, in a low voice, that slightly trembled—

"I saw a house advertised for rent in the city, to-day, which I thought would suit us. It was small, and the rent three hundred dollars. On learning the owner's name, I found that he was an old business friend, with whom I had been quite intimate, and so called upon him. His reception of me was not over cordial. When I mentioned my errand, he hesitated in his replies, and finally hinted something about security for the rent. I left him without a word. To have replied without an exposure of unmanly weakness would have been impossible. Keenly, since my misfortunes, have I felt the change in my relations to the world; but nothing has wounded me so sharply as this! Mr. Willet, your generous interest in my welfare touches my heart! Let me talk with my family on the subject. I doubt not that we will accept your offer thankfully."

CHAPTER XXXVI.

"OUR Father in heaven never leaves us in a pathless desert," said Mrs. Markland, light breaking through her tear-filled eye. Her husband had just related the conversation held with Mr. Willet. "When the sun goes down, stars appear."

"A little while ago, the desert seemed pathless, and no star glittered in the sky," was answered.

"Yet the path was there, Edward; you had not looked close enough to your feet," replied his wife.

"It was so narrow that it would have escaped my vision," he said, faintly sighing.

"If it were not the safest way for you and for all of us, it would not be the only one now permitted our feet to tread."

"Safest it may be for me; but your feet could walk, securely, a pathway strewn with flowers. Ah me! the thought that my folly—"

"Edward," Mrs. Markland interrupted him in a quick, earnest voice, "if you love me, spare me in this. When I laid my hand in yours on that happy day, which was but the beginning of happier ones, I began a new life. All thought, all affection, all joy in the present and hope in the future, were thenceforth to be mingled with your thought, affection, joy, and hope. Our lives became one. It was yours to mark out our way through the world; mine to walk by your side. The path, thus far, has been a flowery one, thanks to your love and care! But no life-path winds always amid soft and fragrant meadows. There are desert places on the road, and steep acclivities; and there are dark, devious valleys, as well as sunny hill-tops. Pilgrims on the way to the Promised Land, we must pass through the Valley and the Shadow of Death, and be imprisoned for a time in Doubting Castle, before the Delectable Mountains are gained. Oh, Edward, murmur not, but thank God for the path he has shown us, and for the clear light that falls so warmly upon it. These friends, whom he has given us in this our darkest hour, are the truest friends we have yet known. Is it not a sweet compensation for all we lose, to be near them still, and to have the good a kind Father dispenses come to us through their hands? Dear husband! in this night of worldly life, a star of celestial beauty has already mirrored itself in my heart, and made light one of its hitherto darkened chambers."

"Sweet philosopher!" murmured her husband, in a softened voice. "A spirit like yours would illuminate a dungeon."

"If it can make the air bright around my husband, its happiness will be complete," was softly answered.

"But these reverses are hard to bear," said Mr. Markland, soberly.

"Harder in anticipation than in reality. They may become to us blessings."

"Blessings? Oh, Agnes! I am not able to see that. It is no light thing for a man to have the hard accumulations of his best years swept from him in a moment, and to find himself, when just passing the meridian of his life, thrown prostrate to the earth."

"There may be richer treasures lying just beneath the surface where he has fallen, than in all the land of Ophir toward which he was pressing in eager haste," said Mrs. Markland.

"It may be so." Markland spoke doubtingly.

"It must be so!" was emphatically rejoined. "Ah, Edward, have I not often warned you against looking far away into the future, instead of stooping to gather the pearls of happiness that a good Providence has scattered so profusely around us? They are around us still."

Markland sighed.

"And you may be richer far than imagination has yet pictured. Look not far away into the shadowy uncertainties of coming time for the heart's fruition. The stones from which its temple of happiness is to be erected, if ever built, lie all along the path your feet are treading. It has been so with you from the beginning—it is so now."

"If I build not this temple, it will be no fault of yours," said Markland, whose perceptions were becoming clearer.

"Let us build it together," answered his wife. "There will be no lack of materials."

CHAPTER XXXVII.

WHEN the offer of Mr. Walker's cottage was made known in the family, there was a passive acquiescence in the change on the part of all but Aunt Grace. Her pride was aroused.

"It's very kind in Mr. Willet," she said—"very kind, but scarcely delicate under the circumstances."

"Why not delicate?" inquired Mr. Markland.

"Did they think we were going into that little pigeon-box, just under the shadow of Woodbine Lodge. If we have to come down so low, it will not be in this neighbourhood. There's too much pride in the Markland blood for that!"

"We have but little to do with pride now," said Mrs. Markland.

Her husband sighed. The remark of his sister had quickened his blood.

"It is the best we can do!" he remarked, sadly.

"Not by any means," said Grace. "There are other neighbourhoods than this, and other houses to be obtained. Let us go from here; not remain the observed of all curious observers—objects of remark and pity!"

Her brother arose while she was speaking, and commenced walking the room in a disturbed manner. The words of Grace had aroused his slumbering pride.

"Rather let us do what is best under the circumstances," said Mrs. Markland, in her quiet way. "People will have their own thoughts, but these should never turn us from a right course."

"The sight of Woodbine Lodge will rebuke me daily," said Mr. Markland.

"You cannot be happy in this neighbourhood." Grace spoke in her emphatic way. "It is impossible!"

"I fear that it is even so," replied her brother.

"Then," said Mrs. Markland, in a firm voice, "we will go hence. I place nothing against the happiness of my husband. If the sight of our old home is to trouble him daily, we will put mountains between, if necessary."

Markland turned toward his wife. She had never looked more beautiful in his eye.

"Is self-negation to be all on her part?" The thought, flashing through his mind, changed the current of his feelings, and gave him truer perceptions.

"No, Agnes," he said, while a faint smile played around his lips, "we will not put mountains between us and this neighbourhood. Pride is a poor counsellor, and they who take heed to her words, sow the seeds of repentance. In reverse of fortune, we stand not alone. Thousands have walked this rugged road before us; and shall we falter, and look weakly back?"

"Not so, Edward!" returned his wife, with enthusiasm; "we will neither falter nor look back. Our good and evil are often made by contrasts. We shall not find the way rugged, unless we compare it too closely with other ways our feet have trodden, and sigh vainly over the past, instead of accepting the good that is awarded us in the present. Let us first make the 'rough paths of peevish nature even,' and the way will be smooth to our feet."

"You will never be happy in this neighbourhood, Edward," said his sister, sharply; for she saw that the pride her words had awakened was dying out.

"If he is not happy here, change of place will work no difference." Mrs. Markland spoke earnestly.

"Why not?" was the quick interrogation of Grace.

"Because happiness is rarely, if ever, produced by a change of external relations. We must have within us the elements of happiness; and then the heart's sunshine will lie across our threshold, whether it be of palace or cottage."

"Truer words were never spoken," said Mr. Markland, "and I feel their better meaning. No, Agnes, we will not go out from this pleasant neighbourhood, nor from among those we have proved to be friends. If Woodbine Lodge ever looks upon me rebukingly, I will try to acknowledge the justice of the rebuke. I will accept Mr. Willet's kind offer to-morrow. But what have you to say, Fanny?" Mr. Markland now turned to his daughter, who had not ventured a word on the subject, though she had listened with apparent interest to the conference. "Shall we take Mr. Walker's cottage?"

"Your judgment must decide that, father," was answered.

"But have you no choice in the case, Fanny? We can remove into the city, or go into some other neighbourhood."

"I will be as happy here as anywhere. Do as seems best, father."

A silence, made in a measure oppressive by Fanny's apparent indifference to all change, followed. Before other words were spoke, Aunt Grace withdrew in a manner that showed a mind disturbed. The conference in regard to the cottage was again resumed, and ended in the cheerful conclusion that it would afford them the pleasantest home, in their changed circumstances, of any that it was possible for them to procure.

CHAPTER XXXVIII.

PREPARATION was at once made for the proposed removal. Mr. Walker went back to the city, and the new owner of the cottage, Mr. Willet, set carpenters and painters at work to make certain additions which he thought needful to secure the comfort of his tenants, and to put every thing in the most thorough repair. Even against the remonstrance of Mr. Markland, who saw that his generous-minded neighbour was providing for his family a house worth almost double the rent that was to be paid, he carried out all his projected improvements.

"You will embarrass me with a sense of obligation," said Mr. Markland, in seeking to turn him from a certain purpose regarding the cottage.

"Do not say so," answered Mr. Willet; "I am only offering inducements for you to remain with us. If obligation should rest anywhere, it will be on our side. I make these improvements because the house is now my own property, and would be defective, to my mind, without them. Pray, don't let your thoughts dwell on these things."

Thus he strove to dissipate the feeling of obligation that began to rest on the mind of his unfortunate neighbour, while he carried out his purpose. In due time, under the assignment which had been made, Woodbine Lodge and a large part of the elegant and costly furniture contained in the mansion, were sold, and the ownership passed into other hands. With a meagre remnant of their household goods, the family retired to a humbler house. Some pitied, and stood at a distance; some felt a selfish pleasure in their fall; and some, who had courted them in their days of prosperity, were among the foremost to speak evil against them. But there were a few, and they the choicest spirits of the neighbourhood, who only drew nearer to these their friends in misfortune. Among them was Mr. Allison, one of those wise old men whose minds grow not dim with advancing years. He had passed through many trying vicissitudes, had suffered, and come up from the ordeal purer than when the fire laid hold upon the dross of nature.

A wise monitor had he been in Markland's brighter days, and now he drew near as a comforter. There is strength in true words kindly spoken. How often was this proved by Mr. and Mrs. Markland, as their venerable friend unlocked for them treasures of wisdom!

The little parlour at "Lawn Cottage," the name of their new home, soon became the scene of frequent reunions among choice spirits, whose aspirations went higher and deeper than the external and visible. In closing around Mr. Markland, they seemed to shut him out, as it were, from the old world in which he had hoped, and suffered, and struggled so vainly; and to open before his purer vision a world of higher beauty. In this world were riches for the toiler, and honour for the noble—riches and honour far more to be desired than the gems and gold of earth or its empty tributes of praise.

A few months of this new life wrought a wonderful change in Markland. All the better elements of his nature were quickened into activity. Useful daily employment tranquillized his spirits; and not unfrequently he found himself repeating the words of Longfellow—

> "Something attempted, something done,
> Had earned a night's repose."

So entirely was every thing of earthly fortune wrecked, and so changed were all his relations to the business world, that hope had yet no power to awaken his mind to ambition. For the present, therefore, he was content to receive the reward of daily toil, and to be thankful that he was yet able to supply the real wants of his family. A cheerful tone of feeling gradually succeeded the state of deep depression from which he had suffered. His spirit, which had walked in darkness, began to perceive that light was breaking in through the hitherto impenetrable gloom, and as it fell upon the path he was treading, a flower was seen here and there, while the roughness his imagination had pictured became not visible.

Nearly a year had glided away since the wreck of Markland's fortune, and little or no change in his worldly prospects was visible. He was sitting late, one evening, reading aloud to his wife from a book which the latter had received from Mrs. Willet. The rest of the family had retired. Mrs. Markland was plying her needle busily. Altered circumstances had made hourly industry on her part a necessity; yet had they in no way dimmed the cheerful brightness of her spirits.

"Come, Agnes," said her husband, closing the book, "it is growing late; and you have worked long enough. I'm afraid your health will suffer."

"Just a few minutes longer," replied Mrs. Markland, smiling. "I must finish this apron for Frank. He will want it in the morning." And her hand moved quicker.

"How true is every word you have been reading!" she added, after a few moments. "Manifold indeed are the ways in which a wise Providence dispenses good to the children of men. Mercy is seen in the cloud as well as in the sunshine. Tears to the spirit are like rain to the earth."

"The descent looked frightful," said Markland, after a pause—"but we reached the lower ground uninjured. Invisible hands seemed to bear us up."

"We have found the land far pleasanter than was imagined; and the sky above of a purer crystal."

"Yes—yes. It is even so. And if the flowers that spring up at our feet are not so brilliant, they have a sweeter perfume and a diviner beauty."

"In this land," said Mrs. Markland, "we see in the visible things that surround us what was rarely seen before—types of the invisible things they represent."

"Ah, yes, yes! Scales have fallen from my eyes. I have learned a new philosophy. In former times, Mr. Allison's words seemed full of beautiful truths, yet so veiled, that I could not see their genuine brightness. Now they are like sudden gleams of sunlight on a darkened landscape."

"Seekers after happiness, like the rest of the world," said Mrs. Markland, resting her hands upon the table by which she sat, and, gazing earnestly into her husband's face, "we had lost our way, and were moving with swift feet in the wrong direction. Suddenly, our kind Father threw up before us an impassable mountain. Then we seemed shut out from the land of promise forever, and were in despair. But he took his weeping, murmuring children by the hand, and led them gently into another path!"

"Into a narrower way"—Mr. Markland took up the words of his wife—"and sought by few; yet, it has already brought us into a pleasant region."

"To speak in less ideal language," said Mrs. Markland, "we have been taught an all-important lesson. It is this: That there is over each one of us an intimate providential care which ever has regard to our eternal good. And the reason of our many and sad disappointments lies in the fact, that we seek only the gratification of natural life, in which are the very elements of dissatisfaction. All mere natural life is selfish life; and natural ends gained only confirm this selfish life, and produce misery instead of happiness."

"There is no rest," said Markland, "to the striving spirit that only seeks for the good of this world. How clearly have I seen this of late, as well in my own case as in that of others! Neither wealth nor honour have in themselves the elements of happiness; and their increase brings but an increase of trouble."

"If sought from merely selfish ends," remarked his wife. "Yet their possession may increase our happiness, if we regard them as the means by which we may rise into a higher life."

There followed a thoughtful pause. Mrs. Markland resumed her work, and her husband leaned his head back and remained for some minutes in a musing attitude.

"Don't you think," he said at length, "that Fanny is growing more cheerful?"

"Oh, yes. I can see that her state of mind is undergoing a gradual elevation."

"Poor child! What a sad experience, for one so young, has been hers! How her whole character has been, to all seeming, transformed. The light-hearted girl suddenly changed to a thoughtful, suffering woman!"

"She may be a happier woman in the end," said Mrs. Markland.

"Is that possible?"

"Yes. Suffering has given her a higher capacity for enjoyment."

"And for pain, also," said Mr. Markland.

"She is wiser for the first experience," was replied.

"Yes, there is so much in her favour. I wish," added Mr. Markland, "that she would go a little more into company. It is not good for any one to live so secluded a life. Companionship is necessary to the spirit's health."

"She is not without companions, or, at least, a companion."

"Flora Willet?"

"Yes."

"Good, as far as it goes. Flora is an excellent girl, and wise beyond her years."

"Can we ask a better companion for our child than one with pure feelings and true thoughts?"

"No. But I am afraid Flora has not the power to bring her out of herself. She is so sedate."

"She does not lack cheerfulness of spirit, Edward."

"Perpetual cheerfulness is too passive."

"Her laugh, at times, is delicious," said Mrs. Markland, "going to your heart like a strain of music, warming it like a golden sunbeam. Flora's character is by no means a passive one, but rather the reverse."

"She is usually very quiet when I see her," replied Markland.

"This arises from an instinctive deference to those who are older."

"Fanny is strongly attached to her, I think."

"Yes; and the attachment I believe to be mutual."

"Would not Flora, at your suggestion, seek to draw her gradually forth from her seclusion?"

"We have talked together on that subject several times," replied Mrs. Markland, "and are now trying to do the very thing you suggest."

"With any prospect of accomplishing the thing desired?"

"I believe so. There is to be company at Mr. Willet's next week, and we have nearly gained Fanny's consent to be present."

"Have you? I am indeed gratified to learn this."

"Flora has set her heart on gaining Fanny's consent, and will leave no influence untried."

"Still, Fanny's promise to go is withheld?"

"Yes; but I have observed her looking over her drawers, and showing more interest in certain articles therein than she has evinced for a long, long time."

"If she goes, she will require a new dress," said Mr. Markland.

"I think not. Such preparation would be too formal at present. But, we can make that all right."

"Oh! it will give me so much pleasure! Do not leave any influence untried."

"You may be sure that we will not," answered Mrs. Markland; "and, what is more, you have little to fear touching our success."

CHAPTER XXXIX.

THE efforts of Flora Willet were successful; and Fanny Markland made one of the company that assembled at her brother's house. Through an almost unconquerable reluctance to come forth into the eye of the world, so to speak, she had broken; and, as one after another of the guests entered the parlours, she could hardly repress an impulse to steal away and hide herself from the crowd of human faces thickly closing around her. Undesired, she found herself an object of attention; and, in some cases, of clearly-expressed sympathy, that was doubly unpleasant.

The evening was drawing to a close, and Fanny had left the company and was standing alone in one of the porticos, when a young man, whose eyes she had several times observed earnestly fixed upon her, passed near, walked a few paces beyond, and then turning, came up and said, in a low voice —"Pardon this slight breach of etiquette, Miss Markland. I failed to get a formal introduction. But, as I have a few words to say that must be said, I am forced to a seeming rudeness."

Both the manner and words of the stranger so startled Fanny, that her heart began to throb wildly and her limbs to tremble. Seeing her clasp the pillar by which she stood, he said, as he offered an arm—

"Walk with me, for a few minutes at the other end of the portico. We will be less observed, and freer from interruption."

But Fanny only shrunk closer to the pillar.

"If you have any thing to say to me, let it be said here," she replied. Her trembling voice betrayed her agitation.

"What I have to say, concerns you deeply," returned the young man, "and you ought to hear it in a calmer mood. Let us remove a little farther from observation, and be less in danger of interruption."

"Speak, or retire!" said Fanny, with assumed firmness, waving her hand as she spoke.

But the stranger only bent nearer.

"I have a word for you from Mr. Lyon," said he, in a low, distinct whisper.

It was some moments before Fanny made answer. There was a wild strife in her spirit. But the tempest was of brief duration. Scarcely a perceptible tremor was in her voice, as she answered,

"It need not be spoken."

"Say not so, Miss Markland. If, in any thing, you have misapprehended him—"

"Go, sir!" And Fanny drew herself up to her full height, and pointed away with her finger.

"Mr. Lyon has ever loved you with the most passionate devotion," said the stranger. "In some degree he is responsible for the misfortune of your father; and now, at the first opportunity for doing so, he is ready to tender a recompense. Partly for this purpose, and partly to bear to you the declaration of Mr. Lyon's unwavering regard, am I here."

"He has wronged, deeply wronged my father," replied Fanny, something of the imperious tone and manner with which she had last spoken abating. "If prepared to make restitution in any degree, the way can easily be opened."

"Circumstances," was answered, "conspired to place him in a false position, and make him the instrument of wrong to those for whom he would at any time have sacrificed largely instead of becoming the minister of evil."

"What does he propose?" asked Fanny.

"To restore your father to his old position. Woodbine Lodge can be purchased from the present owner. It may become your home again."

"It is well," said Fanny. "Let justice be done."

She was now entirely self-possessed, bore herself firmly erect, and spoke without apparent emotion. Standing with her back to the window, through which light came, her own face was in shadow, while that of her companion was clearly seen.

"Justice will be done," replied the young man, slightly embarrassed by the replies of Fanny, the exact meaning of which he did not clearly perceive.

"Is that all you have to communicate?" said the young girl, seeing that he hesitated.

"Not all."

"Say on, then."

"There are conditions."

"Ah! Name them."

"Mr. Lyon still loves you with an undying tenderness."

Fanny waved her hand quickly, as if rejecting the affirmation, and slightly averted her head, but did not speak.

"His letters ceased because he was in no state to write; not because there was any change in his feelings toward you. After the terrible disaster to the Company, for which he has been too sweepingly blamed, he could not write."

"Where is he now?" inquired the maiden.

"I am not yet permitted to answer such a question."

There came a pause.

"What shall I say to him from you?"

"Nothing!" was the firm reply.

"Nothing? Think again, Miss Markland."

"Yes; say to him, that the mirror which once reflected his image in my heart, is shattered forever."

"Think of your father," urged the stranger.

"Go, sir!" And Fanny again waved her hand for him to leave her. "Your words are an offence to me."

A form intercepted at this moment the light which came through one of the doors opening upon the portico, and Fanny stepped forward a pace or two.

"Ah! Miss Markland, I've been looking for you."

It was Mr. Willet. The stranger moved away as the other approached, yet remained near enough to observe them. Fanny made no response.

"There is a bit of moonlight scenery that is very beautiful," said Mr. Willet. "Come with me to the other side of the house."

And he offered his arm, through which Fanny drew hers without hesitation. They stepped from the piazza, and passed in among the fragrant shrubbery, following one of the garden walks, until they were in view of the

175

scene to which Mr. Willet referred. A heavy bank of clouds had fallen in the east, and the moon was just struggling through the upper, broken edges, along which her gleaming silver lay in fringes, broad belts, and fleecy masses, giving to the dark vapours below a deeper blackness. Above all this, the sky was intensely blue, and the stars shone down with a sharp, diamond-like lustre. Beneath the bank of clouds, yet far enough in the foreground of this picture to partly emerge from obscurity, stood, on an eminence, a white marble building, with columns of porticos, like a Grecian temple. Projected against the dark background were its classic outlines, looking more like a vision of the days of Pericles than a modern verity.

"Only once before have I seen it thus," said Mr. Willet, after his companion had gazed for some time upon the scene without speaking, "and ever since, it has been a picture in my memory."

"How singularly beautiful!" Fanny spoke with only a moderate degree of enthusiasm, and with something absent in her manner. Mr. Willet turned to look into her face, but it lay too deeply in shadow. For a short time they stood gazing at the clouds, the sky, and the snowy temple. Then Mr. Willet passed on, with the maiden, threading the bordered garden walks, and lingering among the trees, until they came to one of the pleasant summer-houses, all the time seeking to awaken some interest in her mind. She had answered all his remarks so briefly and in so absent a manner, that he was beginning to despair, when she said, almost abruptly—

"Did you see the person who was with me on the portico, when you came out just now?"

"Yes."

"Do you know him?"

"He's a stranger to me," said Mr. Willet; "and I do not even remember his name. Mr. Ellis introduced him."

"And you invited him to your house?"

"No, Miss Markland. We invited Mr. and Mrs. Ellis, and they brought him as their friend."

"Ah!" There was something of relief in her tone.

"But what of him?" said Mr. Willet. "Why do you inquire about him so earnestly?"

Fanny made no answer.

"Did he in any way intrude upon you?" Mr. Willet spoke in a quicker voice.

"I have no complaint to make against him," replied Fanny. "And yet I ought to know who he is, and where he is from."

"You shall know all you desire," said her companion. "I will obtain from Mr. Ellis full information in regard to him."

"You will do me a very great favour."

The rustling of a branch at this moment caused both of them to turn in the direction from which the sound came. The form of a man was, for an instant, distinctly seen, close to the summer-house. But it vanished, ere more than the dim outline was perceived.

"Who can that be, hovering about in so stealthy a manner?" Mr. Willet spoke with rising indignation, starting to his feet as he uttered the words.

"Probably the very person about whom we were conversing," said Fanny.

"This is an outrage! Come, Miss Markland, let us return to the house, and I will at once make inquiry of Mr. Ellis about this stranger."

Fanny again took the proffered arm of Mr. Willet, and the two went silently back, and joined the company from which they had a little while before retired. The latter at once made inquiry of Mr. Ellis respecting the stranger who had been introduced to him. The answers were far from being satisfactory.

"He is a young man whose acquaintance I made about a year ago. He was then a frequent visitor in my family, and we found him an intelligent, agreeable companion. For several months he has been spending his time at the South. A few weeks ago, he returned and renewed his friendly relations. On learning that we were to be among your guests on this occasion, he expressed so earnest a desire to be present, that we took the liberty sometimes assumed among friends, and brought him along. If we have, in the least, trespassed on our privileges as your guests, we do most deeply regret the circumstance."

And this was all Mr. Willet could learn, at the time, in reference to the stranger, who, on being sought for, was nowhere to be found. He had heard enough of the conversation that passed between Mr. Willet and Fanny, as he listened to them while they sat in the summer-house, to satisfy him that if he remained longer at "Sweetbrier," he would become an object of the host's too careful observation.

CHAPTER XL.

A FEW weeks prior to the time at which the incidents of the preceding chapter occurred, a man, with a rough, neglected exterior, and face almost hidden by an immense beard, landed at New Orleans from one of the Gulf steamers, and was driven to the St. Charles Hotel. His manner was restless, yet wary. He gave his name as Falkner, and repaired at once to the room assigned to him.

"Is there a boarder in the house named Leach?" he made inquiry of the servant who came up with his baggage.

"There is," was replied.

"Will you ascertain if he is in, and say that I wish to see him?"

"What name, sir?" inquired the servant.

"No matter. Give the number of my room."

The servant departed, and in a few minutes conducted a man to the apartment of the stranger.

"Ah! you are here!" exclaimed the former, starting forward, and grasping tightly the hand that was extended to receive him. "When did you arrive?"

"This moment." "From—

?"

"No matter where from, at present. Enough that I am here." The servant had retired, and the closed door was locked. "But there is one thing I don't just like."

"What is that?"

"You penetrated my disguise too easily."

"I expected you, and knew, when inquired for, by whom I was wanted."

"That as far as it goes. But would you have known me if I had passed you in the street?"

The man named Leach took a long, close survey of the other, and then replied—

"I think not, for you are shockingly disfigured. How did you manage to get that deep gash across your forehead?"

"It occurred in an affray with one of the natives; I came near losing my life."

"A narrow escape, I should say."

"It was. But I had the satisfaction of shooting the bloody rascal through the heart." And a grin of savage pleasure showed the man's white teeth gleaming below the jetty moustache.—"Well, you see I am here," he added, "boldly venturing on dangerous ground."

"So I see. And for what? You say that I can serve you again; and I am in New Orleans to do your bidding."

"You can serve me, David," was answered, with some force of expression. "In fact, among the large number of men with whom I have had intercourse, you are the only one who has always been true to me, and" (with a strongly-uttered oath) "I will never fail you, in any extremity."

"I hope never to put your friendship to any perilous test," replied the other, smiling. "But say on."

"I can't give that girl up. Plague on her bewitching face! it has wrought upon me a kind of enchantment. I see it ever before me as a thing of beauty. David! she must be mine at any sacrifice!"

"Who? Markland's pretty daughter?"

"Yes."

"Better start some other game," was bluntly answered. "Your former attempt to run this down came near ruining every thing."

"No danger of that now. The ingots are all safe;" and the man gave a shrug.

"Lyon—"

"My name is Falkner. Don't forget it, if you please!" The speaker contracted his brows.

"Falkner, then. What I want to say is this: Let well enough alone. If the ingots are safe, permit them to remain so. Don't be foolhardy enough to put any one on the scent of them."

"Don't be troubled about that. I have sacrificed too much in gaining the wealth desired ever to hold it with a careless or relaxing grasp. And yet its mere possession brings not the repose of mind, the sense of independence, that were so pleasingly foreshadowed. Something is yet lacking to make the fruition complete. I want a companion; and there is only one, in the wide world, who can be to me what I desire."

"Fanny Markland?"

"Yes."

"You wish to make her your wife?"

"She is too pure to be happy in any other relation. Yes; I wish to gain her for my bride."

"A thing more difficult than you imagine."

"The task may be difficult; but, I will not believe, impossible."

"And it is in this matter you desire my service?"

"Yes."

"I am ready. Point the way, and I will go. Digest the plan, and I am the one to carry it out."

"You must go North."

"Very well."

"Do you know how her father is situated at present?"

"He is a poor clerk in a jobbing-house."

"Indeed! They stripped him of every thing?"

"Yes. Woodbine Lodge vanished from beneath his feet as if it had been an enchanted island."

"Poor man! I am sorry for him. I never contemplated so sweeping a disaster in his case. But no one can tell, when the ball leaves his hand, what sort of a strike will be made. How does he bear it, I wonder?"

"Don't know. It must have been a terrible fall for him."

"And Fanny? Have you learned nothing in regard to her?"

"Nothing."

"Did you keep up a correspondence with the family whose acquaintance you made in—?"

"The family of Mr. Ellis? No; not any regular correspondence. We passed a letter or two, when I made a few inquiries about the Marklands, and particularly mentioned Fanny; but heard no further from them."

"There are no landmarks, then?" said Lyon.

"None."

"You must start immediately for the North. I will remain here until word comes from you. Ascertain, first, if you can, if there is any one connected with the Company who is yet on the alert in regard to myself; and write to me all the facts you learn on this head immediately. If it is not safe to remain in the United States, I will return to the city of Mexico, and we can correspond from there. Lose no time in gaining access to Miss Markland, and learn her state of mind in regard to me. She cannot fail to have taken her father's misfortunes deeply to heart; and your strongest appeal to her may be on his behalf. It is in my power to restore him to his former position, and, for the sake of his daughter, if needful, that will be done."

"I comprehend you; and trust me to accomplish all you desire, if in human power. Yet I cannot help expressing surprise at the singular fascination this girl has wrought upon you. I saw her two or three times, but perceived nothing very remarkable about her. She is pretty enough; yet, in any company of twenty women, you may pick out three far handsomer. What is the peculiar charm she carries about her?"

"It is nameless, but all-potent, and can only be explained psychologically, I suppose. No matter, however. The girl is necessary to my happiness, and I must secure her."

"By fair means, or foul?" His companion spoke inquiringly.

"I never hesitate about the means to be employed when I attempt the accomplishment of an object," was replied. "If she cannot be prevailed upon to come to me willingly, stratagem—even force—must be used. I know that she loves me; for a woman who once loves, loves always. Circumstances may have cooled, even hardened, the surface of her feelings, but her heart beneath is warm toward me still. There may be many reasons why she would not voluntarily leave her home for the one I promised her, however magnificent; but, if removed without her own consent, after the change, she may find in my love the highest felicity her heart could desire."

"My faith is not strong," said Leach, "and never has been, in the stability of love. But you have always manifested a weakness in this direction; and, I suppose, it runs in the blood. Probably, if you carry the girl off, (not so easy a thing, by-the-way, nor a safe operation to attempt,) you can make all smooth with her by doing something handsome for her father."

"No doubt of it. I could restore Woodbine Lodge to his possession, and settle two or three thousand a year on him beside."

"Such arguments might work wonders," said the accomplice.

A plan of operations was settled during the day, and early on the next morning the friend of Mr. Lyon started northward.

CHAPTER XLI.

THE first letter received by Mr. Lyon, gave only a vague account of affairs.

"I arrived yesterday," wrote Leach, "and entered upon my work immediately. The acquaintance with Mr. Ellis has been renewed. Last evening I spent with the family, and learned that the Marklands were living in a pleasant little cottage within sight of Woodbine Lodge; but could glean few particulars in regard to them. Fanny has entirely secluded herself. No one seemed to know any thing of her state of mind, though something about a disappointment in love was distantly intimated."

The next letter produced considerable excitement in the mind of Mr. Lyon. His friend wrote:

"There is a person named Willet living in the neighbourhood, who is very intimate in Markland's family. It is said by some that he more than fancies the daughter. As he is rich, and of good reputation and appearance, he may be a dangerous rival."

About a week later, Leach wrote:

"This Willet, of whom I spoke, is the owner of an elegant seat not far from Markland's. He resides with his mother and sisters, who are especial favourites among all the neighbours. Next week they give a large party. In all probability Miss Markland will be there; and I must contrive to be there also. Mr. Ellis and his family have recently made their acquaintance, and have received invitations. Your humble servant will be on the ground, if asking to go under the shadow of their wings will gain the favour. He is not over modest, you know. If Fanny Markland should be there, depend upon it, the golden opportunity will not pass unimproved. She shall hear from you."

Another week of suspense.

"Don't like the aspect of affairs," wrote the friend. "I was at Mr. Willet's, and saw Miss Markland. The whole family were particularly gracious to her. It was her first appearance in any company since her father's failure. She looked pensive, but charming. In truth, my friend, she is a girl worth the winning, and no mistake. I think her lovely. Well, I tried all the evening to get an introduction to her, but failed, being a stranger. Fortunately, at a late hour, I saw her leave one of the elegant parlours alone, and go out upon the portico. This was the opportunity, and I seized it. Boldly addressing her, I mentioned, after a little play of words, your name. Said I had a message from you, and, as guardedly as possible, declared your undying love. But I could not just make her out. She showed great self-possession under the circumstances, and a disposition to throw me off. I don't think her heart beats very warmly toward you. This was the state of affairs when Mr. Willet made his appearance, and I drew myself away. He said a few words to her, when she placed her arm within his, and they walked into the garden alone. I followed at a distance. After admiring a bit of moon-light fancy-work, they strayed into a summer-house, and I got close enough to hear what they were talking about; I found that she was making particular inquiries as to my identity, and that he was unable to give her the information she desired. I did not feel much encouraged by the tone in which she alluded to me. Unfortunately, I rustled a branch in my eagerness to catch every word, and so discovered myself. Beating a hasty retreat, I went back to the house, took my hat, and quietly retired, walking most of the way to the city, a distance of several miles. I have not called upon the family of Mr. Ellis, and am still in doubt whether it will be wise to do so."

This communication almost maddened Lyon. There was evidently a rival in the field, and one who had over him an immense advantage. Impatiently he waited for the next letter. Three days elapsed before it came. Tearing open the envelope, he read—

"I don't think there is much chance for you. This Willet has been a particular friend of the family since their misfortunes. He bought the cottage in which they live, and offered it to them at a moderate rent, when almost every one else turned from them coldly. The two families have ever since maintained a close intimacy; and it is pretty generally thought that a closer relation will, ere long, exist between them. I called upon the Ellis's yesterday. Their reception was far from cordial. I tried to be self-possessed, and as chatty as usual; but it was uphill work, you may depend on it. Once I ventured an illusion to the party at Willets; but it was received with an embarrassed silence. I left early and without the usual invitation to repeat my visits. To-day I met Mr. Ellis in the street, and received from him the cut direct! So, you see, affairs are not progressing very favourably; and the worst is, I am in total ignorance of the real effect of my interview with Miss Markland upon her own mind. She may yet retain the communication I made as her own secret, or have revealed it to her father. His reception of the matter, if aware of what occurred, is a problem unsolved. I can, therefore, only say, keep as cool as possible, and wait as patiently as possible a few days longer, when you shall know the best or the worst."

A mad imprecation fell from the lips of Mr. Lyon, as he threw this letter from him. He was baffled completely. Two more days of wearying suspense went heavily by, and then another letter came to the impatient waiter.

"This place," so Leach wrote, "will soon be too hot to hold me, I'm afraid. If not mistaken in the signs, there's something brewing. Twice, to-day, I've been inquired for at the hotel. To-morrow morning early I shall prudently change my quarters, and drop down to Washington in the early cars. A little change in the external man can be effected there. On the day after, I will return, and, under cover of my disguised exterior, renew operations. But I can't flatter you with any hope of success. It's pretty generally believed that Willet is going to marry Fanny Markland; and the match is too good a one for a poor girl to decline. He is rich, educated, honourable; and, people say, kind and good. And, to speak out my thoughts on the subject, I think she'd be a fool to decline the arrangement, even against your magnificent proposals. Still, I'm heart and hand with you, and ready to venture even upon the old boy's dominions to serve a long-tried friend. There is one significant fact which I heard to-day that makes strong against you. It is said that Mr. Willet is about making a change in his business, and that Markland is to be associated with him in some new arrangements. That looks as if matters were settled between the two families. In my next letter I hope to communicate something more satisfactory."

On the day after receiving this communication, Lyon, while walking the floor in one of the parlours, saw a man pass in from the street, and go hurriedly along the hall. The form struck him as strangely like that of his friend from whom he was hourly in expectation of another letter. Stepping quickly to the door of the room, he caught a glimpse of the man ascending the staircase. To follow was a natural impulse. Doubt was only of brief continuance.

"David!" he exclaimed, on reaching his own apartment. "In the name of heaven! what does this mean?"

"That you are in danger," was replied, in a tone that made the villain's heart leap.

"What?" The two men retired within the apartment.

"I fear they are on our track," said Leach.

"Who?"

"The law's fierce bloodhounds!"

"No! impossible!" The face of Lyon grew white as ashes, and his limbs shook with a sudden, irrepressible tremor.

"Speak out plainly," he added. "What evidence is there of danger?"

"In my last letter, you will remember, I expressed some fear on this head, and mentioned my purpose to go to Washington and assume a disguise."

"I do, and have felt troubled about it."

"Well, I was off by the early train on the next morning. As good or bad luck would have it, the very man who sat next me in the cars was an individual I had met in the family of Mr. Ellis. He knew me, but played shy for some time. I pretended not to recognise him at first, but turning to him suddenly, after we had been under way for ten minutes or so, I said, as if I had but just become aware of his identity, 'Why, how are you? I did not know that I had an acquaintance by my side.' He returned my warm greeting rather distantly; but there was too much at stake to mind this, and I determined to thaw him out, which I accomplished in due time. I found him a free sort of a man to talk, after he got going, and so I made myself quite familiar, and encouraged him to be outspoken. I knew he had heard something about my adventure at Mr. Willet's, and determined to get from him the stories that were afloat on that subject. All came in good time. But the exaggeration was tremendous. Fanny had concealed nothing from her father, and he nothing from Mr. Willet. I was known as your agent and accomplice, and there was a plan concocting to get possession of my person, and, through me, of yours. 'Take a friend's advice,' said the man to me, as we stepped from the cars at Washington, 'and give—a wide berth in future.' I did take his advice, kept straight on, and am here."

"Confusion!" The pallid face of Lyon had flushed again, and was now dark with congestion.

"When will the next boat leave for Vera Cruz?" inquired Leach.

"Day after to-morrow," was answered.

"We are in peril here every hour."

"But cannot leave earlier. I hope your fears have magnified the danger."

"If there be danger at all, it cannot be magnified. Let them once get you in their hands, and they will demand a fearful retribution."

"I am well aware of that, and do not mean to be left in their power."

"The telegraph has, no doubt, already put the authorities here on the alert. My very arrival may have been noted. It will not do for us to be seen together."

"Ha! I did not think of that!" Lyon was more deeply disturbed. "You had better go from here at once. Where is your baggage?"

"I ordered it to be sent up."

"Let me see after that. At once pass over to the Levee; go on board the first boat that is leaving, whether bound up the river or for Galveston. Only get off from the city, and then make your way to Mexico. You will find me there."

Fear had now seized upon both of the men, and each saw consternation in the other's face.

"I am off at the word," said Leach, as he grasped the hand of his companion.

"Be discreet, self-possessed, and wary." Lyon spoke in a warning voice.

"I will. And you take good heed to the same advice."

The men were yet standing face to face, each grasping the other's hand, when both partly turned their heads to listen. There was a sound of feet at the upper end of the passage, just at the landing, and it came rapidly nearer. A breathless pause marked the deep interest of the listeners. A few moments of suspense, in which Lyon and his companion grew deadly pale, and then the noisy footsteps were silenced at their very door. A smothered sound of voices was followed by a trial of the lock, and then by a decided rapping. But no answer was made to the summons.

Noiselessly, Mr. Lyon drew from a deep side-pocket a loaded revolver; but the hand of his companion was laid quickly upon his arm, and his lips, in dumb show, gave the word—

"Madness!"

Lyon shook him off, and deliberately pointed his weapon toward the door.

"Hallo, there! Are you asleep?"

This loud call came after repeated knocking and rattling. But there was no response, nor the slightest indication of life within the chamber.

"They are here, I am certain." These words were distinctly heard by the anxious inmates.

"Then we must break in the door," was resolutely answered.

"Oh, for heaven's sake, put up that pistol!" hoarsely whispered Leach. "Such resistance will be fatal evidence against us. Better open the door and put a bold face upon it."

"Too late!" was just whispered back, when the door flew open with a crash, and the body of the man who had thrown himself against it with a force greatly beyond the resistance, fell inward upon the floor. At the same instant, Lyon exclaimed, in a quick, savage voice—

"Back, instantly, or you are dead men!"

There was such a will in the words he uttered, that, for a moment, the men, four in number, fell back from the open door, and in that instant Lyon sprung past them, and, ere they could recover themselves, was beyond their reach. His friend made an attempt to follow, but was seized and made prisoner. The time spent in securing him was so much of a diversion in favour of Lyon, who succeeded in getting into the street, ere the alarm extended to the lower part of the house, and passing beyond immediate observation. But escape from the city was impossible. The whole police force was on the alert in half an hour, and in less than an hour he was captured, disguised as a sailor, on board of a vessel ready cleared and making ready to drop down the river. He yielded quietly, and, after being taken before the authorities in the case, was committed for hearing in default of bail. The arrest was on a requisition from the governor of New York.

CHAPTER XLII.

FANNY had not hesitated a moment on the question of communicating to her father the singular occurrence at Mr. Willet's; and Mr. Markland was prompt not only in writing to two or three of the principal sufferers by Lyon in New York, but in drawing the attention of the police to the stranger who had so boldly made propositions to his daughter. Two men were engaged to watch all his movements, and on no pretence whatever to lose sight of him. The New York members of the Company responded instantly to Markland's suggestion, and one of them came on to confer and act in concert with him. A letter delivered at the post office to the stranger, it was ascertained, came by way of New Orleans. A requisition from the governor of New York to deliver up, as a fugitive from justice, the person of Lee Lyon, was next obtained. All things were thus brought into readiness for action, the purpose being to keep two police officers ever on the track of his accomplice, let him go where he would. Inquiries were purposely made for this man at the hotel, in order to excite a suspicion of something wrong, and hasten his flight from the city; and when he fled at last, the officers, unknown to him, were in the cars. The telegraph gave intelligence to the police at New Orleans, and all was in readiness there for the arrival of the party. How promptly action followed has been seen. On the day after Lyon's arrest, he was on his way northward, in custody of two officers, who were already well enough acquainted with his character to be ever on the alert. Several attempts at escape were made, but they succeeded in delivering him safely in New York, where he was committed to prison.

On the day, and almost at the very hour, when the iron doors closed drearily on the criminal, Fanny Markland was alone with Mr. Willet. At the earnest desire of Flora, she had gone over to spend the afternoon at Sweetbriar. The brother came out from the city at dinner-time, and did not return again—the attractions of his fair guest being more than he could resist. There had been music and conversation during the afternoon, and all had been done by the family to render the visit of Fanny as agreeable as possible; but she did not seem in as good spirits as usual—her eyes were dreamy, and her voice had in it a shade of sadness.

Toward evening, she walked out with Flora and her brother. The conversation turned on the beautiful in nature, and Mr. Willet talked in his earnest way—every sentence full of poetry to the ears of at least one absorbed listener. In a pause of the conversation, Flora left them and went back to the house. For a little while the silence continued, and then Mr. Willet said, in a tone so changed that its echo in the maiden's heart made every pulse beat quicker,—

"Fanny, there is one question that I have long desired to ask."

She lifted her eyes to his face timidly, and looked steadily at him for a few moments; then, as they fell to the ground, she replied—

"You can ask no question that it will not give me pleasure to answer."

"But this, I fear, will give you pain," said he.

"Pain, you have taught me, is often a salutary discipline."

"True, and may it be so in the present instance. It is not unknown to me that Mr. Lyon once held a place in your regard—I will go farther, and say in your affections."

Fanny started, and moved a step from him; but he continued—

"The question I wish to ask is, does there yet remain in your heart a single point that gives back a reflection of his image? In plainer words, is he any thing to you?"

"No, nothing!" was the emphatic, almost indignant, answer.

"It is said," resumed Mr. Willet, "that you once loved him."

"He came to me," replied Fanny, "a young, artless, trusting girl, as an angel of light. Nay, I was only a child, whose ears were unused to warmer words than fell from the loving lips of parents. Suddenly, he opened before me a world of enchantment. My whole being was on fire with a delicious passion. I believed him true and good, and loved him, because, in my eyes, he was the embodiment of all human perfections. But time proved that I had only loved an enchanting ideal, and my heart rejected him with intense loathing."

"Enough," said Willet; "I feel that it must be so."

The two remained silent for the space of nearly a minute; Mr. Willet then resumed—

"Forgive me if my question has seemed indelicate, and be assured that I asked it from no idle curiosity. Let me go a little farther; and, my dear young lady, retain your calmness of spirit. Look into your heart, but keep every pulsation under control. Since our first meeting, I have felt a deep interest in you. What you have suffered has pained me seriously; but the pain has given way to pleasure, for out of the fire you have come up pure and strong, Fanny! I have but one word more—there is a sacred place in my heart, and your image has long been the inhabitant. Here is my hand—will you lay your own within it, that I may grasp it as mine for life?"

Willet extended his hand as he spoke. There was only a moment's hesitation on the part of Fanny, who stood with her head bent so far down that the expression of her face could not be seen. Raising her eyes in which joy shone through blinding tears, she extended her hand, which was seized, grasped tightly for an instant, and then covered with kisses.

CHAPTER XLIII.

NO sooner was Lyon completely in the power of the men he had wronged to an extent that left no room for mercy, than he made offers of compromise. A public trial involved not only public disgrace, but he had too good reasons to fear conviction and penal retribution. This was the greatest evil he had to dread, and so he made up his mind to part with at least a portion of his ill-gotten gains. Interview after interview was held with the parties representing the Company for which he had been agent, and a final arrangement made for the restitution of about two hundred thousand dollars—his release not to take place until the money, or its value, was in the hands of his creditors. Nearly three months passed in efforts to consummate this matter, and at last the sum of one hundred and eighty thousand dollars was obtained, and the miserable, disgraced man set free. He went forth into the world again with the bitterness of a life-disappointment at his heart, and a feeling of almost murderous hate against the men whose confidence he had betrayed, and who obtained from him only a partial recompense.

Of the sum restored, there fell to Mr. Markland's share about twenty-five thousand dollars. Its possession quickened in his heart the old ambitious spirit, and he began to revolve in his thoughts the ways and means of recovering, by aid of this remnant of his fortune, the wealth which a scheming villain had wrested from his grasp. Mr. Willet, whose marriage with his daughter was on the eve of taking place, had made to him certain proposals in regard to business, that promised a sure but not particularly brilliant return. All the required capital was to be furnished. He had not yet accepted this offer, but was about doing so, when expectation ended in certainty, and his proportion of the money recovered from Lyon was paid into his hands.

A rapid change of feelings and plans was the consequence. On the day that cheeks covering the whole sum awarded to Mr. Markland were received from New York, he returned early in the afternoon from the city, his mind buoyant with hope in the future. As the cars swept around a particular curve on approaching the station at which he was to alight, "Woodbine Lodge" came in full view, and, with a sudden impulse he exclaimed "It shall be mine again!"

"The man is not all crushed out of me yet!" There was a proud swelling of the heart as Markland said this. He had stepped from the cars at the station, and with a firmer step than usual, and a form more erect, was walking homeward. Lawn Cottage was soon in view, nestling peacefully amid embowering trees. How many times during the past year had a thankful spirit given utterance to words of thankfulness, as, at day's decline, his homeward steps brought in view this pleasant hiding-place from the world! It was different now: the spot wore a changed aspect, and, comparatively, looked small and mean, for his ideas had suddenly been elevated toward "Woodbine Lodge," and a strong desire for its re-possession had seized upon him.

But if, to his disturbed vision, beauty had partially faded from the external of his home, no shadow dimmed the brightness within. The happy voices of children fell in music on his ears, and small arms clasping his neck sent electric thrills of gladness to his heart. And how full of serene joy was the face of his wife, the angel of his home as she greeted his return, and welcomed him with words that never disturbed, but always tranquillized!

"There is a better time coming, Agnes," he said in an exultant voice, when they were alone that evening. He had informed her of the settlement of his affairs in New York, and reception of the sum which had been awarded to him in the division of property recovered from Mr. Lyon.

"A better time, Edward?" said Mrs. Markland. She seemed slightly startled at his words, and looked half timidly into his face.

"Yes, a better time, love. I have too long been powerless in the hands of a stern necessity, which has almost crushed the life out of me; but morning begins to break, the night is passing, and my way in the world grows clear again."

"*In* the world, or *through* the world?" asked Mrs. Markland, in a voice and with an expression of countenance that left her meaning in no doubt.

He looked at her for several moments, his face changing until the light fading left it almost shadowed.

"Edward," said Mrs. Markland, leaning toward him, and speaking earnestly, but, lovingly, "you look for a better time. How better? Are we not happy here? Nay, did we ever know more of true happiness than since we gathered closer together in this pleasant home? Have we not found a better time in a true appreciation of the ends of life? Have we not learned to live, in some feeble degree, that inner and higher life, from the development of which alone comes the soul's tranquillity? Ah, Edward, do not let go of these truths that we have learned. Do not let your eyes become so dazzled by the splendour of the sun of this world as to lose the power to see into the inner world of your spirit, and behold the brighter sun that can make all glorious there."

Markland bent his head, and for a little while a feeling of sadness oppressed him. The hope of worldly elevation, which had sprung up with so sudden and brilliant a flame, faded slowly away, and in its partial death the pains of dissolution were felt. The outer, visible, tangible world had strong attractions for his natural mind; and its wealth, distinctions, luxuries, and honours, looked fascinating in the light of his natural affections; yet glimpses had already been given to him of another world of higher and diviner beauty. He had listened, entranced, to its melodies, that came as from afar off; its fragrant airs had awakened his delighted sense; he had seen, as in a vision, the beauty of its inhabitants, and now the words of his wife restored all to his remembrance.

"The good time for which all are looking, and toiling, and waiting so impatiently," said Mrs. Markland, after a pause, "will never come to any unless in a change of affection."

"The life must be changed."

"Yes, or, in better words, the love. If that be fixed on mere outward and natural things, life will be only a restless seeking after the unattainable—for the natural affections only grow by what they feed upon—desire ever increasing, until the still panting, unsatisfied heart has made for itself a hell of misery."

"Thanks, angel of my life!" returned Markland, as soon as he had, in a measure, recovered himself. "Even the painful lessons I have been taught would fade from my memory, but for thee!"

CHAPTER XLIV.

A FEW weeks later, and "Lawn Cottage" was the scene of an event which made the hearts of its inmates glad even to tears. That event was the marriage of Fanny. From the time of her betrothment to Mr. Willet, a new life seemed born in her spirit and a new beauty stamped upon her countenance. All around her was diffused the heart's warm sunshine. As if from a long, bewildering, painful dream, she had awakened to find the morning breaking in serene beauty, and loving arms gathered protectingly around her. The desolating tempest had swept by; and so brilliant was the sunshine, and so clear the bending azure, that night and storms were both forgotten.

Old Mr. Allison was one of the few guests, outside of the families, who were present at the nuptial ceremonies. The bride—in years, if not in heart-experience, yet too young to enter upon the high duties to which she had solemnly pledged herself—looked the embodied image of purity and loveliness.

"Let me congratulate you," said the old man, sitting down beside Mr. Markland, and grasping his hand, after the beautiful and impressive ceremony was over and the husband's lips had touched the lips of his bride and wife. "And mine is no ordinary congratulation, that goes scarcely deeper than words, for I see in this marriage the beginning of a true marriage; and in these external bonds, the image of those truer spiritual bonds which are to unite them in eternal oneness."

"What an escape she made!" responded the father, a shudder running through his frame, as there arose before him, at that instant, a clear recollection of the past, and of his own strange, consenting blindness.

"The danger was fearful," replied Mr. Allison, who understood the meaning of the words which had just been uttered. "But it is past now."

"Yes, thanks to the infinite wisdom that leads us back into right paths. Oh!

what a life of unimagined wretchedness would have fallen to her lot, if all my plans and hopes had been accomplished! Do you know, Mr. Allison, that I have compared my insane purposes in the past to that of those men of old who made their children pass through the fire to Moloch? I set up an idol—a bloody Moloch—and was about sacrificing to it my child!"

"There is One who sits above the blinding vapours of human passion, and sees all ends from the beginning; One who loves us with an infinite tenderness, and leads us, even through struggling resistance, back to the right paths, let us stray never so often. Happy are we, if, when the right paths are gained, we walk therein with willing feet. Mr. Markland, your experiences have been of a most painful character; almost crushed out has been the natural life that held the soaring spirit fettered to the perishing things of this outer world; but you have felt that a new and better life has been born within you, and have tasted some of its purer pleasures. Oh, sir! let not the life of this world extinguish a fire that is kindled for eternity."

"How wonderfully has the infinite mercy saved me from myself!" returned Mr. Markland. "Wise, skilful in the ways of the world, prudent, and far-seeing in my own estimation, yet was I blind, ignorant, and full of strong self-will. I chose my own way in the world, dazzled by the false glitter of merely external things. I launched my bark, freighted with human souls, boldly upon an unknown sea, and, but for the storms that drove me into a sheltered haven, would have made a fearful wreck."

"Then sail not forth again," said Mr. Allison, "unless you have divine truth as your chart, and heaven's own pilot on board your vessel. It is still freighted with human souls."

"A fearful responsibility is mine." Mr. Markland spoke partly to himself.

"Yes," replied the old man; "for into your keeping immortal spirits have been committed. It is for them, not for yourself, that you are to live. Their good, not your own pleasure, is to be sought."

"Ah, if I had comprehended this truth years ago!" Markland sighed as he uttered the words.

"This is too happy an occasion," said Mr. Allison, in a cheerful voice, "to be marred by regrets for the past. They should never be permitted to bear down our spirits with sadness. The bright future is all before us, and the good time awaiting us if we but look for it in the right direction."

"And where are we to look for it, Mr. Allison? Which is the right direction?"

"Within and heavenward," was answered, with a smile so radiant that it made the wan face of the old man beautiful. "Like the kingdom of heaven, this good time comes not by 'observation;' nor with a 'lo, here!' and a 'lo, there!' It must come within us, in such a change of our ruling affections, that all things good and true, which are real and eternal verities, shall be the highest objects of love; for if we love things that are real and abiding, and obtain as well as love them, our happiness is complete."

"Thanks for the many lessons of wisdom I have received from your lips," replied Mr. Markland. "Well would it have been for me if I had earlier heeded them. But the ground was not hitherto prepared. Now, after the rank weeds have been removed, the surface broken by many furrows, and the ground watered with tears, good seed is falling into its bosom."

"May it bring forth good fruit—some thirty, some sixty, and some an hundred-fold!" was said, low and fervently, by the aged monitor; and, in the pause that followed, his ear caught a whispered "Amen."

And the good seed did spring up in this good ground, and good fruit came in the harvest time. Strongly tempted, indeed, was Mr. Markland, by his love of the world, and the brilliant rewards it promised to the successful, to enter a bold combatant in its crowded arena; but there were wise and loving counsellors around him, and their words were not unheeded. Instead of aspiring after "Woodbine Lodge," he was content to purchase "Lawn Cottage," and invest the remainder of what he had received in property that not only paid him a fair interest, but was increasing in value. The offer of Mr. Willet to enter into business was accepted, and in this his gains were sufficient to give him all needed external comforts, and a reasonable prospect of moderate accumulation.

How peacefully moved on again the pure stream of Mrs. Markland's unambitious life! If her way through the world was not so thickly bordered with brilliant flowers, humbler blossoms lined it, and she gathered as sweet honey from these as ever from their gayer sisters. She, too, had grown wiser, and could read the pages of a book whose leaves she had once turned vainly, searching for truth.

Even Aunt Grace was beginning to feel that there were some things in the world not dreamed of in her common-sense philosophy. She looked on thoughtfully, pondering much of what she heard and saw, in her heart. She had ceased to speak about the annoyance of having "Woodbine Lodge" "forever staring down," with a kind of triumph, upon them; though it was hard for her, at all times, to rise above this weakness. The "Markland blood," as she said, was too strong within her. What puzzled her most was the cheerful heart of her brother, and the interest he took in many things once scarcely noticed. Formerly, when thought went beyond himself, its circumference was limited by the good of his own family; but now, he gave some care to the common good, and manifested a neighbourly regard for others. He was looking in the right direction for "that good time coming," and the light of a better morning was breaking in upon his spirit.

As years progressed, the day grew broader, and the light of the morning became as the light of noonday. And as it was with him and his, so may it be with us all. In each of our hearts is a dissatisfied yearning toward the future, and a looking for a brighter day than any that has yet smiled down upon us. But this brighter day will never dawn except in the world of our spirits. It is created by no natural sun of fire, but by the sun of divine love. In vain, then, do we toil and struggle, and press forward in our journey through the world, fondly believing that in wealth, honour, or some more desired external good, the soul's fruition will be gained. The immortal spirit will ever be satisfied with these things; and the good time will never come to the erring seeker.

THE END.